THE RULES

By Mary Arthur

This is a work of fiction. All characters and events in this novel are a product of the author's imagination and are used fictitiously. Any resemblance to actual events, locales, or people is coincidental.

First edition: April, 2018
Paperback ISBN: 9781980966906

Prologue

Present day

Carly Mancuso walked down Main Street, tugging her jacket closer to shield her against the gentle March wind. As she sipped the steaming cup of coffee she just bought at the little coffee joint in town, she wondered how she had gotten to this place in time.

The breeze blew her fringed chestnut bangs in front of her eyes. She pushed them back as she stopped at the crafter's cooperative to window shop. To anyone watching Carly, she would appear to be admiring the beaded necklace in the display. However, she caught sight of her reflection, which caused her pause. Here she was in this quaint town in Connecticut, living a peaceful life---finally. No one knew who she was, nor did they care. This was exactly the way Carly wanted it.

She did not look forty-two years old. Although, she had to admit there were moments that she felt much older. The past years had taken their toll on her, but she had changed and adapted through it all. If you asked Carly, she would tell you she had finally become the person she always thought lived somewhere deep inside her. Too bad it took so long to find her.

As she continued her walk, she smiled at others, who like herself, were out for a stroll on this brisk Saturday afternoon. She turned the corner to walk up the side street that led to her home, still sipping her coffee along the way. Carly stopped, blinking hard trying to change what her eyes were telling her.

"Hey, Carly," he said. "How've you been?"

Carly Mancuso dropped her coffee cup and stared into the face of the devil.

Chapter 1

June, 10 months earlier

I shouldn't have survived. Sometimes, I wish I didn't. Life is funny though. There I was, thinking I had it all; knowing I could get more. Then, the next minute, I wake up in what I'm pretty sure is a hospital bed. I've got this tube in my mouth that feels like it goes down into my lungs. I figure it's connected to the machine next to me. Its rhythmic sounds appear to coordinate with my breathing. This machine, I suppose, is breathing for me, which is a good thing because I'm just too damn tired to do it myself.

I can hear the muted sound of more machines that beep around me. I want to cover my ears to block the incessant humming, but I discover my hands are tied down. I figure it's so I don't pull on something. Oh, yeah, there are more lines and tubes stuck in various places on my body. Funny that I don't feel any pain. As I try to shift my gaze around, I can see that some are connected to bags hanging on poles. Medicine, probably. Others appear to attach to those damn machines that won't stop beeping. I guess, that's so they'll know if I die.

People. There are people around too. They're talking in low voices with grave looks on their faces. I wonder what's going on. Just then, one of those people walks over to me. She must have seen that I was staring at them. She tells me she's the respiratory therapist. She explains that I've been sick; I'm on a ventilator to help me breath. She continues by saying she's the one who takes care of the ventilator and monitors my lungs. I make a weak attempt to acknowledge that I understand what she said.

Then I hear this really annoying beeping that just won't stop. It sounds like whining. Man, I hate whining. But this is so loud now, it's piercing my ears. I feel like my head my will explode from the sound; my heart is pounding like crazy too. I wonder what the hell is going on. Then I see all those people who were standing at the door, suddenly come flying into my room.

Some guy, who I guess is a doctor starts yelling orders to the others. Someone takes a huge needle and pushes something into one of those tubes. Then that respiratory therapist chick starts beating on my chest. "What the hell?" I think. She pushes up and down with a fast and steady pace. Someone else is squeezing this blue bag; I feel it pushing more air into me. It feels good, I think. But I just can't make the effort to understand what's going on.

I don't feel a thing anymore. It doesn't feel like me this is happening too. I smile to myself as I drift away, praying that I don't wake up dead.

Chapter 2

Suzanne McGregor loved her job. She was a nurse in an intensive care unit at a major trauma hospital in Connecticut. Hartford Hospital presented opportunities for her to stretch her limits to extremes. She was continually immersed in situations which required split second decisions and interventions.

In her ICU, she faced patients whose lives hung on the very fringe of existence. Modern medicine was able to intervene where God left off. Sometimes, she wondered if this was a good thing. The crushing blows her patients had undergone would often leave them debilitated both mentally and physically. She contemplated if this was truly what the fates had wanted. She pondered if it was better if some of them did not survive. After all, God did not create the machines that prolonged the suffering.

It was a mid-summer afternoon when Suzanne arrived for work at 2:45 p.m. She usually worked the day shift, but she had offered to switch with an evening shift nurse who needed the night off. She sat down at the desk in the center of the ICU where she had visual access to all the patient cubicles as well as their monitors. After she received a hand-off report, she decided to begin by assessing her one and only patient.

Normally, her assignment would consist of two or three patients, but this man stood on the precipice of life and death. He required his nurse to be at his bedside for constant observation and care. He was on a multitude of medications for his blood pressure and his heart. He was also receiving hefty doses of antibiotics as well as morphine for pain. Basically, he was in a medically induced coma so he could be treated effectively until he healed—if he didn't die first.

When she entered the room, she smiled at the woman sitting in the corner. Her heart aches for the family members who found themselves in these situations. She thought to herself, how devastating it must be to live through this.

She turned to the woman in the corner. "Hi, I'm Suzanne. I'll be Nick's nurse this evening. Are you his wife?"

"Oh, no, we're uh, that is, I'm his girlfriend. I'm Carly."

"Well, it's nice to meet you. I know this is hard, but if you have any questions, please ask. OK?"

"Thanks, sure, I will." The woman replied.

As she approached the man lying still in the bed, she noted how bloated he looked. She was barely able to make out his features. She knew he received about four liters of fluid to help sustain his blood pressure. Because his kidneys weren't working at this point, his body stored the liquid within. She listened to his heart and his lungs. She could hear distorted breath sounds as the excess fluid moved with each breath. Suzanne, then checked the monitors as well as the medication drips to assure they were running at the correct dosage. She made a note of which ones would need refilling soon.

When Suzanne turned back to her patient to complete her assessment, she attempted to check his eyes for reactivity. It was as if she saw him for the first time; she stopped short. "No, it couldn't be after all this time", she thought in disbelief. She noticed a familiar fading scar on the side of his head. She shook it off, deciding she was imaging things. Many people have scars, for pete's sake.

When she finished her assessment, Suzanne sat at the laptop designated for that room. She felt her face flush and hoped it wasn't obvious that she was flustered; her eyes gravitating towards this patient—this man she thought she knew. She took a few deep breaths to steady herself before she entered her notes in the computer. She thoughtfully typed all of her information into the nursing section. She knew she'd be making more entries each hour of the shift. For now, she had to remain calm no matter who he was.

She conscientiously took care of her patient. She pushed her suspicions about him to the back of her mind. From the hand-off report she had received, she was aware that earlier in the day, he had suffered his second cardiac arrest. He hinged on the edge. His prognosis was grave at best.

She had been off when he was first admitted to the ICU, so Suzanne read his history and hospital course carefully. Mid-way through this exhausting shift, another nurse came to relieve her for a break. She welcomed the relief from the intensity of caring for him. She was also anxious to make a phone call.
She again smiled at the woman who looked so lost and small, sitting in the corner, and left the room. She grabbed her purse and went down to the cafeteria. Suzanne fumbled for her phone, found his number and hit send.

"Hey Susie Q, what's up? I thought you were working."

"Oh Andy, I think it's him. He's here. I'm sure of it. I saw a scar. He's my patient." She spoke so quickly that Andy Gallagher wasn't sure he heard her correctly.

"Wait, slow down. What do mean he's there? You mean Eric? That's impossible." He said, trying to talk her down.

"Yes, Andy, I mean Eric. But that's not what he's calling himself now. Anyway, he's here. I mean I know he can't hurt me anymore. He's near dead, but I can't believe it." She continued to babble.

"Ok, well, do you want me to come down there? I don't know what good that would do, but I will."

She sighed and took a thoughtful breath. "You're so sweet, but you're so right. What good would it do now? I guess I just needed to tell someone who knew."

She could hear the smile in his voice when he said, "I'm your guy, you know...the armor, the white horse....the whole package."

"I do know. I feel better. I'm being silly." Then she realized she probably should have kept the information to herself. She tended to over-react without thinking first. She would pay the price later. "Oh, Andy, I'm probably wrong. Forget I said anything. I'll go grab a bite before I head back up to the floor. I'll see you later, but don't wait up, ok?"

"I'll be here. You have a good night and call if you need anything. Love you"

"Love you too." She pressed end and took another breath. She felt better after talking to Andy. In her heart, she knew it was just too improbable. She was prepared to face the world and this patient whoever he is. She'd try not to mention her reservations again.

Carly sat still in the room, just watching him. He didn't move. His chest rose rhythmically with each breath from the ventilator. The monitor blipped in sync with his heartbeat. She scanned the multitude of IV poles and the many bags hanging from them. She shifted in the hard seat and tried to focus her attention on reading her book. Well, she'd pretend to anyway.

She couldn't believe it had all come to this. His tantrums, his drinking, his bullying and now his life hung by a thread. When had it all begun? If someone told her yesterday that she'd be sitting here today, she would have thought them crazy. But yet, here she was.

She wasn't wild about the idea of sitting in the hospital either. She pushed back the resentment she was feeling. Her surroundings were unfamiliar. She didn't understand much of what was happening. She asked questions, thinking they were becoming annoyed with her. But she didn't care, she had every right to know exactly what was going on. How could she deal with everything if she didn't? She had to fully comprehend the situation for herself and for his family when she called them. A call she dreaded.

As she sat quietly observing, Carly went back and forth in her mind about what happened. She remembered the numerous trips to the emergency room when he had developed atrial fibrillation. Even then, the doctors had cautioned him about his drinking. They told him, in his case, it was the cause of his cardiac status.

Then a few nights ago, she heard him moaning in his room. They had not shared a bed in over a year. From previous experience, she knew Nick to be overly dramatic about everything. She thought to herself, "what now?", as she stomped up the stairs. There, she found him curled up in a ball, clutching at his gut.

"What's wrong?" She asked impatiently, wanting to tell him to stop acting like a baby.
"My stomach. I feel like it's being ripped out of me."

She looked at him, and decided the pain was probably real, but still he was most likely making a bigger deal out of it then necessary. Her patience was wearing thin; her sympathy non-existent. But still, she attempted to show concern and help if she could.

He added, "I've keep having diarrhea too."

"Okay. For how long?" She asked. Her thoughts said, "Oh, dear God, seriously?"

"A week or so." He wailed in agony as if in labor. He caught his breath. "But it's been a few times a day, every time I go."

She stood over him, wishing he would shut up and go to sleep. However, she was concerned and continued, "What color is it?"

"What? Oh, it's black, I guess." He screamed again.

"Come on. We're going to the hospital. You could be bleeding internally."

She recalled how it snowballed from there. Once at the emergency room, they found his blood pressure to be dangerously low. Fluids were started and lab work was begun. The room was a flurry of frenzied activity with each team member doing what they needed to do in order to stabilize his rapidly deteriorating status.

The initial tests indicated acute pancreatitis evidenced by the extreme levels of toxins in his blood. The tests also suggested that his liver as well as his kidneys were failing. These factors were also causing the intense belly pain and most likely the internal bleeding. His heart was pumping overtime as his breathing became labored. In other words, every organ in his body was shutting down.

The treating physician was frank and told Carly that Nicky's condition was life threatening. He said Nick needed to be taken to Hartford Hospital by Lifestar, the medical transport helicopter. Carly remembered thinking that he just didn't look that sick. She didn't understand how this was happening.
Within ten minutes, the transport arrived, and Nick was whisked away along with bags of fluid and blood being infused into him.

They told her he might have died if she hadn't acted when she did. Bewildered, she stood in alone in the emergency room cubicle amidst the empty bags and wrappers of medical equipment that had been used with urgency to sustain his life then tossed to the floor in haste.

Once at Hartford Hospital, he was placed in an observation room. They were infusing insulin to flush the toxins from his pancreas. However, he suffered his first cardiac arrest there. He was intubated with a tube in his throat and attached to a mechanical ventilator which would breath for him. A few hours later, he suffered a second arrest and received CPR for the second time. She wondered how many people survive this.

As she sat, her thoughts were interrupted by the soft pathetic sound of weeping. It was a woman, she realized, most likely the patient next door. She heard the male nurse speak in a soft reassuring voice. He told her he understood how much pain she was in. He offered her dilaudid. He explained it would take the edge off. He also told her it would help when he had to change the dressings on her wounds. Carly heard the catch in the woman's anguished voice when she agreed. Soon after this compassionate nurse administered the medication, the keening had subsided. Carly felt an uncontrollable urge to thank the nurse for helping his patient. But she also wanted to sit with that woman and hold her hand to comfort her. She was all alone. She wondered if Nick was feeling like the woman next door.

Just then, the regular nurse came back to the room after what Carly supposed was a much needed break. Suzanne took a report from her stand-in, then she glanced at Carly. "You doing ok?"

Carly looked up from her book, "Yeah, as well as can be expected, I guess. How's he doing? I mean, he looks the same to me, but is there any change?"

"No, he is about the same. He's a strong guy, holding his own. He still needs all the pressors, which are medications to help his blood pressure, as well as the fluids too. They help keep his pressure from falling. He's on meds to maintain a regular heartbeat too. So hopefully those things will keep him stable until his body heals enough to work on its own. The ventilator is on max settings to also help the process along. You can talk to Taylor about it tomorrow. She's the lead respiratory therapist in this ICU."

"What about the infection?" Carly asked.

Suzanne told her that he was still on the antibiotics for the bacteria in his blood that was causing sepsis. She also told Carly that he may need another plasmapheresis treatment. She explained that it is a procedure similar to dialysis. It would filter the toxins from his pancreas and his blood.

Suzanne thought for a moment, then she asked, "How long have you and Nick been together?" She made it sound as if she was innocently interested. She didn't want to appear as if she was fishing.

"Oh, close to five years now." She answered, not taking her eyes off Nick.

Suzanne really didn't want to pry, but she had questions. However, this certainly wasn't the time or place. "Nick" was her patient, after all, and he deserved her total focus as well as the best possible care she could give. A big rule in healthcare is not to become personal with patients or their families. So, her response to Carly was only, "That's a long time, we'll pull him through."

Chapter 3

As Nick lay there something around him triggered a dream or was it a memory? He heard familiar voices but he couldn't grasp any names. He thought they were angels coming to take him. Or maybe devils keeping him in this hell. He couldn't be sure; everything was a jumble in his mind.

He didn't understand as his thoughts darted back and forth; neurons firing haphazardly creating weird images. He wasn't able to grab onto to one thought and focus. Then a vision took shape in his subconscious mind. In this particular dream, he couldn't control his rage as he tore through the blonde woman's apartment. With his gleaming knife, he sliced across the deep green cushions on her couch, exposing their fleshy foam filling. The glossy blade found its way to the framed photographs of the two of them that remained on her credenza. He took another swallow of tequila. Then he cut her throat in the picture imagining she was standing in front of him.

"Bitch," he thought, "how dare you! You think you're all perfect but you're not. You're just another whore. You're probably with your new boyfriend right now laughing at me." Driven by his insecurities and the need to be center of attention, he barked more false accusations as he cut through another photo.

His building fury had him toppling the bookcase which sent the contents flying through the room. His knife slashed through cover after cover. He moved into the bedroom—"her bedroom now, since she kicked me out", he thought, really getting into the role he was playing. He stabbed relentlessly at the pillows wishing the feathers that were flying all over were her blood splattering as he severed her arteries.

When Suzanne's apartment was no longer the pretty home she had made, he felt satisfied. He kicked the cat out of his way for good measure and shoved himself through the upended kitchen. Possibly overkill, but great dramatic effect. He slammed the door behind him.

Nick shuddered in his bed, his face grimacing. Suzanne noticed an increase in his heartrate at that moment. She wondered what that was all about as she watched it quickly return to normal.

Chapter 4

In the ICU, exceptions were made for visitors; they could stay as long as they needed to. However, Carly decided to leave in the late afternoon. She had been there most of the day and she was exhausted. She really couldn't wait to go home and have some peace.

She picked up her things and started to leave. She knew she'd be back in the morning anyway. She wondered why.

"Go home and get some rest, Carly." Suzanne said as she hung a new bag of something that probably was important, Carly figured. It was wrapped in a brown plastic sheath.

"That's the plan. Thank you. Please call me if anything, well, if you need to talk to me."

"I will. Hey, don't worry. Hopefully, the worst is behind him."

"Yes, hopefully. Carly left the room thinking, "what's next if it is?"

On the way home, she made a few quick calls to update Nick's sister Ann, and his daughter Daniella. Both expressed concern but seemed hesitant to become more involved than a phone call. "Note to self…more bridges burned by Nicky." Carly said when she disconnected the calls.

Before heading home, she decided to make a stop at her parent's house. They were on the way, so she thought it would be a good time to drop in. Her parents, Salvatore and Giovanna Mancuso, had moved to Connecticut from New York many years ago. Sal's company had relocated there; they decided it would be a good place to raise their family. They were blessed with only one child, Carly.

Carly was named after her mother's maiden name of diCarli. She was the light of their life. She had her father's impulsivity and zest for life; from her mother she inherited strength and a strong will. As a child, these qualities posed some difficulties because she always wanted to "go, go, go" even when her parents said "no, no, no". However, these qualities conversely proved to be a good combination as Carly grew into an adult.

As she turned down the street, she noted how picturesque the scene was. The houses were an assortment of conventional styles including colonials, split levels, and capes. They were moderately sized. There was no room for cookie-cutter McMansions in this neighborhood. The homes were not clustered too closely together which provided the residents with space and privacy. Every property had well-manicured green lawns with colorful summer flowers planted and plenty of trees.

When she arrived at her parent's home, her dad was in the driveway vacuuming his car. He was in his early sixties and newly retired.

"Hey little girl! I'm so happy to see you. What a nice surprise!"

"Hi Dad." She gave him a kiss. "I was on my way home from the hospital and figured it was early enough to stop."

"Let's go surprise mom." They walked in together. "Hey Gi, look who I found in the driveway!"

"What Sal? I'm in the bathroom. Be right there." She called. When she came down the stairs, she saw Carly. "Oh sweetie." She threw her arms around her, pushing Carly's hair back to look into her eyes, "How's my girl?"

"Oh mom, I'm ok. Just mentally drained."

"Come on into the kitchen. I'll make some coffee and we can talk."

Sal walked with them. "Hey, Gi, don't we have some of that Entenman's cheese danish in the pantry? I could sure go for that. How 'bout you Carly?"

Smiling she answered, "Yeah dad, that sounds awesome. I haven't had my sugar and carb fix yet today."

Sal took out the pastry and grabbed a few of the brightly printed paper plates that Gi had bought at the Christmas Tree Shop. He set them out as her mother brought the coffee to the table.

For a few minutes they sat silently as they each prepared their coffee. Carly's mother broke the silence first. "So, aside from being exhausted and apparently having a sugar insufficiency, how are you? How's Nick?"

Carly had withheld held some of the details of their relationship from her parents concerning Nick's behavior. She didn't want them to worry but she also feared they might think less of her for not doing something about it sooner.

"Well, I'm handling it. What bothers me is that his family wants no responsibility. So, I'm left to make all the decisions. They won't even come to see him. I feel badly for him but I guess he did it to himself. Anyway, he's still pretty sick. The doctors think if he can make it through this part, he might have a chance."

Sal piped in, "A chance to live, you mean? Wow, that sounds pretty bad."

"Of course, she means a chance to live. What else would she mean? You're so silly sometimes, Sal." Her mother poked him and they laughed.

"Haha, yes, dad. Like mom said. Anyway, I guess we take one day at time and see what happens." She took a sip of her coffee and reached across the table to cut another piece of the danish.

Gi looked at her and said, "Carly, you have always been a strong girl, I know you'll get through this. But just remember that even the strongest people need help once in a while."

"Thanks mom."

Soon, the conversation veered away from Nicky. It was just what they all needed, most of all, Carly. When she left, her spirits were a thousand pounds lighter.

Traffic wasn't too bad, thankfully. She was home from her parents' house in about twenty minutes. When she walked into her own home, tranquility washed over her. It was quiet and seemed to be the most beautiful place on earth. Soft greens and blues set in an eclectic décor with accents of purples; it filled her with calm. It was good to be here.

She didn't feel hungry, although she should be after the past three days and only a few pieces of cheese danish to sustain her. Instead, she poured a small glass of wine and sat on the couch, savoring the quiet. Carly needed things to be organized, so she went over the details of Nicky's illness again and again.

Nick's prognosis was not good. She was aware how close to death he hovered. And as worried as she was about him, she knew she had to think about her own survival. Yes, it was true she had planned to break up with him, but since this happened so suddenly, she just wasn't prepared.

She closed her eyes and tried to remember the night they met all those years ago on that mid-April night.
It all started in West Hartford, Connecticut. Nicky Pellegrino sat at the bar nursing his vodka on the rocks with a twist. He spoke

easily with the bartender about current events. He chatted with the couple sitting next to him, commenting on their meal and the attributes of the chef. Nicky had a relaxed way about him that could make people comfortable in his presence. His twinkling blue eyes added a boyish charm that only enhanced his other endearing qualities.

He always enjoyed his nights at The Pub because here he felt as if he belonged. Yes, there were other more popular spots in West Hartford Center with competitive upscale menus and extensive wine lists, but to Nicky this place offered so much more. It felt intimate and cozy with its dark hardwood floors and subtle lighting. The walls were painted in rustic gold tones. The trim around the glossy oak bar was natural colored stone tile. Mosaic wall lamps cast flattering shadows that illuminated the faces of the patrons.

For Nicky, everyone at The Pub was his friend and captive audience, if only for the night. He always dressed in a stylish jacket with a button-down shirt and jeans when he was there. Nicky wanted to leave the best impression – always. You never knew who you might meet.

The couple sitting next to Nicky introduced themselves as Tom and Barbara. They were visiting their daughter who was attending the University of Hartford. She was a business major.

"Kids. You have any Nick?" Tom asked.

"Yeah, I have a daughter." Nick answered.

"Then you know what I mean. Barb and I drive all the way up from New Jersey to visit for the weekend and she doesn't have time for us."

"Oh, I sure do. Seems like they always have other plans that they can't change. Guess it's not cool to hang with your parents." Nicky agreed.

"You got that right. I know how important their friendships are, but it's tough on Barb and I."

Barbara chimed in, "Oh Tom, it's not that bad. We'll spend the whole day with her tomorrow. It is Friday night and she had a date after all. Give the girl some room."

At that, Nicky laughed with twinkling eyes as Barbara took another bite of her perfectly grilled swordfish.

Nicky excused himself and sauntered over to a table where he noticed a few of his buddies were sitting. "Hey guys." He announced, expecting approval. His best friend, Allan, sat at the head of the table and raised his glass high to Nicky as though this was the round table and Nicky was the last knight to return from the quest.

Allan stood about five inches shorter than Nicky. His body was stocky in comparison. His face was round and harbored small eyes. His stubby fingers were attached to squat arms. All in all, Allan would probably be described as chubby—round and pudgy all over.

"Hey, look it's the mayor." Chubby Allan joked. "Have a seat Nick. What's going on?"

"Just wanted to come over and say hi." He motioned to the bartender. "Jill, the next round for these guys is on me."

Nicky joined his friends for a little while, then feeling satisfied with himself, he went back to his seat at the bar and started his third vodka.

As the piano played softly in the background, the patrons of The Pub were consumed in their conversations. No one saw her slip discretely into a corner booth. She ordered a glass of Malbec, while her friend Sally ordered Merlot. They clinked their glasses and giggled like schoolgirls at the thought of their quiet night out.

When the waitress brought their appetizer of coconut shrimp, she said, "I'm sorry and I don't mean to intrude, but aren't you Carly Mancuso?"

Carly smiled, "You found me out."

"Oh, Carly, I mean Ms. Mancuso, I just love your music."

"Thank you, Amber. That's always great to hear."

It didn't take long for word to spread that Carly Mancuso, the former singer, was in the bar. Pretty soon, she was asked to sing and of course she agreed. She stood from her seat at the table, smoothed her black pencil skirt and took her place next to the piano player. In what seemed like a lifetime ago, Carly had played larger venues, but her favorites were always the informal impromptu intimate gatherings. Even though she had not performed publicly in a very long time, she took the mic and let it flow.

Nicky turned from his seat, seeing Carly for the first time. He was mesmerized. In that first moment, time stood still for him. Her short chestnut hair formed an aura around her small face. She was more petite in person than he would have thought, but her confidence and zest for performing made her seem almost majestic. She glowed.

After three songs, Carly graciously thanked the patrons and returned to her table.

"Ok, now, where were we?" She laughed as she and Sally waited for their meals.

"Never a dull moment when we go out, Carly." Sally shook her head and laughed along with her best friend.

Carly nodded in agreement. "I know, right? Anyway, it felt good to do that. I mean, I know when I stepped back, I said I wouldn't perform for a while. But that wasn't really performing. See, look, there's another guy singing with the piano player now.

So, how are you Sally? It feels like forever since we've both been free at the same time."

Carly and Sally had known each other since they were teenagers. They had even attended the same college. They commiserated through the trials and tribulations of growing up. Carly had become a songwriter turned singer; the singer part happened quite by accident. There were always other things in life that mattered more. In contrast, Sally had pursued a career in psychology. She was now the chief medical officer for the psychology department at the nearby UCONN-John Dempsey hospital. They had one of those enduring friendships where they could pick up where they left off at any point in time.

"I know. I mean we talk enough, but it's so great to be sitting here with you. So, any new man in the picture?"

"Haha, leave it to you to get right to the point." Carly swirled her wine, admiring the body of its legs slide down the glass. "Well, I did meet a nice guy recently."

Sally's blue eyes twinkled with interest, "Oh yeah? Go on."

"Well, I was at the bookstore, just browsing and we started talking about books and authors. Anyway, we had a coffee and exchanged phone numbers. I didn't hear from him for a day or so, so I sent him a text. He texts right back, so I'm thinking that's a good sign. So, we're texting back and forth trying to figure out when to get together. He was flirty too. Cute, right? But I started to see that he was always busy. He had told me he was single. Then the lightbulb went off; he's just not interested enough to make time. Right then and there I just let it go. I'm not gonna get sucked in with a guy who's that wrapped up in himself."

"Wow, I'm proud of you Carly Mancuso. You're finally growing up. How did it feel to just walk away?"

Carly tilted her head at Sally, "It felt good. I felt empowered. I...hey, wait a minute, are you getting all Dr. Sally on me?"

"Oops, me? No, why would I do that?" With that, Sally raised her glass to Carly. They clinked and ordered another.

Chapter 5

After dinner, Sally said she had to leave. Her husband, who was also a doctor was on call at the hospital. She was on call to relieve the babysitter of her two-year old daughter, Alyssa.

Carly decided to stay a little longer and enjoy the music, the down-time, and quite possibly a piece of chocolate molten lava cake. She thought she'd also enjoy some ice cream on the side.

Amber, her waitress, brought her the dessert accompanied by a glass of wine. "This is from the man at bar." She pointed towards Nicky, who was smiling and raising his glass to her.

"Oh, that's so sweet, Amber. But I can't accept it. I've had my limit tonight. Please tell the gentleman I said thank you."

Amber was confused and caught in the middle. People usually don't turn down free drinks, especially when they're from cute guys like Nick. Sheepishly, she delivered the message and slipped back into the kitchen.

Equally perplexed and quite frankly more than a little embarrassed, he smiled and turned back toward the bar. "Hmmm, what now?" He wondered. Nick knew he had this one night to meet this woman who had his heart doing backflips. If he didn't recover his courage, he'd miss this opportunity. He took a deep breath, trying to be casual as he walked towards Carly's table.

"Hi, there," he said, "I don't have a clever line ready, I thought the wine would be my opening."

Waking from her chocolate coma, Carly lifted her head. Nick was grinning at her as he surveyed the devastation of what once was a beautiful dessert. "Looks like you really enjoyed that."

She gazed at his blue eyes which seemed to be dancing with the reflections of light from the candle on her table. "What? Oh this," She answered pointing her fork at the plate. "Yes, I have to say it was completely amazing and absolutely worth the extra time I'll have to put in at the gym tomorrow."

"I should introduce myself. I'm Nicky Pellegrino."

"Not to be rude, but should that mean something to me, Mr. Pellegrino?"

"Damn, you're a tough audience." He raked his hand through his wavy black hair. "That's it, I'm done. I've got nothing else except my natural charm and lively wit."

Carly laughed out loud, he really caught her off guard. "Would you like to sit for a minute, Mr. Pellegrino? And I'll judge for myself just how lively your wit is."

Nicky let out the breath he was holding and slid into the seat across from her. "Thank you. Now at least my pride is intact. That walk back to my seat at the bar can be tough when you've got your tail between your legs."

Carly had to admit that he made her laugh. She also agreed with Amber that he was "pretty cute". Probably six-one, she thought as she sized him up. Lanky, but fit. Yeah, this was fun, she'd play it out. "So, Mr. Pellegrino, what can I do for you?"

"Please call me Nicky. You've already done it. I just wanted to tell you I loved hearing you sing tonight. I needed to meet you before you left. I knew I wouldn't get the opportunity again. I would really like a chance to get to know you better. That about sums it up."

"Nicky, ok. That's kind of you to say. You seem nice too. Since the waitress knows you, I figure you come here often. But I have to get going, so maybe I'll see you again sometime."

"Wait, can we talk some more? Maybe make plans to have dinner sometime?"

"Nicky, listen, you seem nice and all, but I don't feel comfortable making plans with someone I've met at a bar after a few drinks. That my first rule—never date someone you just met at a bar. It's never as rosy the next day."

"Ok, then, how about we meet for breakfast?"

Carly laughed again. "I'll let you know." She grabbed her jacket as she stood to leave. "Good-night, Nick."

He watched her leave with a smile on his face. He felt there was promise in her voice. Then all at once, he slapped his hand on his forehead. "How is she gonna let me know? She doesn't have my number. Damn-it, that was a pretty slick move." Nicky knew he just had to see her again, but how?

Innocent Beginnings. As Carly reflected on those sweet memories, she remembered how magical the dawn of a new relationship could be. "He was quite the charmer that night. Where did it go so terribly wrong?"

Chapter 6

Carly woke to a bright sun beginning to peek through the slats of the blinds in her bedroom; the sounds of a summer morning lofting through the window. She stretched out in her bed finally feeling rested. She was nervous to check her phone, but relieved when there were no missed calls. "Seven a.m., wow, I slept late." she thought. Carly rarely allowed herself to sleep past six.

She got up and went down to the kitchen to start the coffee pot she had set up the night before. While it brewed, she checked the list she had started. She planned to sit vigil at the hospital, but not until later. First, she wanted to spend some time at the shelter.

When Carly decided to put her singing career on hold at the age of thirty-one, she decided to travel. She wanted to actually experience the world rather than breeze through it in a night. She needed to get away but she also needed to live. She had enough money in the bank and had invested wisely. She was also receiving royalties from her songs as well as songs she had written for other performers.

After her extensive five year adventure, she decided it was time to give back. She began to volunteer at a women's shelter, a cause that was near and dear to her heart. One of her closest friends had been beaten and had lapsed into a coma caused by domestic violence. She later died. Her volunteering began about the same time she met Nick.

As she drank that first cup of coffee, she figured she should call the hospital and check in. She knew it could go either way. It could put her mind at ease or Nicky could reach out from his death bed, commanding her to be there.

She dialed the phone and asked to speak with the nurse who was taking care of Nick. After a very brief conversation, Carly was satisfied that there was no change. No change for someone in Nick's condition was better than the kinds of changes he'd been having recently. The nurse assured Carly it would be fine for her to come later in the day. She also told her she'd call if anything should happen.

Relieved, Carly did a little dance in the kitchen and headed up to the shower.

Chapter 7

The house was an old Victorian set high on the hill along with the others in the Prospect historical district. It was a Queen Anne style home constructed with all the intricate detail utilized in the Victorian era. It had two floors of living space with a third floor attic that had been converted into an office and storage area. The exterior stayed true to the "five color scheme" of the times.

The first floor was painted deep burgundy red. The trim on the front turret that rose taller than the house was autumn gold. The turret itself was dark green. The second floor had been rendered in a breezy shade of blue. Not as dark and thundering as the typical blue of the period which might overshadow the house giving it the appearance of toppling over. Instead, it balanced the proportions. The Eastlake spindle trim around the wide front porch was accented in purple hues, alternating with the colors of the rest of the home. The color scheme flowed. The home had been restored to its original specifications. It bore the plaque revealing the date and name of the original occupant from the National Registry of Historic Homes.

Nathanial Turner had built this house in 1870. From its vantage point up on that hill he could look down onto the town and monitor his factory. His business was silk thread, which the town of Willimantic had become famous for.

In its day, Willimantic was a major industrial hub. The trains, which still run today, would transport goods between Boston, Providence, Hartford, and New York. This little town prospered and the factory owners became wealthy.

Eventually known as "Thread City", Willimantic, Connecticut, continued to thrive. The factory owners imported silk worms from China and learned how to cultivate them. They also were one of the first cities to use steam power from the river to produce electricity. However, abundance and wealth like this for some usually breed poverty and despair for others.

Because of its link to the major cities, over time a transient population had begun to reside there. Prostitution and racketeering grew as the economy changed. The small town of Willimantic stood on the precipice of becoming a major industrial city. However, because it was small, it just couldn't keep up the pace with the quick growth other major cities were enjoying. In the sixties, people forgot about its rich history and affluent beginnings. It then bore the stigma as a city of heroin users. These days, decades later, Willimantic has transitioned into a quaint artsy town consisting of unique eateries and distinctive boutiques.

Eight women lived in this house on Prospect Hill. Because of its size, they each had their own bedroom. They took great care of this home, routinely doing household chores. They maintained it meticulously. Sometimes, they could be seen rocking on the covered front porch sipping coffee. Outwardly, they appeared carefree, enjoying a comfortable bond with each other.

They took pride in this house because for them it was more than just a place to live. It was a safe-haven that provided sanctuary from the circumstances that brought them here. If they let down their guard or upkeep for even a moment, they feared their security would crumble with it.

Jennifer Diaz stood on the porch watching the sunrise beyond the spires of the church that sat at the base of the hill. She lit another cigarette and smiled. Jennifer had a big personality which matched her size. Her wiry raven hair hung loose around her broad shoulders; but her leopard spandex pants, which she fondly referred to as "active wear", were quite tight. She completed her ensemble with a black t-shirt cinched by a gold belt.

Lucy Owens joined her on the porch. Lucy was dressed in baggy flannel pants, sneakers, and an oversized sweatshirt. She was average size but appeared dwarfed when standing next to Jennifer. "Good Morning, gorgeous." She said to Jenn.

Jenn swung her hair back over one shoulder. "Well, hey. How are you today? It's so quiet, is everyone sleeping in?"

Lucy set her coffee on the railing and zipped the sweatshirt over her pregnant belly. "I saw a few of the girls going into the kitchen when I was coming out. Irene said she'd start breakfast soon. Beautiful out here today, huh?"

"Yeah, it sure is. I love it when Irene cooks and I'm starving."

"You're always starving, Jenn." Lucy joked.

For a few minutes, they stood in silence watching and waiting as the sun now stood high in the sky above them on this summer morning.

Chapter 8

Carly usually walked to the shelter; it was just up the hill from her house. Today, she decided to drive since she would be going directly to the hospital after her morning there. She also lived in a Victorian, however, it was a smaller farmhouse style. She loved the details. The stained-glass windows added a whimsical effect. She never thought she would have ended up in this home in this town. Yet here she was.

She reflected that somewhere along the line, Nick had started to think of himself as a real estate mogul when in fact he hadn't done anything in real estate except talk. He thought he could buy and flip properties as was the current craze. Carly let herself be bullied into buying the house and financing the project. "Shame on me," she thought. She had hoped this might give Nick his big start. It turned out that although Nicky had lofty ideas, he couldn't restore it himself. Instead he enlisted the help of Chubby Allan who was a good carpenter despite his stubby fingers. However, Nick never finished paying Chubby Allan thus putting a wrench in that friendship as well.

After the house was finished, Nick realized he couldn't sell it for a profit. He hadn't done his homework when he purchased the property. Although it was a good buy, it wasn't a good buy in this town. Add to that, how much money he borrowed from Carly for the restoration and he was still underwater. He knew he would take a loss if he sold it. Nicky never learned the golden rule of buying property---location, location, location.

At that point in their relationship, Carly needed to get away from him if only in locale, so she moved into the house. After all, she was the actual owner. It turned out to be one of the best decisions she had made. She had fallen in love with this home, her first home, and this eccentric little town with its crazy history. Unfortunately, Nick didn't get the memo and joined her shortly thereafter.

She pulled into the driveway and waved at Jenn and Lucy who were waiting for her on the porch. Jenn ran down the stairs to meet her, barely giving her time to get out of the car. She nearly lifted her off the ground when she wrapped her big arms around Carly in a giant bear hug. That was Jenn, through and through—no holds barred.

"Carly, let me help you with your bag. It's so good to see you see. Are you ok? You look great. I love those skinny little jeans on you. Those beige suede boots are just fabulous. You really rock them, girl! Oh, I'm so happy to see you. We all are." Jennifer let go enough for Carly to catch her breath.

"It's great to see you too. But Jenn, it's only been a couple of days. You're just too cute, you know."

They walked arm in arm up the stairs, where Carly gave Lucy a big hug and patted her belly. "How are you feeling, Lucy? Is that little one easing up on the morning sickness?"

"Yeah, and it's about time. Three months is way too long for morning sickness for this girl, right?" Lucy was more reserved than Jennifer, so she didn't pry. None of the women did. Carly had been there to help them and had become their friend. They all knew Carly was having some difficulties, but Lucy also knew Carly would tell them about it, if it was appropriate.

Once inside, Carly could smell the bacon that Irene was cooking. "I think I am hungry." She called into the kitchen. "I'm just going to visit Jackson first."

"Don't you be too long." Irene yelled back.

Lucy and Jennifer joined Irene in the kitchen with some of the other women to help with the finishing touches. Eating any meal together should be a special occasion—a family occasion.

Carly climbed the stairs to the third floor office where she found Jackson Foley sitting at his desk. He was the manager of this shelter but also had become Carly's friend. Simply put, he was a kind man. With his degree in counseling, he was able to help the women who lived in this house. There were other staff members who worked different shifts to oversee the operations of the house as well as maintain the safety of the occupants. To all of them, Jackson was their hero.

After Carly's adventures during her initial retirement, she had volunteered at a few shelters in the Hartford area. Even after she met Nick, she continued to volunteer when time -his time- allowed. She had been so fortunate, but she felt she the need to give back.

When she moved to Willimantic, she read an article about the loss of funding for some of the special services. She discovered that this particular shelter program would be terminated. The house would be put up for sale because the rent and upkeep were not in the city budget. Nobody had considered what would happen to the women who needed these services. She knew in her heart, she could not let that happen.

Carly felt badly about the situation. She did some research and with the help of her accountant, she purchased this house. She also set up a fund that she would contribute to annually for its upkeep along with the staff's salary. She included provisions to maintain another shelter that was operating in town. The contracts were signed by all parties involved. A trust was initiated to ensure that her endowment was used appropriately. Her part in this was to remain anonymous.

The women who lived at this shelter became permanent residents. They had all lived there for a few years with Lucy being the most recent to join the crew. The other home was more of an emergency crisis sanctuary when a woman had to get out in a hurry.

Carly began to volunteer and to her it was a second home. She didn't counsel, she listened. She helped them fill out applications and find jobs. She had her accountant, Michael, assist them with financial planning so they could learn to save and build something for themselves.

"Hey, Jack, it's breakfast time. Are you going to join us?" She said as she poked her head in the door.

"Carly, how are you? How's Nick? I didn't want to call and bother you when I got your text." He took his glasses off and set them down.

"He's still pretty bad. They don't think he'll survive." She realized unconsciously she was fiddling with the paper clips on his desk.

"Do you want to talk about it?"

"Ha, no, I just want some normal time. After the last few days, counting today, I need to mentally get away from it." She did her best to be upbeat. She didn't want to expose herself or her limitations to anyone.

"Understood. So how about we go have some of that breakfast? Irene won't be happy if we're late." They both smiled and headed down to the kitchen to join the others. They knew how much this family meant to Irene, really, to all of them.

When they arrived, they found the kitchen bustling with activity. Irene was wearing her favorite sunny yellow apron while she scrambled a huge skillet of eggs. Meghan was making a fresh pot of coffee while DeeDee and Gracie set the table. Mai helped Joanie with the biscuits. Meanwhile, Lucy was removing the pancakes and bacon from the warmer handing them off to Jennifer who placed them on the table.

"Don't forget the syrup and butter." Irene told Joanie with the egg coated spatula in her hand.

"I'm on it." Joanie saluted.

All the food reached the table hot and steaming. The aroma filled the air with comfort. As everyone took their seat, Irene said grace and thanks reverently with her head bowed. Now it was officially time to eat.

Chapter 9

Suzanne McGregor and Andy Gallagher had known each other for many years before they became a couple. They had each felt the initial attraction but the fear of losing their friendship prevented them from acting on it until recently. They met during an investigation a little over eight years ago when Suzanne had arrived home to find her apartment vandalized. Andy was one of the detectives who presided over the case.

When she arrived home from the hospital at midnight after her shift, she crawled into bed with Andy. She had told him not to wait up. They could talk in the morning. She was still disturbed by this new patient, this man who went by the name of Nicky Pellegrino. As she tried to shut her mind down and find some sleep, she snuggled against Andy; her brain bringing up those vivid details of that night so long ago. Until today, those memories had faded into an area of her brain she never visited again.

Suzanne recalled the day she found herself sitting in a dingy interview room in the Stonington Police Department. She pushed her unruly blonde curls away from her face as she dabbed her eyes with a tissue. She had composed herself enough to speak with the detective. However, in her head, she was screaming with grief and horror at the sight of the malicious destruction in her home. The red paint splattered on the walls mimicking blood. The image of her cat lying dead in her living room freeze-framed in her brain.

"Yes, Detective Fritch, that's exactly what I'm saying."

"Ok, take a breath, Suzanne, and start at the beginning again." He hit the record button once again. He had jotted some thoughts on the pad that lay on the table. He would come back to those later. His partner, Andy Gallagher observed while standing off to the side.

Suzanne told her story once again. "Eric and I had been together for about five years. The first year was great. I really loved him. But during that time, there were some red flags that I should have paid more attention to. Then, he really started to change-or maybe his true self was coming out. Either way, I should have paid attention"

"For instance, Suzanne?" the detective interjected.

"Well, like he quit his job out of the blue. Normal people don't just quit their jobs like that. Normal people usually have a plan. So, I thought something had happened. But, when I asked him, he got really angry and started talking all over the place. I just couldn't follow what he was saying; he was so scattered. It was like he was crazy. I should have been more in-tune to his temper too. Then, it seemed like he always had wild ideas to make money. For him, money was the holy grail. He'd watch those infomercials and believe everything those actors were saying. But the thing was, he was convincing me of it as well.

I have worked hard my whole life and I know that there aren't any 'get rich quick' schemes. You need to be diligent, I know that in my head. I should have paid attention. The only people who make money that way are the people who sell those informercials. Anyway, he was always looking for the easy way out. Then when things went south or required too much effort, he'd either give up or put it on me to do the work."

"So, did you?"

"Well, yeah. At the time, I thought I was working towards our goals. You know helping to make a future together. Anyway, I began to realize that anytime I had an interest in something on my own, he'd either get angry about it because it didn't concern him or he'd figure a way to capitalize on it to make money. Soon, my friends were a distant memory and the things I used to enjoy became a chore because it turned into a job."

Searching for some clarity behind what she was saying, Fritch pressed on. "Ok, Suzanne, I'm just curious, why did you stay with him? And why are you so convinced it was him?"

"I had grown to be afraid of him as time went on. He had a terrible temper which was worse when he drank. He drank more and more. If people didn't do what he wanted, he would yell and carry on like a spoiled child. I watched him bully people into doing what he wanted—even his parents. Many times, he would just start screaming at me out of the blue. I kept my mouth shut because if I said anything back, it would only get worse." Appearing frightened and vulnerable, she continued. "The few times I tried to break it off, he got almost violent. Many times, I would plan a safe way to break it to him, but I was always worried about the aftermath. Don't they say that breaking up is the easy part; the aftermath is what's scary. Anyway, somehow, I found the strength to break it off. That was a few days ago. He got so mad. He threatened me and called me horrible names. He said I should watch my back. He started slamming the doors so hard, one of the hinges broke. I thought he was going to hurt me. He didn't leave at first, but finally he did. He grabbed me by the arm and he told me to have a nice life in his sarcastic voice. I knew he wouldn't just go away quietly." She concluded dramatically.

"So, let's get back to this incident. What happened and why do you think it was Eric?" Detective Fritch asked as he turned the page on his notes.

"Well, he wouldn't stop calling me. He would just start shouting again. He would threaten me and call me names, just like before. I went to police, but they couldn't really do anything. I tried to get a restraining order, but the judge said there wasn't enough evidence of a threat and I couldn't prove anything. Eventually, I just stopped answering the phone, then I changed the number.

"When I got home tonight after work, I was just drained. I walked into my apartment and I saw it was in shambles. I kept blinking, not really believing what I was seeing. My whole life ripped to shreds. I could only think of one person who would have done this. Then, then I found Lily, my cat, dead. She was in the living room." Suzanne took a deep breath and tried to compose herself once again. In a shaky voice she said, "Her head was twisted in angle that I knew wasn't natural. That's when I called you."

"Ok, Suzanne, I know this must be hard to talk about. I think we've got enough information to start an investigation. If you find that anything has been stolen, you'll need to let us know. We'll look into Eric Popper, but we're also going to explore the possibility of it being a random act." Detective Fritch explained as he pushed his glasses up on his nose.

Suzanne mumbled, fighting back the tears again. "It was him, Detective. I know it. I'm afraid he's going to come back to kill me next. He's crazy! This was just a warning. You have to help me." She burst in a building panic.

Chapter 10

After an extensive investigation, the break-in at Suzanne's apartment had yielded no clues. Eric was still the prime suspect. However, because he had spent most of his time there, no one was surprised to find his fingerprints at the scene. Nothing could be proven, and no new leads were discovered.

Eric Popper had been found and questioned. He presented himself in a charming manner as he spoke to the detectives. He showed concern when he said he didn't understand why Suzanne would point the finger at him. He eluded to the fact that he had broken up with her because she was unstable. He also planted seeds of doubt when he guessed out loud that maybe she had done this herself to get back at him for the break up.

Detectives Fritch and Gallagher wondered if Eric might be telling the truth. But they just couldn't be sure. Suzanne appeared to be a very normal and well adjusted woman. Her reactions to the incident seemed genuine. No one could act that well, unless she was a sociopath. Or maybe he was. Their stories were in direct conflict, although, Suzanne appeared to be the more credible of the two.

Erring on the side of caution, and with the help of Detectives Fritch and his partner Gallagher, Suzanne secured a restraining order. The judge was reluctant to grant it at first since there was no proof it had been Eric who posed a threat. However, after hearing Suzanne's account along with the detective's report, Judge Harrison agreed it might be prudent.

Suzanne knew this order was only as good as the person who had it. She knew she had to be diligent and aware of her surroundings at every moment. She also knew there was a strong possibility that Eric would not be found again and therefore, not served with the order. He would continue to be a silent threat to her for a long time.

For safety sake, she moved from her apartment in the quiet seaside community of Stonington, Connecticut, leaving no forwarding address. She also left her nursing job at the small community hospital. She moved north to the small town of Farmington and began work at a local hospital there. Although she would miss her friends and her lovely home, she would make a new life in her new hometown, safely away from Eric Popper. The plan would work.

Suzanne turned over again in the bed wondering, "Could Nick really be Eric?" She admitted it had been a while since she'd seen him. In his current state, his appearance did not render any clues.

Chapter 11

Suzanne didn't sleep much and to make matters worse, she had to be up at 5:30 a.m., to work her normal day shift. When she stumbled into the kitchen wrapped in her fluffy blue robe, she looked at Andy through puffy eyes, tousled curls going every which way.

"Good morning," He said. "I guess I don't have to ask how you slept."

"Oh, I'm so sorry I kept you up, didn't I?" She said as she poured some coffee into her giant mug.

"I was awake when you came in. I was hoping if I didn't talk you'd be able to sleep."

"Thanks, but, uh, no such luck."

"Are you still thinking that patient of yours is Eric?"

"I wasn't until I saw the scar. Then I took a good look at his face. Could be. Oh Andy, how could it be after all this time?"

"I could come over to the hospital today if you still want me too. Check things out?" He offered. He put a plate down in front of Suzanne. "Here, have some eggs, you need the protein."

"I'm not really hungry, but I should eat. I need the energy. I hate doing these back to back shifts. Remind me next time I volunteer for one." Suzanne tried to laugh as she put a forkful into her mouth. "You know, I'll be alright at the hospital. After all, the guy is in a coma. It's just all those memories..." She tried to shake it off.

"I know. I remember a lot of it too. Just offering my services." Always the optimist, he continued, "Ok, then here's the deal. The minute he wakes up, I'll call Fritch just to let him know. I'll fill Shaker in this morning when I get to station." Phil Shaker was Andy's new partner in Farmington. "I mean, at his point, the most we could do is press charges for assault. But, at least it would be something."

Wishing she could put the cover back on the can of worms she'd just opened, Suzanne agreed, "That sounds like a good plan." She headed to the shower feeling more hopeful that everything would be fine.

Andy, however, was not so sure. He wondered how this guy could come back into their lives after all this time. It just didn't seem possible. But yet, Suzanne was seemed to think so. He rubbed his chin noting the stubble. "Time to go," he thought. After giving Suzanne a kiss, he left for work.

When he arrived at the police station, he briefed Shaker on the situation. "Are you going to reopen the case?" Shaker asked.

Andy draped his jacket over the back of chair and pushed up his sleeves. "I don't think so. Not yet anyway. Sounds like the guy could die. But I am going to do a search for this Nicky Pellegrino guy just to find out if there's any connection."

"Yeah, that's a smart move. This way if he makes it, we'll be one step ahead." Shaker agreed. "Remember that old football rule---'The best defense is a good offense', right?"

"Yeah, hey who said that anyway? Andy asked.

"Are you kidding me? Do you live under a rock or something? How could you even ask that question?" Shaker said incredulously.

"Oh brother, You're a football expert now."

"Come on Andy, everyone knows this. It was Vince Lombardi. How could you not know that?"

"I give, ok. I didn't know. I'm sorry I am not a trivia expert like you. I'll make sure in the future I google that stuff first."

"This is not just trivia, my friend. This is an important rule that applies to all of life not just football." Shaker blew out an exasperated breath. "Jeez!"

The captain poked his head out of his office in the corner. "Will you two knock it off! Shaker, did you fill Andy in on the body?"

"Uh, yeah cap. We're getting to it now."

"Good, let me know when you make some headway." The captain disappeared back into the office in the corner.

Andy took a sip from his coffee. "He's kind of like a turtle, isn't he? Pops his head out from his shell, then pops it right back in."

"I heard that." Cap called.

Shaker briefed Andy on the body that had been found in the muck on an isolated part of the Farmington River. It had been discovered by a couple of kids looking for a place to get high. It appeared to have been there a while. Meanwhile, Andy was preoccupied, googling Nicky Pellegrino and only half listening.

On her way to the hospital, Suzanne remembered the night she and Andy admitted their feelings had become more than friendship. She believed she was lucky to have found him in the midst of everything that had happened.

Although two years had passed since the vandalism to her apartment, the fear wasn't as fresh. However, Suzanne McGregor was still careful. The restraining order had long since expired. Her attempts at leading a normal life were almost successful. Her new friends would describe her as happy but somewhat guarded.

She had not heard from Eric these past years, however there were times when she would swear he was nearby. She'd catch the whiff of a familiar scent or a glimpse of a profile in a crowd that reminded her of him. Suzanne often wondered if he was stalking her or if perhaps she was just going crazy. Because of these nagging suspicions, she made sure she never was out alone.

Suzanne loved her new job. She was challenged on a daily basis while working in the intensive care unit. Her co-workers respected her knowledge and her thirst to learn more from those around her. She felt great satisfaction at the role she played in preserving life; she grieved deeply when she lost one. Her job had become her purpose and her reason for remaining centered.

After a long shift at the hospital that night so long ago, Suzanne pulled into her driveway. Her heart pounded as it always did in anticipation of seeing a strange car on the street or something askew on her porch. She took a deep breath of relaxation after a quick scan. She knew she was being silly, but she couldn't keep those feelings at bay.

She turned off her engine and locked her car. Slinging her tote over her shoulder, she walked to the door as her curly blonde ponytail swung in circles behind her. She could hear the house phone ringing, so she hastily unlocked the door to answer it before the caller hung up.

"Hello?" She heard herself say breathlessly. She did another quick scan around the small foyer. She should have been more careful when she walked in. She forgot her rule when she rushed for the phone, the caller will call back if it's important. She had been careless.

"Andy! Hi! Wow, it's so good to hear your voice. It's been a while." She threw her jacket over the railing on the stairs, kicked off her shoes, and poured a glass of wine while they chatted.

Andy Gallagher was Detective Fritch's partner. During the investigation, he and Suzanne had struck up a friendship. They kept in touch ever since. Even with her nagging fears and anxieties, Suzanne remained a strong woman. She could take care of herself, but knowing Andy had her back, provided her with what she called her secret weapon.

"Hey Suzie Q, what's new?" Yeah, Andy had a way with words, but hearing Suzanne laugh was worth every ounce of silly he could muster.

"Oh Andy, I can always count on you. Are you coming up this way soon? I haven't seen you in a while."

"I'm hoping to head up tomorrow. I thought we could grab an early dinner and catch up. What do you think?"

"Well, I think you're in luck. I'm working a short shift, just filling in for someone, so, yes, I'm free."

"Then I guess it's true what they say—timing is everything. How about I pick you up about four?"

"How about, --sure that's great! I'll be ready." Suzanne hung up the phone smiling. It felt good to be normal.

On the darkened street, Eric Popper drove past the cute little cape watching her shadow glide by the bay window. "She really should change up her routine. It's no fun being so predictable. I'll catch up with her some other time." He smirked.

"Ok, time to head home." He picked up speed and drove away.

Eric had too much time on his hands- again. He frequently found himself in this situation. He thought he was pretty smart but once again when things didn't go his way and the boss wouldn't listen to Eric, he lost both his cool and his job. Add one more name to that list of people who needed payback, please.

If properly diagnosed, Eric would most likely fit the profile of a sociopath. He could blend in with society. He had allure, that in many cases, drew people to him. He had an ability to convince others to see things his way. His only concern was himself. However, if someone crossed him, his lack of conscience took over.

As he drove, he downed another shot, "So now what?" He glanced at the clock, thinking he'd grab some Chinese takeout then head home and watch a movie. "The Godfather must be playing again on some channel. Perfect night for this boy."

Chapter 12

Suzanne always looked forward to seeing Andy. He had become her one true friend. Sometimes she felt a romantic inclination towards him, but those feelings faded when they each returned to own lives. She knew he felt the attraction as well—like those times when the "hello hug" lasted a little longer than the customary friendship hug. She swore she could hear him make that small sound that was almost a sigh. Or maybe that was her.

Although they talked about once a week, it had been about six months since they'd actually gotten together. She always looked great, but today she felt compelled to look better than her best. Rummaging through the acres of clothing in her closet, she settled on a sleek black top with skinny jeans. It was still chilly outside in April, so a tall pair of hand-tooled cowboy boots would be perfect.

She looked at herself in the mirror and thought she really looked good. She left her hair down because it allowed her to have something to hide behind if she needed to. Sipping the cool remnants of her afternoon coffee, she peaked out the window to watch for his arrival.

Andy took his usual route to see Suzanne. He drove down I-95 connected to route 2, then sailed onto I-84 which would bring him right into Farmington.

Farmington was a cute town with an old history. It was first settled back in the 1640's when the English arrived. It had a rich history, inhabited originally by the Tunxis Indians along the banks of Farmington River. The English settlers had retained it as a farm community. They lived in beautiful colonial homes, many of which still stand.

George Washington visited the town many times during the Revolutionary War. He called it one of his favorite places. As time went on, the small farming community also became a famous place for prestigious prep schools and the Hill-Stead museum.

Now as Andy drove down route 4 toward Suzanne's home, he couldn't help but be a little disturbed by the sight of the grand Mormon temple that now adorned this once quiet stretch of road. He'd seen it many times before, but it never ceased to amaze him. The towering gold spires rose into the blue sky, dancing in the sunlight shining down. It was a mesmerizing vision that might inspire awe in some; Andy's reaction was unsettled.

He laughed to himself at the inappropriateness of the temple in this otherwise quaint New England setting. "Oh well, what are you gonna do?" he thought as he drove past.

He glanced in the mirror for a second to be sure he looked good. His hair was closely cropped and freshly trimmed. The flecks of gray were becoming more prominent. He had what he referred to as laugh lines around his eyes now too. Yeah, age was creeping up on him as he turned the corner into his forties. Funny thing about it; he was okay with that.

He lit one more cigarette before he'd arrive at Suzanne's house. She didn't mind that he still smoked, but he didn't like to do it around her. As he took one more puff, he put it out and opened the window to let the fresh air eradicate the smell. He turned the corner and parked in her driveway.

When Suzanne saw him pull in, she opened the door and stood on the porch to wait for him. She was beaming as he walked up the path to her. She remembered how handsome he looked. He was five foot ten, about three inches taller than her, and solidly built. He wore jeans with a polo shirt and short black leather jacket. His wide grin let her know he as happy to see her as she was to see him.

They hugged on the porch, when he broke away and looked at her. Her amber-brown eyes glistened from feelings that overwhelmed her at this moment. He simply said, "I feel the same."

"Andy." They embraced each other again and shared a deep kiss that would have melted ice. It was their first kiss.

"I guess this means, this is our official first date?"
She smiled, "I guess it does."

"By the way, you're gorgeous." He kissed her forehead, took her hand in his as they walked to his car. Along the way, they stole knowing glances at each other. Let the date begin.

They did not notice Eric watching from his car, parked down the street. "How sweet, she's got a boyfriend." He followed them to the restaurant.

After her trip down memory lane, Suzanne arrived at the hospital on time. She was in much better spirits feeling ready to take on the day.

Chapter 13

That same morning, Carly helped clean up the breakfast plates. She was feeling fat and happy. Her normal routine in the house was to spend some time alone with each woman. She was not a trained counselor, but the informal talks helped them as well as her. She could apply so much of what was said to her own experiences with Nicky. Funny how she never realized it before. They would also sit as a group and chat. Sometimes, they went on shopping trips or out to lunch. This was the new normal.

With Carly's assistance, many of them had good jobs. They had learned to handle their money without relying on anyone but themselves. This increased their confidence and self-worth. There had been a few women who were able to move into their own places and start new lives as whole human beings—no longer victims. Although the rules of the house were that the women could stay indefinitely, the ultimate goal was to foster growth and independence, so they could leave the nest.

Gracie Parrish, a small woman in her early thirties, remained at the kitchen table. She had been living here about two years now after her ex-husband had thrown her into the wall for the last time. She finally stood up and said, "no more!" She pressed charges and moved out for good.

Gracie was now enrolled at the local community college in the medical assistant program. Her books lay open in front of her as she concentrated on her studying. Her sleek black hair was pulled tightly in braid that hung down her back. Her new glasses perched on her nose making her look like a perfect college student. If anyone had told Gracie, that she would soon be earning an associate degree, she would have told them they were crazy. She was the first in her family to attempt higher education.

"Hey Carly, when you have a minute, can you quiz me on this? I have that exam tomorrow."

"Oh sure Gracie, which class is that?"

"Medical terminology. I think I've got it down, but some of the symbols are confusing."

"Sounds interesting."

"Well, it's not as interesting as the assessment class was, but it's stuff I have to know for charting and probably for talking to doctors too. It's like a whole new language."

Carly sat next to Gracie, "How are your clinical assignments going? Do you like them?"

She put her highlighter down, "Yeah, I really do. As much as I'm learning real world stuff, it helps because I'm in different settings. So I'll know where I like working when the time comes. I've been in the emergency room, clinics, and different types of doctor's offices. I like the clinics the best, I think."

"Oh yeah, how come?" Carly asked with interest.

"Well, all kinds of patients come in. Most aren't there for emergencies, they need all sorts of things. It's more diverse then a doctor's office and not as gory as the ER." They both laughed as they began to study together.

Jackson stood by the window with his coffee cup in his hand. He listened to the interchange between Carly and Gracie. He thought how lucky they had been that Carly had become part of this family. He often wondered why she had chosen this avenue. He knew there was more to the story than she let on. He noticed a certain contentment come over her when she walked through the door. Her entire face seemed to relax. Her petite slouched frame would become weightless as she stood tall without whatever it was that weighed her down. Whatever it was, he was happy she was there too. Her positive spirit was contagious.

Finally, around noon, Carly said she had to leave. It was time to get back to her own reality. She was feeling better about everything. Being here always had a grounding effect on her.

Chapter 14

I can't seem to open my eyes, but I don't feel dead. I guess I don't know what dead feels like to be honest. I can hear the same beeping that I remember from before. I'm guessing there's no beeping in heaven; yeah, of course I'd go to heaven.

My body feels so heavy, I just can't seem to move anything. I don't have pain so that's a good thing. I just feel a dull uncomfortable twinge where I guess the tubes go into me. I still have that damn tube in my throat. I can feel the breaths going in and out of my lungs. The rhythmic sound the machine makes is almost hypnotic.

I hear a woman's voice say, "Mr. Pellegrino, good morning. I'm Taylor, your respiratory therapist. I'm going to listen to your lungs." She positions her stethoscope on various parts of my chest as she listens to my breathing. Why are those things always so cold? "Ok, Mr. Pellegrino, you sound a little junky, so I'm going to suction." I feel something else go into my lungs through the tube, I want to gag, but I can't. Then I have this sensation of a vacuum cleaner as she pulls the smaller tube out through the tube still in my mouth. I can hear what I'm figuring is the mucous move out of my lungs. Yeah, that was a fun experience. "I'm just going to listen to you again to make sure I cleared it." After she's finished, she tells me I sound pretty good. "Mr. Pellegrino, I'm just checking your ventilator now, I just wanted you to know I'm still here."

She sounds nice enough; I wish I could thank her, but it's too much effort. I drift off again to that familiar droning of the machines around me. I hear the muffled voices of others I think are in the room. Their voices are comforting to me. I recognize them as the people who take care of me.

I wish I knew what the hell was happening to me. I can't remember anything. I want to know why I'm here. Even though I feel so weak, my mind takes me to a dark place where I think maybe they've done this to me. Yeah, that must be it. Somehow, these people who I thought were taking care of me, are really doing bad things to me. They've drugged me and tied me down. They're the ones who took away my breath and made a machine do it for me. Now I want to smash that respiratory girl in the face. How could I let myself get sucked into it all? Why though? I have to get out of here. I have to make a plan. I have to get hold of...damn, what's her name? I can't remember her name. I should though, right? I think she was important to me. I know she'll help me if she knows what they're doing to me. God, I wish I could remember her name. Now, I hear one of those people yell something about my heart. Oh, shit, what are they doing now?

Chapter 15

Suzanne had been sitting at the laptop, charting the results of her last assessment. She glanced at Nicky to see he was beginning to stir, struggling against the restraints. She saw his face contort. Thinking he was having pain, she checked to see when he was due for medication. As she approached the bed, his heart rate rose drastically; its normal rhythm had become erratic.

She called for help. Dr. Bennett and Taylor were the first to rush into the room. Dr. Bennett looked at the ECG. "Suzanne, add another fluid bolus. Let's try an extra dose of Ativan too. Maybe if he calms down, his heart rate will too."

Suzanne adjusted the Ativan drip to increase the dose he was receiving. She knew Ativan is an effective anti-anxiety drug. If he had begun to wake and panic, that should do the trick. They needed to get his heart under control so he wouldn't arrest again— for the third time. The quick onset of the Ativan would yield results soon. The three stood by the bed and watched as Nicky began to relax. His fists were no longer clenched, his facial muscles seemed to ease right before their eyes.

"That could have been bad. I don't know if he would have survived another cardiac insult." Dr. Bennett muttered gravely. "We'll need to keep him calm. Suzanne, I'll write an order for additional Ativan as needed for anxiety. I think you can hold the extra fluid too."

"Sounds good, thank you." She dialed the dose back to his normal infusion and wondered what the heck was going on in his head.

Carly walked into the room as Dr. Bennett was leaving. "Oh, doctor, how is he today?"

He stopped, choosing his words carefully. "Well, he's still about the same. He's on all the blood pressure medications and antibiotics. He's still needing a lot of fluids to support his blood pressure and cardiac function. We just had to give him some extra Ativan for anxiety. He seemed distressed. That helped."

"Oh," she said thoughtfully. "Is this bad that he's not improving after these few days? I mean shouldn't he be getting a little better by now?"

"I would think so, but his body is trying to come back from some serious insults to all his major organs. I wish I could give a more positive prognosis, but it really is wait and see at this point. I'm sorry, Carly"

"I understand, thank you doctor. "She said.

When she entered the room, she took baby steps to the bed where Nick slept. He was really bloated. And there were so many tubes. She looked at the IV poles, noticing that nothing had changed since last night. She touched his hand and said, "Hi Nick, it's Carly. How are you today? I'm going to sit a while, I'll be right over there." She pointed to the chair as if he could see.

She sipped her coffee and took out her book. She supposed that she had had more than her share of coffee over the last few days. She should have been jittery from it, but instead it was having a soothing effect. She wished she still smoked. A cigarette would feel pretty good right about now. "Nope, not going down that road again," she thought.

She was happy that the nurse wasn't talking to her now too. Probably because the doctor had laid out the gloom and doom; there was no need for the nurse to repeat it. She felt her own anxiety coupled with some anger simmering under the surface. She tried to calm herself by attempting to recognize the route of it as she'd been taught.

"Ok, maybe the anger is coming from the fact that he did this to himself. He was always such a drama queen. It's from all the alcohol. No human should consume the amounts that he did. So, now I'm stuck sitting here. I shouldn't think that way, he could be dying, but I can't help it. He makes it so hard to be sympathetic. It makes me mad. But I do care, I don't want him to die. I just don't want him to come back." She took another sip, trying to dissuade more thoughts like that.

Carly was also embarrassed. She worried that everyone thought she was a drunk like him. People assumed you're like the people you associate with. On admission she even made a point to tell them how many times she brought him to rehab. She shouldn't have cared what they thought, but she didn't want to be judged either. She was most certainly not like him. She continued to stare at her book.

Wearing the standard issue navy blue hospital scrubs, an attractive woman with an optimistic bounce in her step approached her. "Hi Carly? I'm Taylor, Nick's respiratory therapist. Suzanne said it might be helpful if we talked about the ventilator."

"Can't they just leave me alone?" she thought. "Sure, why not. I'm going to be upfront with you, Taylor. I'm exhausted so if I seem a little frustrated and disinterested, that's why."

"Ok, I completely understand. This is so much to deal with. Did Suzanne explain about the meds he's on and why?"

"Yeah. She said they're supporting his low blood pressure with fluids and a bunch of medications to keep it up. She also told me he's on some cardiac medications, steroids, insulin, vitamins, and lots of fluids. Is that about right?"

"You got it. Any questions about any of that?"

"No, I looked a lot of it up last night. But why is it taking so long for him to get better?"

Taylor continued, "Well, remember he was pretty sick when he first got here. He didn't really crash til the day before yesterday. We think some of it was due to the alcohol withdrawal. As you probably know, that can cause seizures and cardiac arrest too. So, add that to the damage his body had been going through and well, it makes for a long road ahead."

"Yes, the doctor explained that to me too." Carly agreed. "What about the breathing machine?"

"Well, his lungs took a big hit too. I'll try to put it simply and I apologize if any of this sounds like I'm talking to a fifth grader. I always find it better to be basic. Ok, so, if his heart wasn't working right, his lungs won't either. So his breathing became compromised. If he's not breathing well, he's not getting enough oxygen and he's building up unsafe levels of carbon dioxide. Both of those things signal a dangerous scenario. He's also being given so much fluid too to raise his blood pressure. But his kidneys are also shutting down, so his body isn't getting rid of it. But at the same time, his body needs the fluid. See how puffy he is?" Carly nodded. "Well he's just as puffy on the inside. A lot of that fluid is around his lungs too, making it hard for them to expand. So the vent is set to give him the breaths he needs in order to get oxygen and get rid of carbon dioxide, while at the same time minimizing damage to his lungs by overinflating them. Does that make sense? Is it too much information?"

Carly remained silent for a minute then nodded again. "Yeah, that makes sense, I guess. When will he be able to breathe without the machine?"

"Well, that all depends on him. Once they're able to decrease the fluids and pressors safely, I'll be able to start changing the settings. It's a process and it's not cookie cutter. We'll move it along depending on how he responds."

"Thank you, Taylor, I appreciate that. I really didn't know what the breathing machine was doing."

"I know. Most people don't. Basically, it does the breathing for him, so he can safely rest and heal. That's the simple explanation." Taylor smiled in her laidback way. She had spoken to so many family members over the years, so she was always careful not to overwhelm them with too much technical jargon. The basics were all they needed and most likely all they could comprehend at times like these. "I'll be in and out of here, so if you have any questions, please ask, ok?"

"I will, thanks again." Carly watched Taylor leave the room and move on to her next patient in the ICU. "Come on Nicky," she thought. "You've got to get better."

Chapter 16

Shaker was trying to get Andy up to speed with what they knew so far about the body those kids had found. Dead bodies were a rarity in Farmington. "Andy, buddy, will you shut down that damn computer and pay attention. We got a body out there."

"What? Oh, yeah, sorry. I'm a little preoccupied."

"File that away for now, we've gotta take a look at this. It sounds like it's been there a while. You ready to head out?"

"Sure, let's go. I promise to be good." Andy joked.

Andy and Phil Shaker pulled their police issued Ford Explorer into one of the parking areas along the Farmington River. This particular parking lot led to a path where hikers could walk. Many of the town's kids used this path to go to a favorite hangout spot around a massive old oak that hinged right on the river bank. A homemade rope swing dangled from the branches.

Trudging along in his heavy hikers, Andy followed Shaker to where the others waited. Dr. Oates, the medical examiner, was scowling. The scowl was permanently affixed to his large face, but at this moment it seemed more intimidating. "Glad you boys could finally make it. We've been waiting for you so we could move the body."

"Sorry Doc, we got hung up. So, what's the deal?" Shaker asked.

"Well, I'm afraid it's going to take a while to make an ID or even find anything definitive. I can tell you it's a male, probably late thirties, early forties. I don't know yet how long he's been in the water, but my guess from the decomposition is about eighteen months. It's remarkable that the body didn't surface sooner. He's tangled up in the muck and he's got a couple of bricks stuffed in his pockets—probably helped keep him down. My guess is that he was dumped somewhere else and the current brought him here. Because the body's pretty badly decomposed, the autopsy will take a while. Identification will have to be DNA from the bones. Not much left of facial recognition. Looks like the bass got to him too."

"Mind if we take a closer look? Then you can take him and do what you do best." Andy said.

They approached the body, careful not to disturb anything. They greeted the crime scene techs who were looking for anything that might mean something. Even though they all knew this was probably not where the body was dumped, care still had to be taken on the off chance something important might be found.

The ME was right, there was really nothing recognizable about the guy, except that it was a guy. He was a bloated mass of blueish flubber; his skin had separated from most of his body; his fingers and toes had been snapped off.
"Poor bastard," Andy thought, "Hey Doc, any idea yet how he died?" he called.

"Aside from the obvious choice of drowning, you mean? He shook his head. "I'm hoping to find something when I get him on the table."

After about a half hour of searching what was left of the body and it's clothing, they gave Dr. Oates the okay to move the it. Andy and Shaker stayed behind to go over the area and take more photos. Their initial assessment of the area yielded no tangible results as they expected. They would have to be patient and wait for the autopsy.

"You ready to rock and roll, Andy?" Shaker motioned his head toward the path that led to the car.

"Yep, let's go. Feeling hungry too. Let's grab some sandwiches on the way."

Chapter 17

Carly was feeling fried and needed a change of scenery. She decided to go outside and get some fresh air, maybe some quiet too. She let Suzanne know she'd be back. She grabbed a cup of soup and an apple at the café in the hospital lobby. "Perfect," she thought. From there, she walked away from the main entrance. The warm breeze was like magic in contrast to stagnant air conditioning she had been sitting inside. She found a spot away from all the hub-bub, where she sat on a stone wall next to the valet parking lot. She closed her eyes and soaked in the sun along with all the peace it brought to her.

She thought about calling Sally, but she just didn't know where to start. They had chatted when Nicky was first admitted, sending only brief texts since then. Carly kept Sally abreast of things, but she just didn't have the mindset to talk about it. That's the great thing about having a best friend, Sally understood.

As angry and fed up with Nick as Carly was, she couldn't help but smile as she remembered when she finally decided to date him. It had been two days after they first met. The image of those sparkling blue eyes continued to make their way into her consciousness. She recalled the way his jacket hung on his lankly frame. He was actually adorable when she was giving him a hard time and he didn't know what to make of it. She decided she should go to The Pub and maybe run into him again.

Carly wore a pair of jeans with a sleeveless tunic and light sweater. She chose a pair of boots with a heel to give some height to her petite frame. She also considered that he was much taller than she was, so she could definitely get away with heels. When she arrived, she walked in, chose a seat at the bar, and ordered a glass of wine. She did a quick scan of the room; Nicky wasn't there.

"Well, it's early," she thought, so she ordered an appetizer of bacon wrapped dates stuffed with gruyere cheese. When her food was brought to her, she added another appetizer of the lobster and crab spring rolls. "I guess I'm hungrier than I thought." She told the bartender.

"Wow, woman, where do you put it all?" came an amused voice from behind her.

She knew that voice and turned to see him standing there. "Mind if I sit next to you?"

"I think that would be okay. Nicky, right?" she said pretending to be uncertain.

"Yes, Nicky. Or Mr. Pellegrino to you."

"I think tonight you can be Nicky. Do you want some of the dates, they're amazing." She offered.

His vodka martini in a rocks glass arrived. He took a sip and said, "Maybe one, but I'm going to order some food too. I've been thinking about the hanger steak all day."

"Yeah, that looks yummy too." She raised her glass to clink his. "I have a rule that if I'm sharing a drink with someone, we have to 'cheers'. It's good luck."

"So, we're sharing a drink now? Next you'll be saying we're on a date." He was giving her a taste of her own medicine and she knew it.

"Ok, ok, I give. Look, since we've already met, you're here and I'm here. I see no problem in us chatting while we have a drink and some food."

"Haha, I guess there's no rule against that." He teased.

Carly and Nick enjoyed their time together. She loved his curly mop of unruly hair. It had no rhyme or reason and enhanced his ruddy complexion. He was easy to be with, making her laugh with his silly stories. He wasn't one of those guys who bemoaned his former girlfriends or problems with his job. It was evident that he enjoyed life, embracing the opportunities presented to him.

Nick told Carly that he was the owner of the local hardware store near the old metal bridge. It had been in his family for years and was a mainstay in Farmington. He enjoyed his work because of the regular customers as well as the new more infrequent ones. She could understand his love of the place because for him it was a social experience; part its charm, she supposed.

Nick wanted to understand why Carly had abandoned her singing career. She explained that it just wasn't fulfilling; she never really wanted to be a singer. Yeah, she loved to sing and perform, but her passion had really been about the writing. She had discovered that for her, the process of writing was cathartic. She felt by understanding herself in this way, she might be able to help others. So, she just up and retired. She moved back to Connecticut, hoping to find some way to give back as well as provide a meaningful life for herself. She took a few classes in counseling and began to volunteer at women's shelters. She didn't want to talk about her friend at this point.

"Are you going to continue with counseling? He asked.

"I'm not sure. I still write a bit but I haven't really thought that much ahead about those other things. Right now, I like the volunteering. Plus, I need the break. Those ten years took away part of my life that I'll never get back. Who knows?"

After the food, they shared another drink. They paid for their meals and Nicky walked Carly to her car. His eyes shimmered in the moonlight. "Carly, I'd like to see you again. Is that possible? I mean like a real date."

"Yeah, I'd like that too. I really had a nice time tonight." She was feeling shy about this part of night. It had been a long time since she found herself with a man she whose company she enjoyed as well as being attracted to. She was definitely rusty.

"Lunch tomorrow? Nothing fancy, maybe a pizza??

"That sounds perfect. Lunch is a no pressure type date." She giggled.

"I'll call you tomorrow morning and we'll set a time, OK?" And before she had time to add anything to the thought, he took her face in his hands and kissed her goodnight.

That night, almost five years ago, Nick had charmed his way into Carly's heart. They spent more and more time together. They made plans for a shared future. At the age of thirty-seven, Carly had never really entertained the idea of having children; Nick had changed that as well.

"Boy, was I a stupid little girl," she thought as she opened her eyes to the reality of where she was right now—sitting in front of a hospital, eating an apple. "How could I let myself get sucked in?" Although, Carly still cared for Nicky and felt compassion for him, she remembered that she had been trying to figure out a safe way to get Nick out her life and her house. She knew this was her opportunity; she had been mulling it over since that night she brought him to the ER. As cruel at it sounded, she knew she could never allow him to come back should he survive.

While she made this decision consciously, she could feel her spirits lift as the heaviness she felt in her heart disappeared. "Here I was stressing over being stuck with him now forever. Well, I don't have to be. Divine intervention," she mused.

"Someone was certainly looking after me and gave me this chance. The window will close if I don't go through."

Carly tossed her apple core and the empty soup container in the trash and headed back to ICU. She knew she didn't need to disclose her decision to anyone until he started to improve—that is if he didn't die first.

Chapter 18

The women at the house on Prospect Hill, ranged in ages and background. However, they shared their reason for being there. They had all been victims of domestic violence. When they had each said, "enough", they were sheltered in a transition home—a safe place, where they could receive victim counseling and not worry that someone might hurt them. They also learned about their options for the future. Those with money or jobs were aided in finding housing where they could support themselves. Some eventually moved in with family while they got back on their feet.

But there were others, like these women, who had become dependent on their abusers, believing they deserved the cruelty which forced their self-esteem to plummet to untold depths. Eventually, these two factors resulted in the inability to secure employment or live independently. Instead, they were offered a home at Prospect Hill, where the counseling continued. They were also taught job skills with the hopes that they would ultimately have the tools to be on their own.

Jackson Foley had been in charge of this house for a few years now. He was very proud of the group that resided there. They had formed a family. Although, most of them had acquired decent jobs, they chose to remain here with each other. This had become a support system.

Lucy Owens was the newest arrival. When she first arrived, she was withdrawn and cautious to be close to anyone. Jackson knew the others in the house would help bring her around, allowing her to slowly gain their trust. Shortly thereafter, at twenty-one, she found out she was pregnant with her first child. Now, just completing her third month, she could finally admit that she was very excited to have this baby. Her housemates were equally as excited.

They helped prepare a nursery and watched over Lucy with doting protective eyes; especially Jenn who had adopted the role of bodyguard. Irene, who was in her mid-sixties, had volunteered to baby-sit so Lucy could work after the birth. Irene already had three grandchildren; she was ready to take on a fourth.

After what she had endured at the hands of her ex-boyfriend, she felt so blessed that her child would be born into a house filled with so much love. She now understood that a true family can come in different shapes and sizes.

The house was quiet today, after everyone left for their various jobs or errands. Jack had some paperwork to catch up on. His day shift assistant counselor was downstairs, prepping for the late afternoon group meeting that she took charge of on a weekly basis. All the women would be back in time. Aside from the routine progress updates, they all had concerns about Carly and how to handle the situation. Jackson would be attending the meeting today as well.

Chapter 19

While Carly was on her break from her vigil, Suzanne continued to take care of Nick. She stood by his bedside, listening to his heart and lungs. She examined IV sites to inspect for any signs of infection. She spoke in a low voice, that only he could hear, "Eric? Is it really you?"

In that instant, he opened his eyes and glared right at her. He struggled against the restraints on his hands, trying to free himself. Suzanne jumped back away from the bed, terrified that his sudden rage would allow him to break free. He managed a disgusting smile around the tube in his mouth and it fastenings. His eyes abruptly closed as his body relaxed.

Trembling, Suzanne stood frozen at the foot of the bed. "Oh my god," she shook, "Did that really just happen?" She quickly scanned the monitors as she tried to gain her composure. Suzanne wondered what would happen if she held one of his cardiac meds. Quickly, she dismissed the thought. It was against everything she believed in

When she turned back toward the doorway, she noticed Dr. Bennett sitting at the desk located in the center of the ICU. He appeared to be studying the computer in front of him. Suzanne knew he had other patients here, but since Nick was the sickest, it was probably a safe guess he was going over Nick's daily lab reports.

He approached her, "Suzanne, I think we can stop the fluids for now. His blood pressure seems to be holding. His BUN is coming down too so I think his kidney function might be improving. Has the urine output increased?"

She thought for a moment, then checked the nursing notes in the chart over the last day for a comparison. "Well, it looks like he is putting out a little more and the color isn't as amber or cloudy."

"Ok, then let's back off on the fluid for now. I also want to wean the Levophed. He's been on it for close to three days. We'll keep the other two pressors for now, but I want to see how he does without this one."

Suzanne was happy to start the weaning process on his medications. If he could safely come off the pressors which helped improve his blood pressure, he'd be on the right track. The fluids had been reduced over the last day and a half, so it was another good sign to temporarily stop them to assess his status.

While Nick seemed so much worse in the morning, it was becoming evident that perhaps, his body was signally a turn in the right direction. He was showing signs of improvement in a short span of time. His will to live had become stronger than his body's need to die.

After her two hour break, Carly found herself reluctantly walking back to Nick's room. She felt the air being sucked out of her as she got closer. As she approached, she had the building sensation that weights were tied to her legs challenging each step she took. The heaviness was suffocating. She secretly wished she could go home or shop or be anywhere that was not here.

When she was buzzed into the ICU, she found Nick's room and sat in her little chair in the corner pretending to read. "No change," she thought as she glanced at him lying there. "Hi Nick, I'm back."

Suzanne walked into the room, "Oh Carly, hi. I've got some news for you."

Noticing Suzanne's smile and tone, Carly asked, "What's going on? Did something happen?"

"Well, to keep it brief, Nick's bloodwork shows improvement. Dr. Bennett thinks some of the setback he had this morning may have been anxiety driven. We started decreasing the fluids last night, but today we're going to stop them. We've also stopped one of the blood pressure meds. It's been a couple hours and he's handling it. So those are good things."

Carly brightened, "What next?" she asked.

"Well, we watch him and see if we can reduce some of the other meds. Next respiratory will work with the ventilator to see if some of the settings can be weaned also."

"Oh, that sounds good. Is it?"

"Yes, it's definitely moving in the right direction." Suzanne assured her.

Chapter 20

Carly decided she needed a night off from all of this. She left the hospital early that day. The news she received was promising. She also was aware that they would call her should anything change. On the drive home, she decided she needed a night with Sally. She gave her car instructions to make the call.

"Carly! Is everything ok?" Sally asked when she picked up.

"Hi there, and yes, everything is good. But I wanted to know if you're free to grab a wine and some apps. Then we can catch up."

"Oh, that sounds fabulous. Listen, let me check with Dan to make sure he'll be home. I'll call you right back."

Carly disconnected the call and turned up the volume on the CD she was listening too. She knew so many people didn't listen to CD's anymore, but she still loved them. Among her favorites was the Rock and Roll Hall of Fame, 25th Anniversary CD. It was live performances with all of her favorite musicians. They played together on each other's songs as if they'd been doing it forever. It always put her in a great mood. As she sang along with John Fogerty and Bruce Springsteen performing an incredible rendition of Roy Orbison's "Pretty Woman", her phone rang through.

Seeing it was Sally, she answered. "Hey, so?"

"Hey, well we're in luck. Dan is already on his way home. He had a late appointment which was cancelled. So he's going to grab Alyssa from his mom and bring her home. I am free to meet you—Yay!"

"Oh wonderful! When can you leave?"

"I could be out of here in about twenty minutes. Where do you want to meet?

"How about at Evergreen Walk? I'm almost to South Windsor now. I could grab us seats and wait for you." Carly offered.

"That sounds great. Since it's early, I probably shouldn't hit too much traffic through Hartford."

"Perfect. Since I'm early, I'll probably shop a little too." Carly decided.

"I wouldn't expect anything less from you." Sally laughed. "Ok, let me wrap things up and I'll head right out. See you soon."

"Okay, bye." Carly hung up and went back to singing with her CD.

It was only three-thirty when she arrived, so she had plenty of time to do some shopping. Evergreen was an open-air shopping center. Carly loved the vibrant flowers lining the stone walkways. She thought it was a soothing but elegant touch that speakers were placed among the plants to play soft upbeat songs for the shoppers. She browsed in the Gap and the Loft. She stopped at Sephora where she bought a deep vivid red lipstick and an eyeliner. "Wonderful," she thought. She put on the lipstick before she bopped over to the restaurant. She was really feeling great.

She found a high-top table in the bar area and settled down with her favorite red wine, a spicy deep syrah. The first solitary sip warmed her as she toasted herself for making it to this point. Nick would be okay and so would she --without him. Carly smiled at some other professionals who were also stopping for a happy hour cocktail celebrating the end of their work day. She studied the menu without really seeing it. She was so deep in thought that she didn't see Sally approaching her.

"You in there?" Sally nudged as she sat down.

"I sure am. It's so good to see you, you look great as always! Order your wine so we can talk. I need to eat too. I'm starving."

"That's nothing new." Sally ordered her usual merlot and in their customary fashion, they clinked their glasses.

They sat in silence for a few minutes when Sally finally said, "So, what's going on? You seem to be in a good place."

"Yeah, you know, I really am. Well, first, Nick is improving. It was kind of a quick turnaround. No matter how I feel about him, that's good. But before I knew that, I had a revelation. It had been simmering in the back of my mind, but then I realized, when he's good enough to be discharged, he doesn't ever have to come back to my house."

"Yes, you're right. That's pretty great. Ok, so where will he go?"

"Well, I suppose he could live in the apartment above the hardware store or go to the house he rents out. But the point is, I was struggling with how to end it and how would I get him out of my house. And now he's out, it's like someone was watching over me to make it easy."

Sally took a bite of the grilled chicken slider. "Mmm, this is good. Ok, so I'm gonna be the devil's advocate. Yeah, he's out of your house, but you still have to talk to him. Do you think he's going to just stand down and fade away?"

"Well, I guess not, but telling him while he's in hospital keeps it safe. I know, I know, that's cold of me. I'm a coward, I admit it. But you know what, at this point, I don't care what anyone thinks of me. You're probably the only one who knows what's it's been like." Sally nodded and Carly continued, "I'm sick of it, the bullying, the name calling, the stupid accusations. All the money he took from me- yeah, I take responsibility for not calling him out on that. He had a great job, his own business that he almost lost. How could he do that? It was the family business. Anyway, it was good his sister stepped up." Carly looked around, she thought she was losing her cool and getting loud. She spoke quietly again, "Sorry, I hope I wasn't talking to loudly."

"No, you're fine, sweetie. Listen, you are not a coward. Remember, I know you. You are strong and you follow your heart. You make up your mind and you stick to it. Remember, you gave up a big career because you felt it wasn't right for you. So, stick to your guns on this one too. I just want you to be aware that there might be some pushback from him. Don't ever back down."

"I know, Sally. But for now, I just want to be happy. I feel free. I can breathe again. The air is fresh and clean all around me." Carly bit into a slider, "Mmm, this is good. Anyway, I'm in a good place, this is finally the right time."

"Then I'm happy too. And I'm here if you need anything, you know that too."

"I sure do. Now, let's celebrate."

It was great to spend time with Sally. It felt like forever since they'd been able to kick back for a couple of hours. When she reached her house at seven, she was still smiling. She grabbed her keys as she walked onto the porch ready to settle in for a quiet evening.

Chapter 21

The next morning, Nicky had improved so much that Suzanne was assigned two patients in the ICU. Her second patient was a long-term ventilator patient who was admitted from a nearby respiratory hospital. The patient was a woman who was one hundred years old. She had been living on this life support for five years following a catastrophic stroke. She was admitted to the ICU because she was now requiring blood and dialysis. Suzanne wondered if this woman was aware of what was happening to her or if she even wanted it at this point in her life.

"Wow, Sadie, you do look fabulous for your age." She told her. "Ok, let's get that blood started. Dr. Bennett is talking to your son to explain the dialysis process to see if he really wants to go through with it. What do you want, Sadie?"

Suzanne checked the blood for the proper type and cross to confirm it was correct. She also went through the procedural standards of identification before she hung it. Once everything was in order, she started the IV and blood started flowing into Sadie.

She would need to monitor Sadie closely for signs of rejection as well as fluid overload which is always a possibility. After she recorded the first set of vital signs. She went over to Nick's cubicle which was next door. He looked great. Overnight, they weaned the one of the other blood pressure medications. His cardiac drugs had also been reduced, however, he still needed the Cardizem to regulate his heart beat. He probably always would.

Taylor was standing at the ventilator making changes as well. "Good Morning, Sue," She said.

"Hey, Taylor. I heard you were able to get him down to more normal settings. Is he tolerating that?"

They walked to the door to talk out of earshot from Nicky. "Yeah, it's really amazing how fast he turned around. I'm actually going to see if he can breathe a little on his own. Dr. Bennett was talking about waking him up to trial that. I think he may want to decrease the Propofol."

"That is fast, considering the past few days. I'll go talk to him about the plans. I've been next door with Sadie."

"Oh, yeah, that's a sad one. One hundred, amazing. It makes me wonder if this is how she wanted to spend the last years of her life."

"I know." Suzanne agreed. "The son is talking to Dr. Bennet now. I get the impression he's a little unrealistic about his mother's situation. Anyway, I'll wait until they're done, then I'll find out about our plans for Nick.

Suzanne did her assessment of Nick, still wondering if this could be Eric. She had taken care of him objectively, the way she would any patient. But there were moments she had to admit, that the memories would simmer under the surface.

As she charted, she heard a man's voice coming from Sadie's room, "Mama, you look beautiful. Are they taking good care of you?" He asked in a high pitched sing-song voice as if he were talking to an infant. "Oh, that's good to hear. I brought your favorite sweater. See, it's the pink one with the fuzzy rose appliques."

As sad as this was, knowing her son was in denial, Suzanne and Taylor glanced at each other with a look that said "seriously?".

The order was given to stop the Propofol. This quick acting drug leaves the body soon after the drip is shut off. It would allow Nicky to wake up enough to determine if he could breathe without the aid of the machine. One more step in his recovery.

Once he became easily arousable, Taylor told Nick she was checking his breathing. He stared at her, finally able to match the face to voice he had been hearing. He remained on the ventilator, but the settings were adjusted to support him while he did most of the breathing without the aid of the machine. He would be monitored closely. If he was successful and remained stable throughout the day, she might be able to remove the endotracheal tube tomorrow.

Chapter 22

The next day as Suzanne was pressing the elevator button that would take her to her floor, she felt a flicker of dread that Nicky might be extubated today. She would have to face him. She silently prayed on the way up that he wouldn't make a scene. Maybe she should take a different patient today or maybe she could sedate him. "No, don't be silly, that's just wrong," she told herself. She knew she couldn't let the anticipation she was feeling was overshadow her ethics.

She took her report from the night nurse who told her Sadie had done well with her blood and was scheduled to begin bedside dialysis at ten. She then told Suzanne that Nicky had also done very well with minimal support from the ventilator until about midnight. At that point, they rested him with full support. Taylor would most likely pull the breathing tube.

"Oh, that's great," Sue said as her heart began to beat a little faster. "Thanks, enjoy your day off." She added.

This was it, she thought as she approached the bed. She whispered in a quiet voice, "Nicky, if that's you Eric, please don't make a scene. It's Suzanne. I'm your nurse and I'm taking good care of you. Please."

He opened his eyes and stared at her. He seemed lucid, appearing to understand what she had said. He winked and shut his eyes again.

Carly woke early with a smile on her face. She knew this would be a good day. As she went downstairs to the kitchen, she was filled with the wonderful aroma of her coffee brewing. She was happy she had remembered to set the timer. She decided to make a list of things she needed to get done today. She had spent so much time at the hospital the last few days, she felt her normalcy needed to get back on track.

There was laundry to do, food to buy, and cleaning. Carly also wanted to stop at the house for a quick visit, she felt it was time to be truthful with her friends about her situation. She had come to realize her situation was not that much different from theirs. She had also been contemplating a part time job or maybe enrolling in the local college. She would research both options and go where her heart told her.

But she knew the first thing she needed to do was to call the hospital. As she waited to be connected to Nick's nurse, she crossed her fingers. If all went well, she could set her plans in motion to separate him from her life. She would tell the nurse as well as his discharge planner. Then she would tell him.

Finally, Suzanne picked up the phone, "Hello, this is Sue," she said.

"Hi Sue, this is Carly Mancuso. I'm calling to see how Nick Pellegrino is doing today." She held her breath.

"Oh hi, Carly. I was going to call you. He's actually doing very well today. The blood pressure drugs and fluids have been stopped. He's also been breathing on his own, but he's still connected to the machine. He's awake and seems to understand what we've told him. Taylor is hoping to extubate him in a little while."

"Really? That's great news!" Carly exhaled. "That was so fast."

"It was, he really turned around quickly. Are you coming in today?"

"Yes, I'll be in around noon, I think. Thanks again."

"You're welcome, I'll see you later."

Carly pressed end on her phone and brought her coffee to her front porch. She sat quietly, sipping her coffee. In her mind, she reviewed what she was going to say.

Taylor walked over to Nicky. "Good morning." She said. "Today, I get to do one of the best parts of my job. I get to take that tube out of your mouth. You'll be able to breathe without any help. You'll need oxygen for a little while, so I'll be putting this nasal cannula in your nose to help with that. OK?"

Nick smiled and nodded that he understood. He seemed calm, he knew he could do it. He didn't remember much of what had happened. Even now he was fuzzy around the edges. But he had this vague impression that he had cheated death.

Taylor told him to take a deep breath and as he exhaled, she pulled the long tube from his mouth that had extended into his lungs. She put the oxygen in his nose and turned off the ventilator. She listened to his breathing, then checked his oxygen level and heart rate on the monitor. "Perfect." She told him. "You're doing great. Nicky, can you say hi? I need to hear your voice."

He looked at her and tried to clear his throat. "Hi." He finally managed in weak raspy voice.

"That's great. Don't worry, your voice will come back. The tube goes through your vocal chords, so they just need to get strong again."

"Thank you." He smiled and felt almost human again. He closed his eyes in pure satisfaction, still wondering what the hell had happened to him.

Tentatively, Suzanne approached his bed. "Hi Nick. How are you feeling?" She asked bravely, not knowing what to expect.

He opened his eyes and winked again. "I feel ok. But I want to talk to you. I think you want to talk to me too."

"Ok, later. You get some rest now. Let me know if you have any pain or discomfort. I'll be nearby." As he closed his eyes again, she felt a rush of relief.

Chapter 23

Andy sat at his desk, waiting for Shaker to arrive with his Starbucks fix. He had been searching for information on Nicky Pellegrino but came up with virtually nothing worthwhile. There were some background pieces about a hardware store, but no pictures to accompany any of it. He did not have an online presence—no Facebook, no Twitter, and no LinkedIn. He also searched the police data bases—again nothing. All he had was Suzanne's description and the scar that he remembered all too well. He really thought Eric had disappeared for good that night if he had survived.

He remembered the date he and Suzanne had. It was the first night that they admitted how they felt about each other. When they arrived back at Suzanne's house, they walked to the front door holding hands. It had been a wonderful evening. They talked openly about how their feelings for each other had grown. Andy told her he had wanted to tell her so many times before, but he worried that she would reject his affection. He couldn't deal with losing her friendship if that happened. Much to his relief, he realized that she was feeling the same way with the same apprehension.

Suzanne unlocked the door and invited Andy in. "Just for a little while, is that okay with you?" He asked.

"Yeah, I want to savor this night for a little while longer." She smiled, "I'll go make us some coffee."

"That sounds good. It'll get me through the drive home. No, I'm not staying over."

Wickedly, she countered, "Why would you think I'd say that?"

"No comment. I'll light the fireplace, Ok?"

They snuggled on the floor in front of the fire and drank coffee. Suzanne had also put out a plate of Italian cookies.

Eric parked his car down the road. Wearing a dark sweatshirt, he skulked around the back of Suzanne's house. "Damnit," he thought when he saw the car in the driveway, "that cop's still there." He peered in the window, careful not to be noticed. His anger grew as he watched the scene play out in front of him. "Bitch, I'll teach you who's directing this show." He silently opened the sliding door on the back deck and crept in. He became infuriated at the sounds of their laughter, her laughter. Undetected, he walked into the living room.

"Hi Sue, how you doing?" Eric smirked.

She jumped up, "Oh my god, Eric?" Then she saw the glimmer of the knife. It was the knife she had envisioned from all those years ago.

Startled, Andy calmly intervened, "Eric, hi. I'm Andy. Why don't you put the knife down. There's no need..."

At that instant, Eric lunged for Andy with the knife taking on a life of its own. His fury building into a blindness that took over his mind. "I'll kill you." The blade found Andy's hand as he tried to grab Eric's wrist.

Suzanne screamed, "NO, STOP!" She charged at Eric and pushed him down. The knife flew to the ground next to them. He pushed her off, trying to get the knife, but her determination had given her inhuman strength as she grabbed the knife first. He dove at her just as she sliced in the air connecting with his head. The blood gushed.

"You bitch, what the hell? Why'd you do that?"

Andy roused, holding his bloody wrist and tackled Eric. "Suzanne, I've got him, call 911!"

She just stood there in a trance, watching the blood flow. Her mind was racing, trying to make sense of things.

"SUZANNE!" Andy shouted, "Call 911!"

In the moment of her hesitation, Eric toppled Andy, kicked him in the gut, forcing him to the ground heaving for air. He ripped the knife from Suzanne's hand, blood still gushing from his wound. He escaped through the back door and sprinted to his car. He sped away only to discover that she had slashed his arm when he took the knife back. He had not felt a thing.

Andy tried to stand but he was dizzy and doubled over from the pain. He thought he must have a broken rib or two. He looked up at Suzanne, and with short breathless words, he said, "Why didn't you call 911?" He reached for his cell and made the call himself.

When the police arrived, Suzanne had regained her composure. She had wrapped Andy's wound until he could be taken to the hospital. It was wide open and would require many stitches. Luckily, no serious damage had been done except that Eric had escaped. From that moment on, he had gone underground.

"Hey buddy, you in there?" Shaker said. "Here's your coffee."

"What? Oh yeah, thanks. Need this right about now." He sipped. "I was just thinking about that night Popper showed up with the knife."

"Figured something like that. You looked pretty grim. Oh, but on a bright note, the ME has some information about that body. He's pretty sure it was a homicide and not just a drowning. He wants us to head down there."

Andy grabbed his cup, "Great, a diversion, let's get the hell out of here."

Chapter 24

July

Following two and a half weeks in the ICU, Nicky had been transferred to a step-down unit where he was closely observed. His medical status was still tenuous. Three weeks later he was progressing well enough to be moved to a regular floor.

Carly had visited Nick frequently during that time. However, she didn't stay too long. During those visits, she spoke with his nurse and discharge planner. She made it clear, that when it was time for him to be released, he would NOT be going to her house. Instead, he should go to a rehab facility closer to his apartment and to his family. She also discussed with them that she would remain the point person until that time. His family including his daughter, had not been to see him and in fact had pretty much written him off; although Carly had kept them informed of his progress.

After she was sure her wishes would be honored, she muscled up her courage and decided it was time to talk to him about those plans. He was still trying to regain a clear thought process, but he was clear enough that he would be able to understand.

She entered his room and was pleased to find him sitting in a recliner, eating his lunch. But he looked like a mess. His once twinkling eyes were glazed over and dilated, probably from all the medications he was still on. His fit body, now sagging, was bruised from the IV's. He looked beat up and fragile in his oversized johnny. His hair was greasy and flat with a bad case of bed head.

"Hey there, you're looking good. How's the food going down?" She said in her most upbeat voice.

He looked up from his plate of mush, "Well, hi." He managed in a hoarse voice. "Better. As long as I take my time, I'm swallowing ok." The breathing tube had also interfered with his swallow reflex. Hopefully, that too would come back with time. "I should sue them for this."

She waited until he was finished, then said, "They told me you're doing well enough to be discharged next week to rehab "

"Yeah, I guess. This all sucks. I can't wait to get out of this fucking place."

"I know," she said, thinking 'you did this to yourself.' "but it's a good thing considering how sick you were."

"Whatever."

She thought, "Man, he still doesn't get it. He should be on his knees thanking the powers that be that he survived, instead he's pissed off at everyone." She went on, "So Nick, there's a few things we need to talk about. Are you up for it?"

"Yeah, sure. What's going on, Carly?"

She knew the only way to say it, was just to say it. Following a deep breath, she blurt it out. "Nick, I don't want us to be together anymore. This has been building for a long time, but there was never a good time to talk. When you get out of here and rehab, you'll be moving to the apartment over the store. I've already cleared that with your sister. I will keep in touch to follow your progress and make sure you get what you need. Do you understand?" There, she did it.

He just glared at her unable to comprehend that she had just broken up with him. Here, when he almost died. "Are you kidding me? You're a cold-hearted bitch, you know that! I can't believe you're doing this!" As quickly as his anger had escalated, it had dropped. "Ok, I understand. I'll be moving back to the apartment."

When she played out this scene in her mind, she imagined that another screaming match would have ensued. She wondered if she missed something. She decided to go on. "Ok, there are a few more things to go over. First, once you're in rehab, I'm going to take you off my insurance. I've already checked and you can get a Husky plan that the state will pay for. You'll need to start paying your cell phone also. I had suspended it when you got sick. So, when you're ready, I'll have it reinstated. There are a few other things, but those were the most important."

"Wow, you really are a manipulative bitch. So, who is he, Carly? Who are you screwing now?" Nick could not fathom that Carly would leave him because of him. He rationalized that there must be another guy in the picture.

"Come on Nicky, you know that's not the case." She answered, trying to keep her cool. "We've been in this spiral for a long time. Yeah, it was great for a while, but then..." she tapered off.

"but then what?" he challenged.

"Look, this is not the time to get into all of this. You need to heal and so do I. I will be here for you. I'd like this to be a decent split."

He slumped back in the chair, his mind ping-ponging back and forth through lapses in concentration. He was struggling to make sense of what she was telling him. She looked at his frail shape and felt sorry for him. However, she knew this was not her fault. None of this would have happened if he hadn't become so aggressive and manipulative. His excessive drinking only amplified matters.

Finally, he said, "You really have this all planned out. Wow, I can't believe you. I'll think it over and let you know my decision. Why don't you just leave now. I can't even look at you. GO!"

"Guilt?" She asked. "Nope, you're not going to lay guilt on me. And there's nothing to think over. I've made up my mind. I will help if I can. We can still talk." In her mind, she was thinking, "lord knows, I'm the only one still talking to you."

"Please leave." He said more forcefully.

Carly decided it was a good time to go. He would have a chance to process things. "Ok, I'll call later. I probably won't come every day, but I will check in with the nurses. I'll see you."

She grabbed her satchel and walked out the door. Moments later she heard the crashing sound as he hurled his lunch tray across the room.

On her ride down in the elevator, Carly remembered how happy and in love they once were. They laughed and enjoyed each other since that first night they met. She couldn't pinpoint when things went wrong. Had the build-up been so gradual that she hadn't seen it coming? Or was it sudden? Right now it felt like one minute he had a great business with a happy-go-lucky attitude; the next he had a chip on shoulder accompanied by a violent temper.

In a short time, he risked losing the family business. He began to take more and more from her. At first, she gave in to his whims to aid him to find whatever it was he was looking for. She thought he loved the store, but she understood he may have needed some success of his own. She just wanted her Nicky back.

Soon, she began to see him drinking excessively. His unprovoked anger became the norm. The final blow came the night he slapped her across the face because she suggested he boil the water before adding the pasta. He had been so drunk, he couldn't remember how to do it.

"If only I knew what happened, maybe we wouldn't be in this place now," she thought as the elevator doors opened. Realizing that she couldn't change the past, she knew she had to move forward and save herself. Obligation or not, soon, Nicky would be out of her life.

Chapter 25

While Nick was recovering, Suzanne had been to visit. Although, he had been her primary patient for about two weeks, at this point, her motives leaned more towards selfishness than caring. He had behaved while in intensive care, but now she needed to gauge his mental status in hopes of diverting any problems he might cause her from here on out. The very act of her caring for him in the ICU could have jeopardized her job should their tumultuous relationship come to light. Considering their past, it might be looked upon as a conflict of interest that may have prejudiced her objectivity and judgement because of her secrecy. Her professionalism was subject to scrutiny. She could not allow that to happen.

She knew Carly visited usually early afternoon, so she timed her visit accordingly to avoid an encounter. She stopped in the doorway and peeked in. "Hi, how are you doing?"

He shifted his gaze away from the TV which seemed to have a hypnotic effect on him. Glassy-eyed and stoned from the Percocet he'd been taking for pain, he said sarcastically, "Suzanne. Great."

"Yeah, it's me. I heard you're going to be discharged next week. That's great news."

"I guess. Why don't you stop the chit-chat and tell me why you're really here."

"Ok, Eric or should I still call you Nicky?" she asked.

"It's Nicky."

"Ok, here's the deal," she continued, "I haven't told anyone that we knew each other or anything about the past for that matter. I was hoping we could keep it that way."

"You're still crazy, you know that? Why would I tell anyone? I'd be just as screwed as you would."

She considered that for a moment, unsure if she should trust anything he said. "Yeah, right, I guess that's true. Okay, then, I guess that's it. I'm sorry about Carly. She seemed nice."

"You're kidding, right? She told you she was going to kick me out? She's more of a bitch than I thought." He answered in disbelief.

"Look I don't know what happened and I really don't care at this point."

"Yeah, yeah, it's all about you. Always covering your ass." He laughed. "Anyway, I've got more important plans to make. All that money, I'm not gonna let her just cut me off."

Suzanne stared at him, wondering what to say. "Just be careful, Eric, don't do anything stupid."

"I told you, my name is Nicky."

She calmly left the room, hoping that the past would stay there. She contemplated what to tell Andy. She had promised him she would let him know when Eric woke up. She didn't exactly break the promise, she just diverted it for a while. She knew he was in the middle of some important investigation which made it easy for her to put things off temporarily.

On her way home, she decided she would simply tell Andy that the patient, Nick Pellegrino, just resembled Eric Popper. True, he had a scar, but she supposed that a scar is not by itself an identifying mark. Many people had scars, after all. Andy had not seen the patient for himself either, so he wouldn't know about the resemblance. Her plan made sense to her. Suzanne didn't want to lie, but this way they could all move on and no one would get hurt.

Later that night, Andy and Suzanne settled in with their first fire of the season. Fall was slowly creeping in, tempting them to begin the hibernation process that accompanied this approaching time of year. In the background, Sting could be heard singing "Brand New Day". Perfect.

"This is great, Andy. It feels so good to kick back. Plus, I'm off the next two days plus the weekend. So, I'm doubly relaxed."

"Don't rub it in." He teased "I gotta tell you, I'm relieved that patient of yours wasn't Eric. What a nightmare that would have been."

"I know, I guess I over-reacted." Changing the subject, she added, "How's your case?"

"I can't really talk about it, but I can tell you it's slow going. Not much evidence left because it's so old."

"That must make it hard." She agreed.

"Yeah, the good thing is our other assignments are keeping us busy. Hey, Suzanne, here's an idea. How about we get away for the weekend? I was thinking of Cape Cod. It should be great this time of year. What do you think?"

She didn't have to think too long. "Yes, let's do it! We could both use a break."

"Then it's settled. I'll make reservations for the Chatham Tides. Let's leave Friday."

Suzanne twirled in the living room. "Yay!!!!."

Chapter 26

At the house on Prospect Hill, Jennifer Diaz sat on the porch with Carly. Of all the women in the house, Carly felt a kinship to Jenn even though they came from different worlds. Jenn had come from an inner city background with a struggling family that had no regard for anything. In contrast, she had focused on earning an associate degree in education. She never had the chance to finish when her life took the turn that brought her to this refuge.

She admired her father and followed in his footsteps. He had a tough life and was sucked into a street gang culture as a young man. Somehow, he managed to pull himself out and find work to support his family when Jenn was in high school. Along with her formal schooling, she had inherited innate street smarts and a unique perceptive nature from her dad. She was able to read people effectively and sniff out friend or foe. Jenn was also equipped with the tools to deal with it. Another inherited trait.

Jenn had known from their first meeting that Carly was exactly who she portrayed herself to be. She wasn't just some famous rich girl looking for a tax break or sympathetic publicity. Her motives were true and ran deep. Jenn liked her instantly.

As they sat, they witnessed a breathtaking sunset. The muted shades of blues and purples melted together, illuminating subtle tones of reds as the sun descended.

Carly said, "You know I thought the most beautiful sunrise I'd ever seen was in Maui. We were 11,000 feet above sea level on the Haleakala volcano. It was magnificent and even spiritual.

A local woman sang a haunting welcome to the sun as it peeked its way above the clouds. I cried, it was so moving. But this sunset tonight just proves that sunrises and sunsets are amazing everywhere."

"You still have a knack for saying things in a way that gets you thinking. But, yeah, you're right, it is a pretty thing to behold." Jenn sat back and took a chance. "So, Carly, I'm gonna be blunt, tell me if I'm over-stepping. What happens now with Nick?"

"Oh, it's ok, Jenn. Well, as far as I know he went to rehab a few days ago. I haven't heard from him, but I do need to call the social worker there to check in."

"Haha, keep your enemies close, as they say, right?"

Carly laughed at Jenn's revelation. "I hate to admit it, but yeah, a good rule to remember."

"Seriously, be firm and don't let him bully you. We both know he'll try."

"I know, I keep waiting for something. I think as long as I know where he is and what he's doing, I can keep on top of it."

Jenn added, "Just remember, you were a victim too, whether or not you knew it. Abuse comes in many forms. Just because he didn't beat the crap out of you doesn't mean you weren't abused. Maybe you should talk to someone, you know, a professional, like we all do. It really helps."

"Yeah, maybe. I never really thought of myself that way, until he was out of my house and I could think clearly and feel free. It's almost like I was brainwashed or something. I hate talking about it because no one gets it. The fear of not knowing what he'd do and what he's capable of is just as big as if he actually did hurt me. I was afraid of every confrontation and where it would lead." Carly shuddered and remembered the constant shouting and name calling. There were also times he tried to grab her after a few too many tequilas. "He bullied everyone, including me. I can't believe I let myself be so sucked in. I feel so ashamed sometimes."

"Just remember, it's not your fault. He chose to drink and to be violent. You didn't make him do those things. And you certainly didn't deserve it"

Carly understood what Jenn was trying to tell her. But she felt uneasy talking about it anymore. Nick had been such a great guy at one time. They had a great relationship. He was attentive to her needs and she to his. Then, he started changing. He was drinking more and more. The temper he held in check became volatile. She never knew what would trigger it. His outbursts were mainly directed at Carly. He lost many friends and most of his family because of this as well. She had learned to tread lightly around him.

"What about Lucy's shower? She's due in December, shouldn't we start planning?"

Jenn smiled at Carly, "Ok, we're changing the subject...got it. Yes, we definitely need to get some planning done. Irene thought we should have it here and of course she volunteered to cook. Gotta love her."

Together, they jotted down a few ideas that Jennifer would talk over with the others when they were all home.

Carly gave Jenn a big hug when she stood to leave. "Thanks for the advice."

THE RULES

Chapter 27

It had been a over a month since the discovery of the body in the river. Andy and Shaker had been waiting for the DNA results. Unlike television, DNA results could take weeks, especially if the situation wasn't dire. Therefore, after patiently waiting, they were understandably anxious to know who this guy was. From the autopsy, Dr. Oates was able to confirm that it was indeed a male in his late thirties. Because of the condition of his organs or lack thereof, the growth status of his bones and teeth was used as a marker for his age.

Dr. Oates also confirmed that the body had been in the water for close to eighteen months. This was incredible since there would normally be extensive deterioration of a body in water. However, the ME stated that because the temperature of the river was unusually cold, decay had been slowed. The bricks they had found on the body also kept his bloated body from bobbing to the surface.

There had been some interesting discoveries during the autopsy. A few broken ribs were found. The radius bone in the victim's arm was broken. There had also been a large crack in the skull close to where the eyes once were. According to Dr. Oates, it appeared the victim had been punched or kicked in the mid-section, grabbed by the arm, then hit in the head with a blunt object. He further explained that due to the severity of the head injury, hemorrhaging probably followed, contributing to the death. Doc Oates ruled the death a homicide. Although, drowning was at the root, the injuries indicated the victim would have probably succumbed anyway.

Dr. Oates led Andy and Shaker to his desk to go over the DNA results, which had arrived that morning. "Ok, here is the final report. I was able to get a few good DNA samples from this unfortunate man's bones. We were lucky to get a match. As you know, not everyone's DNA is in the system."

"The suspense is killing me Doc," Andy said, "who is he?"

"The victim's name is Eric Popper."

Shaker and Andy walked silently to their car after receiving the news. Shaker finally broke the quiet. "What do you think? I don't get it."

"This is all a weird coincidence. The guy's name keeps coming up after all this time; in the hospital and now this body. And you know what? I don't believe in coincidences." Andy agreed, rubbing his forehead.

"I know what you mean. Big rule in investigation; there are no coincidences."

Sitting the car, Andy and Shaker talked over their game plan. Searching the riverbank and currents for the area the body may have been dropped wouldn't help because of the time frame involved. Instead, they needed to do some extensive background research on Eric Popper. It was going to be a long process, but they had to start with the past to learn about this man and what happened to get him to this point.

Chapter 28

August

Carly arrived at the sub-acute nursing facility where Nick was doing his rehab following his discharge from the hospital. After a few days of silence, Nicky had begun badgering her to bring him things he needed. He wanted his laptop and some clothes, along with other personal items. She complied much against her better judgement. She was tentative as she sat in the car, thinking about how to handle this. Her final decision was that she just couldn't face him; she really didn't want to either. She felt her stomach settle the moment she knew she would just bring his stuff to the desk and drop it off with the social worker. She had a choice, after all.

The social worker had told her he would be receiving psychological counseling as well as extensive physical therapy to prepare him for release. Carly hoped he would be accepting of the help. But she knew Nick better than anyone. He would play the game and play it to win. He would convince everyone that he was fine. He would be charming and agreeable; he'd be sure that everyone thought he was smart and basically amazing.

Carly grabbed the boxes from the back of her car. In two trips, she brought them to the desk and requested to see the social worker. On their phone calls, Carly surmised that she would be young. Although she spoke professionally, her voice still had the twang of youth. However, Carly was taken aback when a gaunt female with an anorexic appearance approached her.

The "girl/woman" had reddish burgundy hair; a color that is not acquired naturally. She wore a tiny silver ring in her pointy nose. Her tunic style sweater hung on her elfin frame as though she were playing dress-up in her mother's clothes. In her rational mind, Carly knew she shouldn't judge by appearance. She also knew that this "girl/woman" had to be over twenty-five, at least, to have earned her credentials. Still, she looked about twelve.

"Carly, hi, I'm Kendall." She said as she extended her outstretched hand to Carly.

"Of course you are." Carly inadvertently said out loud. "It's very nice to meet you." Carly was determined to hold her ground and be firm yet friendly. "I brought some things that Nicky had requested. I was hoping you could see that he gets them."

Kendall stared at Carly for a moment in an attempt to make a quick appraisal. "You could bring them to him yourself. I know he's anxious to see you."

Carly thought, "yeah, I bet." She held her ground. "I'd prefer not to see him right now. It's only been a few days. I think he needs to adjust to not having me around."

"Hmm, well, ok, I guess." Although she was a professional by age and schooling, Kendall did not possess the maturity or experience to adequately understand situations such as this. Kendall promptly decided that Carly was basically a bitch as Nicky had described. "Well, suit yourself." She said flatly as she continued to play with her hair.

Carly took note of the attitude in her voice. "Is there a problem here?" She asked at point blank range.

"Um, well, I think as his girlfriend, you need to be more supportive..."

Carly interrupted, "Former girlfriend. I thought I made that clear."

"Oh yeah, sorry, 'former' girlfriend. Anyway, you should still be more compassionate of everything Nick's been through and the road he has ahead of him."

Carly tried to conceal her temper. "take a breath first." She said to herself as the anxiety started its ritualistic ascent from her belly to her chest.

Kendall continued without giving Carly a chance to speak. "It might even be a good idea if the two of you attended counseling together. Nick said how happy and in love you were. Maybe you could even get back together. He's so confused where things went wrong. He's such a great guy, Carly. He's really a delight You know, you shouldn't be so cold-hearted towards him. Have some sympathy."

Carly glared at Kendall in disbelief. "Sympathy?? Are we talking about the same person? Oh, yeah, of course we are. He's bamboozled you already, Kendall. Nicky can appear very charismatic. He uses this talent to get you in his corner. Look, already, you're doing and thinking exactly what he wants. I'm not the bad guy here, Kendall." Carly took another breath and continued speaking, using a tone which resembled the voice of Julia Sugarbaker from Designing Women. It was that flat eloquent way that could cut someone down without them even realizing what happened. "Perhaps, if you were a little older and more experienced, you'd be able to see through all of this. In your position, I would expect objectivity—isn't that one of the rules? Please give these things to Nicky. I'll be in touch with you regarding any insurance documentation I receive as well as discharge plans. I will expect our interaction to be courteous and professional from this point on. I do not want to hear your opinions with regards to my actions. You do not know me, nor will I allow that to occur. I also suggest that if you are going to portray yourself as a social worker and patient advocate, you dress and act the part. No one is going to a trust a twelve-year old's advice in these matters. Good-bye."

Carly dropped the boxes at Kendall's feet and turned toward the door. She tossed her floral scarf over her shoulder for dramatic effect. Kendall stood with her purple painted mouth agape as she watched Carly leave.

Once in her car, Carly knew had to get away from that place. She drove to the Starbucks down the street. She parked and tried to control the shaking. "Well, that was just great," she thought. "Now what?" Once she felt slightly more in control, she calmly walked into Starbucks and ordered her usual –a hot Americano with very little water. At this point, she realized there wasn't any "now what". She would deal with Nick on her own terms in her own way. It became evident that Nicky would portray her as the bad one; unstable, uncaring, and the cause for his situation. The problem was that people would most likely believe him.

"Damn him. He brings out the worst in me. I am not that person at all!"

Chapter 29

Nicky was satisfied to have some of his personal items in his possession. He set up his laptop on the desk in the corner of his room. He had so much work to do. He began searching the internet for income opportunities. He piled up all the crumpled scraps of paper he had been taking meticulous notes on. He scribbled more ideas on the yellow lined legal pad that had just arrived. He quickly wrote down the names and phone numbers that he would need to contact.

He was still having concentration issues which interfered with his focus. He continued to need Percocet which by now had replaced the alcohol portion of his addictive personality. He frequently found his thought process interrupted with thoughts about Carly. His rage still festering.

He appeared disheveled in his baggy flannels and stained tee shirt. Carly had bought him new comfortable clothes, but he preferred these old ones. He sat hunched over the computer, writing, planning, and thinking. To some, he would resemble Wyle E. Coyote, plotting and planning the demise of the roadrunner. He feverishly jotted notes with accompanying charts and nodded to himself in victory for his brilliant ideas. The only thing missing was the ACME supply company and their devious devices. He paid no attention to the fact that those devices usually backfired.

"Yes!" he grinned.

When Carly arrived home, she was still annoyed with the whole "Kendall" thing. She walked in her home, happy to have the peace again. She took a few deep breaths to regain her composure and put Kendall behind her.

On her way into the kitchen, she stopped to straighten her good luck elephants that were on an end table. They usually faced the front door which meant good energy would enter her home. Now they were pointed away.

"I must have knocked them when I was dusting," she thought.

She poured a glass of wine, thinking about what she might make for dinner. She decided to fix a chicken and pepper dish with quinoa and broccoli. It was one of her favorites. As she started preparation for her dinner, she opened a cabinet to grab a saucepan. It wasn't there. "Where the heck did I put it?" she wondered. She opened a few more cabinets and ended up finding it in the dishwasher.

"I never use the dishwasher for this," she thought. "I must be losing it with this Nicky crap." She pulled it out, grabbed an apron and started dicing the peppers.

Later that evening when she opened her closet to put away her shoes, she discovered that her normally organized boots had been rearranged. A chill washed over her. "Someone's been here. Is that possible?"

Chapter 30

Andy arrived home later that evening, happy to see Suzanne. He stood quietly in the doorway watching her. She was chopping vegetables for the pasta dish she would prepare for dinner. Her Pandora station was playing Steve Winwood tunes. She sipped her wine and sang along. Suzanne was satisfied with the knowledge that this perfect little life would continue exactly that way. The short upheaval of Eric's reappearance was now put to rest. She felt confident she would not hear from him again. And Andy would never know.

Andy smiled taking in the scene of how content Suzanne was at this moment. He knew he would have to break the spell, but not just yet. "Hey, babe," He said sneaking up behind her. "I was just going to grab you and smother you with kisses, but I thought I'd probably end up giving you a heart attack." They both laughed.

"Either that or I'd have beat you silly with my skillet." Taking a sip of her wine, she offered him a beer. She knew he looked forward to that beer at the end of the day.

Andy helped her with the food prep which took longer than it should have. They were interrupted by impromptu impulses to dance in the kitchen. Finally, together, they put their meals on their plates and brought them to the table.

"Wow, this is awesome." Andy declared as he licked his lips.

"It did come out good. It was a joint effort."

They laughed and talked as they ate, but Andy's news was lurking in the back of his mind. When they were done, they began to clean up. He knew it had to be now.

"So, Suzanne, I've got something serious to talk to you about." He said as he put the leftovers in the plastic containers.

"Oh no, what Andy? I don't like that tone of voice." She continued to wash the pots feeling apprehensive.

"Well, here it is. Remember that body that was washed up a couple of weeks ago?

"Yeah, what about it?" The relief she felt was instant.

"We ID'd it. I don't know how else to say this. The body is Eric Popper."

The dread she felt was instant. "What? Eric? How is this possible?"

"Well, that's what we have to find out. Anyway, there was no evidence at the scene since first, it's so old and second, it looks like he only washed up there. So, Shaker and I have to start at the beginning. We need to trace Eric up to this point." He continued, "I hate to ask this, but I need you to come down to the station tomorrow to give a statement."

Suzanne turned pale. "A statement? About what?"

"Well, background, stuff like that. Maybe something will jog your memory that might help lead to something else. That's the best we can do for now."

Closing the dishwasher, she took a gulp rather than a sip of her wine. "I thought this was behind me...us. It was so long ago." Her heart was saying no way, to Andy, but out loud, she heard herself say, "I guess that makes sense. Sure, what time should I be there?" she added reluctantly.

Later that evening while Andy was in the shower, Suzanne grabbed one of his cigarettes and her sweatshirt. She stepped out onto the back deck and lit up. At this point she was grateful that Andy still smoked. Suzanne had not smoked since she was in college so many years ago. She coughed and gagged a little with the first puff, but soon enough, the ritual became instinctual.

"How could this be?" she analyzed. "Eric's body? It just doesn't add up. I wish I knew what was going on. Maybe I was wrong about Eric saying he was that Nicky guy. No, I'm sure he admitted it. I should have talked to the girlfriend more. I have to talk to him but I guess I should wait until after I talk to the police." She threw the cigarette butt in the can that Andy used as his ashtray. With her logic in panic mode, she said, "Damn-it-all! What a freakin' mess."

Chapter 31

Suzanne called her supervisor and explained that she would need to take a personal day; an emergency of sorts had come up. Her supervisor was sympathetic and assured her it would be fine. She also told Suzanne to call her if she needed anything.

Suzanne parked at the police station in the visitor lot. She arrived a few minutes early so she sat in the car, trying to stay calm. She wasn't sure what they would ask her, but she wasn't naïve enough to think they wouldn't ask about their past together. She dreaded having to rehash that period in her life.

When she decided to go inside, she approached the window and told the dispatcher she had an appointment to make a statement with Andy Gallagher and Phil Shaker. The dispatcher asked her to have a seat while she waited for an escort to take her through the mysterious locked doors leading to the squad room.

While she sat, she couldn't help but feel guilty. She supposed it was natural to feel this way in the police station waiting room. Suzanne assumed that by merely sitting in the green vinyl chair, she was presumed guilty of something. She found herself trying extra hard to look normal. She risked a smile when she realized how silly she was being. She stared at the door, willing it to open. The more she stared, the more massive it became until it loomed over her like the gates of Mordor. She needed this to be over. After what seemed like days, it was actually only ten minutes, Andy opened the door.

"Hey there. Ready?"

She nodded and stood silently, following him through the guarded entrance into the unknown.

Andy led Suzanne to a musty interview room where she was greeted by Shaker. He motioned for her to sit. She was surprised when she realized it looked exactly the way she envisioned from the cop shows she watched on TV. There was an old metal desk in the center with two uncomfortable chairs on each side. She expected that it would be more upscale in a town like Farmington with all of its money. But it also brought back memories of the police station she had been in before when she reported Eric's vandalism. She supposed that was the point.

Andy and Shaker asked questions and took notes. Andy reviewed the past reports including the night that Eric attacked both of them. He was hoping some new information would come to light from locked memories.

Shaker attempted to approach the interview from a different angle. Instead, he asked Suzanne about Eric's friends and family. He thought that if they could learn more about his connections, he might unearth someone with a grudge. As Suzanne spoke, Shaker realized that Eric had several dealings that should be pursued. It sounded like he had a way of pissing people off, if things didn't go his way.

At last the interview was over. Suzanne stood to leave. She was eager to go home. Andy walked her to her car.

"You did great in there. I know it was hard. But now we've got a few names to follow up on. And that's more than we had before. Thank you for doing that."

"I wanted to help." She stopped short of saying anything more.

He opened her car door and gave her a kiss before she pulled away. Suzanne checked her rearview mirror and watched

Andy disappear into the station. She pulled out her phone and made the call.

"Hey, we have to talk."

"What now? I'm kind of busy."

"Yeah, well, I'm busy too. But something happened and I'm a little confused."

"Well, you can come here if you want. There's room on my guest list." He smirked.

"Absolutely not. I can't be seen there. Can we meet somewhere. Can't you get a pass or something?"

"Geez, you're something else. No, I can't get a pass, not yet anyway. But I can meet you outside, say top of the driveway?"

"Fine, I'll be there in about twenty minutes."
"Hey, bring me a double cheeseburger and some fries too. The food here sucks."

She ended the call and drove towards the highway.

Chapter 32

Andy and Shaker split the list of names Suzanne had given them. They would contact the individuals to categorize those who warranted more in-depth interviews.

Suzanne had revealed that Eric was adopted, so Shaker started by searching for Eric's adoptive parents, Sam and Millie Popper. They were in their forties when they were granted the adoption. It was the happiest day of their lives. They had tried for years to have a child of their own. They loved Eric and provided him with everything he needed to grow strong, happy, and well adjusted.

Shaker discovered that Sam had passed away a few years ago from pneumonia at the age of seventy. Millie was residing in an assisted living facility, following Sam's death. She was still healthy, but this residence provided her with her own private apartment and no maintenance. The biggest plus was the social opportunities that she was afforded. If she had remained in her modest home, she would have become another isolated shut-in.

After speaking with Millie on the phone, she agreed to a visit. When Shaker arrived, he was pleasantly surprised to find Millie waiting for him, smiling. She had a pot of coffee brewing while she placed a plate of homemade banana bread on the table. She motioned for him to sit.

As she prepared the cups, he quickly glanced around the apartment. It was impeccably clean and furnished traditionally in neutral tones. He judged that it was always kept this way and not just a quick cleanup job for his benefit. He noticed some photos on the credenza where the television perched.

Millie herself, was tall; probably considered statuesque in her younger days. She dressed in black slacks and a plain beige cardigan. She also maintained her appearance wearing a chin length hairstyle and light makeup.

"Detective Shaker, what exactly can I do for you?" She sat across from him.

"Well, Mrs. Popper..."

"Please call me Millie." She interrupted.

"Okay, Millie, first I have to deliver some bad news. It's about Eric."

"What's that boy done now?" She asked as though he were a teenager who had just thrown a baseball through a window.

"Well, we found a body in the river, and the identification indicated that it's Eric." He paused a moment to let that sink in. Shaker always hated this part of his job.

Millie put her cup down and stood up. She turned from Shaker and walked towards the photos. Picking one up, she asked, "Are you sure it was him?"

"Yes, we are. The body had been in the water a long time, so the DNA was all we had to go on. It was conclusive." He paused. "Are you ok?"

She replaced the picture frame near the tv. "Yes, I'm fine. I can't say I wasn't expecting this."

"If you don't mind me saying this, that's not the reaction I was expecting. When was the last time you heard from Eric"

She thought for a moment. "Probably about three or four years ago. Before that, he would call every few months. Usually he wanted money."

"Did you give it to him?"

"Of course I did. I'm his mother. Eric was not a very affectionate boy. It was his nature—aloof, I guess you'd call it. I guess I figured giving him the money was a way to know he still needed me. But I have to tell you that if I ever refused, he would become quite angry with me like I owed him. So I didn't mind. Sam and I had it and if it kept our boy in touch with us, well that was ok."

"Did you see him during that time?"

"No, I would deposit what he wanted into his account. The last time I actually saw him was about three or four years ago."

"So, that was the last time you heard from him too. Do you have any idea why?" Shaker questioned.

"Not really. I just figured he didn't need me anymore."

Millie took a deep breath that she exhaled with a sigh.

"Detective, how did Eric die?"

"I'm sorry, Millie, it looks like a homicide. I was hoping maybe you knew what he'd been involved in. Or maybe you'd know some of his friends."

She shook her head and looked down at the coffee that was now cold. "I see. I didn't really know his friends. I did worry that he'd fall in with the wrong crowd as he got older. I can tell you that growing up, he didn't have many. The friends he did have were kids that could do things for him."

"What kind of things?"

"Oh homework, give him rides, lend him money—things like that."

Shaker asked, "What about when he was older?"

"No friends that I know of. I'm sorry, I'm not being much help here."

"You're doing great, Millie. I'm getting a good idea of who Eric was.

Let's get back to the money for a minute. Do you know why he needed it? Didn't he work?"

"Yes, he worked at an insurance company. I can't remember which one. But he also had other jobs. (H)worked at a car dealership, as a bartender, and he even drove a bus for a while. He'd always have a reason for needing money. It was always to help pay bills or start a new venture, buy a car."

"Millie, what about the adoption? What agency handled it? Anything unusual about the process?" He asked changing subjects.

"Detective, I had not adopted before, so I really can't say if anything was unusual." Shaker nodded and she continued, "We went through a private attorney. The adoption agencies were skeptical about handling us because of our age. We were in our early forties at the time."

"Do you remember the attorney's name? Do you have the documents?"

"I have the paperwork, but it will take some doing to find it since I've moved. The attorney? Hmm, it was so long ago, his name was Gustave or Gustin...something like that."

"Will you call me if you find the papers? It might be helpful."

"Ok, I'll take a look around."

"Thank you, Millie. I know this was hard, but I appreciate your time."

"You're welcome, Detective. I wish I could tell you more."

As he stood to leave, Shaker added, "I'll be in touch with any information that comes up." He gave her his card in case she remembered something else.

When she closed the door behind Shaker, Millie thought, "Well, Eric, I guess someone finally paid you back."

Chapter 33

The next evening, Carly heard her phone ping with an incoming text. She was still on edge. She feared it was the police with news. Realistically, she knew they wouldn't text her. They probably wouldn't call her either. They acted like they thought she was a nutcase calling about a misplaced saucepan and some disorganized shoes. Maybe she was. Hesitantly, she looked at her phone and saw it was from Nick:

Hey, thanks for bringing me all that stuff.

She thought it sounded ok and replied:

You're welcome. I'm glad you got it.

Instantly, he responded:

Why couldn't you take the time to see me?

She typed her answer in the form of a white lie:

I had an appointment, but I wanted to be sure you had what you needed.

He added:

What I need is to see you. It would be nice if you could spare a few minutes for me from your busy schedule.

Oh boy, she thought but did not respond. He wrote again:

> There are some other things I need. I'll send you another list.

She wondered what else he could possibly need, but realized it was his way of getting her to come back.

She replied:

> Ok, lmk what you want. I'll bring it when I can.

She closed the texts and within minutes, she received an email from him with a few more items. Carly usually faced things head-on, but right now, her protective instincts told her to avoid reading the email. She couldn't even think about it.

Instead, she picked up the phone and called his sister to give her an update. Although, they had spoken frequently during Nick's hospitalization, she had not been to visit Nick. Carly knew Ann felt bad about the circumstances, but she also knew that Ann was fed up by Nick's antics. He had mismanaged the family business almost causing it to close. Thankfully, Ann and her husband had stepped in and were able to salvage it. They had to pay vendors, creditors, and staff out of their own pockets to stay afloat. Finally, they were back on track and seeing a profit again. Ann did not want anything to do with her brother at this point.

Carly figured she was on a roll and should touch base with his daughter again. Daniella was nineteen and attending a local college. Their conversation was brief. His daughter had also written him off. Although Nicky thought he was being funny, she was tired of the way he always ridiculed her with his stupid put-down jokes and belittled her mother. She made a conscious decision that her life was better at this point without her father.

Carly checked the obligations off her list. Exhausted, she grabbed a book and went to bed.

Chapter 34

While Shaker was interviewing Millie Popper, Andy was checking a list of previous employers for Eric. He made a few phone calls to weed out anyone that would merit a personal visit. The list was extensive, comprised of about ten businesses to call. His former bosses had little information to give Andy. There were no red flags, only the usual comments about his temper when he didn't get his way. However, two of the bosses gave names of coworkers that had had altercations with Eric. Andy jotted down the names.

His first call was to Josh Dunning. Josh agreed to meet with Andy that afternoon. When Andy arrived at the coffee shop, he was met by a beefy guy with hairy arms and a thick neck. He had tufts of black hair poking out from the collar on his shirt. Andy figured he had a hairy back as well. Josh spoke with a Brooklyn accent that sounded to Andy as if it were phony. Probably to render the appearance of a tough guy to match his size. He also tried to sound intelligent when he spoke. However, he often used the wrong words in context or mispronounced them which signaled to Andy that he had a limited vocabulary and most likely limited intelligence.

It seemed that Eric and Josh had been friends at one point at a local bar where they worked together. At some point Josh indicated that there had been an argument ---or as Josh had said, "they had altercated". Andy thought, "What?" But he figured out what Josh was getting at.

When he asked more questions, it seemed likely a friendly competition had begun. Andy continued, "So tell me about the contest, Josh."

"Well, you know, it was like one of those drink contests. Martinis. There's like so many fancy ones out there these days. Our boss thought it would bring in the customers if we um, had a contest." He sipped his coffee.

"Go on Josh." Andy said, as he remained quiet and allowed Josh to keep talking. One of the rules of investigation is to create uncomfortable silences so the interviewee feels the need to fill it.

"Well, um, we're goin' along, having fun. The customers was eatin' it up. Ya know, they got to vote and all. Anyways, Eric got a little serious on me. I'm pretty sure he was like hoking' stuff in my drinks to make 'em taste bad. Guess he wanted to win bad. So, then this one night, he put some real hot jalapeno sauce in the martini I was makin'. Man, it would have been an epic drink. Ya know, it was like a drink with a kick. A little spicy but sweet. I used some cinnamon. I was callin' it the 'cinnamatini'. Anyway, this chick tastes it and starts hoking'. They had to take her the hospital. Turned out she was like allergic to jalapenos. So the contest stopped and I um, never forgave Popper for 'sabaturing' my drink. I coulda won, ya know. Man, I hated that guy after that."

"Ok Josh. When was the last time you saw Eric?'

"hmm, jeez, I guess the last time we 'conversated' was about five years ago. He quit that bar and I never seen him again."

"Dead end, telling the truth," Andy thought. "Ok, Josh, thanks for meeting me. Here's my card. If you think of anything else, give me a call." Andy paid the bill and they each went their separate way.

Andy met Shaker back at the precinct to compare notes. They had known a lot about Eric from Suzanne's relationship with him. The others they spoke with confirmed their picture of Eric. The problem was they had not gathered any information that would lead to motive or a person of interest. So far, all they knew was that Eric Popper was not a nice guy.

"So what now, buddy?" Shaker asked.

Scratching his head, Andy thought for a moment. "I'm at a loss. Is it worth looking at the adoption stuff? Maybe he found his birth parents and he was trying to get money from them to keep quiet."

Shaker grinned, "I think you watch too much TV, but I guess it wouldn't hurt. I mean it's not like we've got anything else. Man, I wish this wasn't so old, you know? We'd at least be able to find some physical evidence."

"I know what you mean. The techs have been combing the riverbank going all the way up to New Hartford. But we seriously can't expect them to find anything at this point."

Frowning, Shaker said, "So, let's get over and check the adoption records. Millie Popper said it was a private adoption through an attorney. She couldn't remember his name. Maybe we can find it in the records."

"You're on, let's get out of here."

Andy and Shaker started to leave when the captain approached them. "Guys, any progress on the river homicide?"

"Hey cap. No, we don't have any leads. Seems like after the incident with Suzanne and me, he went underground. From the people we talked to, no one had seen or heard from him since about that time." Andy told him.

"Alright, so that was what four years ago? And he died about eighteen months ago. So, what the hell was he into in those two years between?"

"Don't know, but yeah, we've got a time frame narrowed down. We were going over to take a look at the adoption records. It's probably another dead end, but at least we'll know we've covered all the bases." Shaker added.

"You're probably right, but go ahead." The captain agreed that every piece of information should be scrutinized.

After comparing notes, Andy and Shaker made entries into their laptops and headed out. On the way, Shaker said, "Andy, I've got an idea. I know we're going to look into this attorney, but I read something recently that might come in handy if we don't get anywhere with him."

"Ok, go on."

"Well, you know those websites where you can find your genealogy and family trees? Andy nodded. "So some of them have you submit a DNA sample and they tell you where your heritage is from. Anyway, there were a few stories about people who found they had siblings they didn't know about. Seems that the DNA samples flagged other samples that showed strong matches."

"You're kidding, right?"

Shaker shook his head, "No, I'm serious. There was one story where the family found out there was another kid out there because the father had an affair. The kid from the affair and one of the kids from the family had submitted their DNA. The results came back with a strong match and the site sent a message to both sides saying, 'hey, here's some family you might want to contact'. Shit storm, right?"

"That's incredible. And I see where you're going."

"Yeah, I wonder if Doc Oates could submit Popper's sample to the site. I guess we'd have to check if that's even legal. But how cool would that be if there was a hit?"

"Leave it to you to know about this, let alone think of this plan."

Shaker continued, "Well, I thought maybe it could be a backup plan. You know in case we get nowhere with the attorney."

"Oh mighty, Shaker, master of trivia, I love the plan. I think we should do it anyway. Let's talk to the DA first." Andy said.

Chapter 35

Nicky worked hard at rehab. His desire to get better was motivated by his need to get back to business. He complied with the counseling he was receiving as well as the physical therapy. Each day, he was stronger than the day before. He vowed he wouldn't be stuck there too long. He had come so far in a brief period. The doctors had written him off for dead, but somehow, he survived. He would make it the rest of the way.

He was feeling quite smug at the prospect of being a nuisance to Suzanne. "Just a little payback," he thought. He smiled, thinking how stressed and angry she was when she came to meet him yesterday. He was getting a kick out of seeing her squirm. He played innocent, claiming he had no idea what she was ranting on about. But he did really enjoy the greasy cheeseburger she brought.

Then there was Carly. She was the one who would pay. Things were going so well. They really had a good thing. Then the selfish bitch tosses him out because he got sick and she didn't want to take care of him. He thought about how she had all the details worked out, nice and pat. Well, he'd be damned if he'd go live in that crappy apartment above the store, answering to his condescending arrogant sister. Accepting help from Ann and her pompous husband was not an option.

He knew he'd have to work the angle of Kendall, the social worker. She was quickly becoming one of his fans. He just wanted her to speed up the discharge process which included a state funded apartment of his choosing, and a monthly income. Sweet. Yep, Nicky Pellegrino would be coming back.

"'The Future's So Bright I Gotta Wear Shades.' That'll be my new theme song. Yes, it will! Who sang that, anyway?" His brain short-circuited for a minute, then bingo! "ZZ Top, how could I forget?"

Chapter 36

Suzanne was confused after her meeting with Nicky. She didn't understand what was happening. She wanted answers, but he was being evasive. He also appeared to enjoy her distress. She decided she would do some investigating of her own to figure things out.

Since receiving the text from Nicky last night, Carly shuddered every time the phone rang. She knew she'd have to answer it at some point. Ignoring it would only make his anger fester. So dutifully, she packed up another box of the things he insisted he needed. She had no idea why he wanted some of the items since he was in the nursing home. For example, what would he need a kettle bell for? She decided that having those personal items probably gave him a modicum of control and a sense that he still owned something. Whatever the reason, she would comply if only to maintain the status quo, preserving peace.

The ringing jarred her from her thoughts. She took a breath and answered, seeing that it was him---again.

"Hi Nick, I was just getting those things packed up for you." She told him, attempting to sound upbeat.

"Oh good, that's what I was calling about. I need you to deposit about $500 into my account too. I need to have some cash until they get my disability started."

Carly frowned, "What happened to the money I deposited when you first got there? I can't keep giving you money."

He burst in, "It's the least you can do after you kicked me out."

Not wanting to start anything, she said, "Fine, I'll stop at the bank on my way. I'm thinking of heading up there about two this afternoon."

"Oh, that's great, I'm really looking forward to seeing you, Carly. Maybe we can grab lunch or something. You know, like a first date. What do you think?"

"Oh man," she thought. "I'll think about lunch. Don't you have to get a pass or something?"

"Yeah, true, maybe just bring me food. Yeah, that'll work."

They hung up with Carly thinking she handled it ok, especially the date part. She hated giving him more money. It felt like she was paying blackmail to pacify him. She also sensed that his emotions and reactions were all over the place—up and down. She wondered what medications he was taking. He seemed so erratic.

She packed up two more boxes and threw them in the car. The fact that she had to play along in this game was just stupid. It was making her crazy. She should just tell him what he could do with his freaking kettle balls. She was so sick and tired of it all. Maybe he should have died. "No, that's not very nice of me." She scolded herself. But she couldn't deny that the thought had crossed her mind. However, that was more than likely the problem. In her attempts to be "nice" and avoid confrontation, she contributed to the creation of the situation. After this visit, she promised herself she would not go there again. She could be strong. No more being a victim, as Jenn had put it.

On her way to see Nicky, Carly stopped at the Prospect house. When she arrived, she found no one there except for

Jackson. He was standing at the kitchen counter, heating up a plate that Irene had made for him. He had pushed his readers on top of his head, so they'd be ready in an instant, should something require reading. The sleeves of his long sleeve polo shirt were pushed up to his elbows. He watched the microwave carousel turn as the aroma of the chicken parm wafted through the room. Carly smiled, as she watched him impatiently tap his fork on the counter.

Carly always thought Jack was an attractive man in bookish sort of way. She liked his gentle manner and calming presence. He also had an unpredictable sense of humor that came out of nowhere. She didn't know much about him personally, except for his work here. Nonetheless, she always relished the talks they had.

Jack didn't realize Carly had been standing in the doorway until the microwave signaled that his food was finally ready. He heard clapping coming from behind him and turned to see her smiling at him.

"Well, it's finally done." She said. "I was worried you might starve."

He pushed his sleeves up again, feeling embarrassed, "Yes it is, thank god. How long have you been standing there? I hope I didn't do anything silly. I wouldn't want you think less of me."

"Haha, no, you just looked like a hungry guy waiting for his food."

"Whew, that's a relief. Hey, you want some? Irene left a big container in the fridge."

"Oh yeah, maybe just a little. It really does smell great." Carly grabbed a plate and loaded it up.

"That's a little? Jack asked. "Where do you put it?"

Carly thought for a minute and replied, "I've been asked that before."

When her food was warm, she took her plate and sat with Jack at the table. For a few minutes, they ate in silence. Carly noticed how relaxed she was feeling.

"This is amazing. Irene is a fabulous cook." She commented.

"Yeah she is. I keep telling her she should do something with it."

Carly was surprised by this. "Like what? You mean a restaurant?"

He put down his fork and took a sip of his water. "I don't know about a restaurant. But maybe catering or something along those lines."

"What an interesting idea, Jack. Do you think it's something we should think more seriously about?"

"Oh, I don't know Carly. I guess we could talk to her." He took another bite. "So, I didn't expect to see you today. Everyone is out."

"I know, I forgot that everyone would be gone by now."

"Well, since it's just us," he said, "how are you? What's going on?"

"Oh I'm good. Just trying to deal with everything. It's really a pain, you know. He always wants something."

Nodding Jack said, "I know, but you have to be firm and just tell him not to call anymore. This is his way of keeping his control over you. It's classic."

"Yeah, I guess I do know that, but I feel sorry for him. I'm the only one he has to talk to. Plus, it helps me to know what he's up to and if I do what he wants, he won't hurt me."

"Carly, did you hear what you just said? You shouldn't have to do what he wants. You broke up with him—end of story, right? I know you feel sorry for him on some level, but think of yourself now too. Look, I've only known you for what, one, two years? Anyway, you strike me as someone who digs in to get things done. You're determined. So, don't let this guy take that away from you. Pick yourself up and face it head on. That's the Carly Mancuso I know."

"You're right. I know you are, Jack. He just makes me feel so wishy-washy. Have you ever had to deal with anything like this?"

"Well, not personally. But I counsel a lot of victims who like you, keep getting sucked back in for different reasons." Trying to keep it light, he added, "But, hey, I did have an ex-girlfriend once who stalked me."

She smiled and asked, "So what did you do?"

"I stalked her right back. She didn't like it much and finally she stopped. Guess she got sick of seeing me."

They both laughed as Jack helped Carly bring the dishes to the sink.

"Jack," she said, "thanks for your honesty. I appreciate it. It's a real eye opener to hear someone else's impression." Looking at her watch, she added, "oh man, I'd better get going so I can – what did you say? -face it head on." She grabbed her purse and called to him from the door, "sorry to leave you with the dishes."

Jackson just laughed as he turned on the faucet. He hoped she could stay strong enough to get away once and for all.

As Carly drove off, she smiled thinking about Jack's pep talk. She knew he was right, everyone was. She just didn't understand why she let Nick control her like he did. She realized part of it stemmed from her dislike of confrontation with a little fear thrown in. The other part was probably attributed to the desire of preserving his feelings. That is, if he had any.

She reminisced about other parts of her life. She had always been a goal setter. She was unique in that she was usually able to see those goals to completion and success. How did that saying go? "She believed she could, so she did." She smiled at that thought, appreciating that it had been one of her life rules.

Sally had pointed out how she just walked away from a promising singing career because her dreams were bigger than that. True, she spent a few years after that exploiting life as a way to find herself. She needed to do it that way. After all, she had spent all of her twenties in the spotlight, speeding through life but not really living it.

She would never forget the first time she traveled alone with her own agenda. It was an exhilarating experience when she walked off the plane in Seattle. She had made her own arrangements, knowing she could do whatever she wanted without any time constraints. The first few hours of that trip proved somewhat bewildering.

Carly had telephoned her hotel and asked them to send the town car to pick her up. When the car arrived, she confirmed with the driver that she was sent by the Executive Hotel. She threw her bags in the trunk. When she got in the car, there was another passenger joining her. Carly attempted to make conversation with the tall cocky blonde of twenty-something.

The blonde acted smug and superior when she spoke to Carly. She told Carly that her fabulous boyfriend had sent the car for her. He owned a computer business on the Lake Forrest side of Seattle. As the conversation continued, and Carly saw what she thought was downtown Seattle pass her by, she finally spoke up. Something was not right.

"Excuse me," she asked the driver. "My hotel is downtown. Where are we going?"

Simultaneously, the driver and blonde girl looked at Carly in disbelief. The driver hedged the question but finally proceeded to inform Carly, that this was an independent ride service.

"So, you're not from the Executive Hotel? Why didn't you say that when I asked you?"

Snapping her compact shut, blonde girl glared at Carly. "Are you kidding?"

The driver apologized. "Don't worry, I'll bring you to the hotel."

Carly snapped, "That's not the point. The point is you picked me up and said you were from the hotel when I asked. Now I'm spending an extra hour or more in your car when I could have been settling in at my hotel already. The point is I had a ride, who by the way, is probably waiting for me at the airport. Now I'm also going to have to pay you. Or is that why you did it? I just can't believe this. I'll just get out when you drop her off."

"No, no," the driver said. "I'll bring you to the hotel."

"Listen, I can call my own taxi."

In the end, blonde girl was dropped off and sauntered off to the waiting arms of blonde guy. Carly assumed that was her fabulous boyfriend who owned his own computer business. He didn't look so fabulous to her.

Carly conceded that this shady independent driver could bring her to the hotel. Unfortunately, that trip took another hour. The driver had problems navigating the traffic and the one-way streets. She circled around the hotel many times. "So near and yet so far", Carly thought each time they passed it.

Ultimately, at a stop sign, Carly declared, "I'm getting out here. I can walk to the hotel."

"Oh no, I can bring you." The driver explained.

"Don't bother. At the rate you're going, I'll be ready to go back to the airport by the time you figure it out. Please open the trunk." Carly got out, grabbed her suitcases and trudged up the steep hill in downtown Seattle to her hotel.

It was totally worth all of that initial aggravation. The hotel was fantastic. The city itself was full of hidden treasures. The views were spectacular as was the food and of course the coffee. Although it was a funny story, Carly did, however, learn a valuable lesson on this first trip alone. Don't take anything for granted—check and recheck. She figured she was lucky that time, but man-oh-man, that driver could have been anyone. Note to self--next time, check ID.

"Yep," she smiled, "that about sums it up. I really did have a terrific time." She looked up and noticed she was coming up on the exit for Nick's rehab. "If I can handle that, I can handle this."

Chapter 37

Carly arrived at the Lakeside Rehabilitation facility just before two p.m. as planned. She sucked in a deep breath and promised herself that this would be it. She would be cordial, as always, not wanting to provoke him. However, she would be firm and stand her ground.

When she walked in she found Nick pacing back and forth in the lobby. His methodical stride conveyed the appearance of a caged animal plotting escape. For someone who was anticipating a visitor, he seemed much too preoccupied with his own agenda. He never even noticed when the door dinged, signaling that someone had entered.

"Nick?" She said cautiously as though she were waking someone from a nightmare.

He turned and focused his glassy eyed stare on her. "Finally, I've been waiting for you."

"I'm right on time. It's just two o'clock. How are you?"

"Whatever. I'm just great." He sarcastically replied. He took a moment to return to reality. "It's really nice to see you. You look great."

Feeling somewhat relieved, but still on guard, Carly said, "Thanks. So, I've got the rest of your stuff. I'll run out and get it."

"I'll help you, honey. The boxes are probably heavy."

"Hmmm, why is he being so nice?" she thought and said, "Oh, thanks, that would be great."

They quickly picked up the boxes from her car and carried them to Nick's room. The patient area where he was living smelled, to put it bluntly. The pungent stench of mold, sweat, with undertones of urine smacked Carly in the face when she walked on the floor. She took slow breaths attempting to quell the rising nausea she was feeling.

Nick was fortunate to have a private room. It was musty and old, badly in need of renovation as was the rest of the place. Placing the boxes on the cracked linoleum floor, he told her to sit. Trying to be nonchalant, she took a seat on the plastic desk chair, avoiding anything with fabric where bodily fluids and sickening bacteria might be colonizing.

Nick started going through the boxes when Carly asked how things were going. He told her he was feeling strong. He said Kendall, the social worker, was working on paperwork for housing, furniture, and services that he might need. He hoped to be out in a couple of weeks.

"Wow, that sounds great, Nick. I'm happy you're doing so well."

"Yeah, I am. Hey, do you think once I'm out we could go out? Maybe lunch or a nice dinner? What do you think?"

She hesitated and gave herself a pep-talk. "Nick, let's get you better first. We'll talk about that later." She said. But she was thinking, "Coward. Be firm."

He continued to rummage through the boxes. "Where's the real estate investment DVD? I see the book, but no DVD."

"Oh, I couldn't find it. I looked where you told me to look. I even checked the file cabinet. Aren't some of the other DVD' similar?"

"That's not the point. I wanted that one! Jeez, Carly, I ask you to do one thing and you can't even get that right. I can't believe you!"

"What?" She asked as she felt herself starting to seethe.

"Never mind, never mind, I think I lent it to Allan." He said, scratching his head. He looked confused, liked he forgot what he was doing. Suddenly, he added in excitement, "Oh, great, my workout DVD," as if he just found a big wad of cash."

Carly sat and watched for a few minutes, tentatively sitting still. She could see how unfocused he was as he continued pawing through the boxes. She was careful not to say anything that might agitate him.

After a few minutes, he said, "This is great. There are a few more things I need. I'll put a list together for you."
Carly scrunched her eyebrows in confusion, unaware that he saw it. "What's the matter?" he asked.

"Huh? Oh, I was just thinking that I brought you just about everything."

"Oh, well I'll let you know. Hey, it was great talking to you. I'll walk you out."

Now she was really puzzled. They hadn't talked at all and now he was ushering her out. "I'll just go with it," she thought. "Ok, take care." She said.

"You're leaving?" He asked.

"I'm sorry, I thought you said you'd walk me out."

"Don't tell me what I said, I know what I said! That's your problem, Carly, you always think you're right. You really piss me off sometimes!"

"Well, I can stay a little longer, maybe I misunderstood." She answered.

"No, that's ok. I have a lot to do now. I'll call you later, ok?" He bent over to give her a kiss; she shuddered. "Love you." "See you later, Nick."

When Carly started to drive away, she thought, "Wow, that was really weird. He's crazier than ever. I am not going back."

Nick stood at this window and watched her drive off. He thought, "That went well. I kept my cool. She'll come back."

Chapter 38

Suzanne felt grateful to have this day off. She had a few errands to take care of. But she also had some items that needed to be addressed when Andy wasn't around. Suzanne wished she had a friend. Although, she could confide in Andy about most things, she couldn't tell him about this. At first, she thought Nicky was Eric, which posed problems, however, now she wasn't so sure. Nicky seemed nicer, but still, something didn't feel right. She really had no place to go with her instincts.

She thought about calling Carly Mancuso, but that might just be weird. Still, she might be able to find information about Carly's Nicky that would be helpful to her. She'd have to think about it. This was all so confusing.

Maybe she could suggest in a subtle way that Andy contact her. But there would be no reason. She had already told Andy that she was mistaken about her patient's identity. Suzanne knew that wouldn't work either. Her conclusion was to investigate for herself.

She rushed through her morning, cleaning her home. She darted through the grocery store in record time. When she was back home, she haphazardly tossed a few things in the slow cooker. This way, she could have a decent dinner prepared. A pork roast, onions, carrots, adobo, cumin, and oregano sounded like a tasty combination. As an afterthought, she shoved a few cloves of garlic into the pork. She'd roast up potatoes later. So now, for the rest of day, she was free.

Suzanne brought her peanut butter and jelly sandwich to the table; she opened her laptop. She really had no idea where to start. She decided the first step would be to organize a list of the things she needed to know. She opened a word document, thinking it would be more secure than having handwritten notes lying around. Notes that Andy might find.

As she made her inventory of the items she was looking for, she toggled back and forth through Google searches. Intermittently, she would think of something new to add to list. During this time, she had another revelation. Her phone and her emails. Surely, there would be some clues there

She opened the old email account she used when she and Eric were together and began reading them. She smiled at some of the memories that were evoked, realizing that Eric was a good guy some of the time. Then there were the cryptic exchanges between them. She understood their meaning which led her to add other items to her growing list. She found a few names from their past that warranted a follow-up as well. One name in particular might provide some beneficial information. Satisfied, she opened her phone and began going through the texts. She had logged his identity as "pop" in her directory. She couldn't remember why she even saved them. "Maybe for insurance at some later date." She thought.

As she scanned them, many details that were long forgotten became fresh again in her mind. "What a crazy time." She said out loud.

Suzanne checked the time. It was close to four already. She had been at this for three hours. She wasn't worried about Andy walking in on her at this point. He was deep into his investigation which meant, he probably wouldn't surface until after seven tonight. At any rate, he usually sent a text on the way home to see if she needed anything.

She took a break and made some coffee. Pacing around the kitchen, while it brewed, she recapped what she learned so far. Not much, just a review of the past. She decided at this point, she had enough material to begin a more educated search. She felt equipped to approach this methodically.

She started with a search for Eric Popper. She had lost track of him over the past two years, even though it wasn't for lack of trying. Much of what she found was what she already knew. She decided to check out Nicky Pellegrino. To her disappointment, minimal information cropped up. No pictures, no social media; there was only a small mention of his little hardware store connected to a fundraiser for the local little league.

Ok," she thought, "what now? Maybe I should make that phone call." She hesitantly picked up her phone.

"Why are you calling me?" A gruff voice barked from the other end.

"Listen, we need to talk, but not over the phone. Can we meet somewhere?"

"Are you out of your freakin' mind? No way, darlin'!"

"It's about pop. They found a body and think it's his. I'm not so sure."

There was silence, but she could hear his breathing. "Ok, listen, I'll meet you tomorrow morning, bright and early. Whole Foods at eight sharp. Prepared foods."

"But, I …." She heard the click as the line went dead.

"Shit, I'll have to call out of work again. This is not good."

Suzanne was still sitting at her laptop when Andy walked in at six o'clock. Startled, she shut the top reflexively. He didn't call first.

"Hey Suzie Q, what are you doing?" He said as he bent over and kissed her.

Fearing that she would stumble over her words, she said, "Oh, just doing a search for this disease one of my patients has."

"Always working. You know, your patients are lucky to have you. So, what is it?"

"What's what?" she questioned back.

"The disease, what is it?"

Hastily, she said. "Stiff Person Syndrome."

"Really? There's such a thing?"

"Oh yeah, there are a whole bunch of these weird syndromes out there. This one is very rare. It's a neurological thing that causes muscles to contract and stiffen bringing on intense pain. Some people have been badly injured because of the stiffening. Sometimes, it's so severe that organs themselves shut down during an exacerbation."

He just stared at her. "Wow, that's just crazy."

"I know, right? But it's real and there's even testing that confirms it." She found she couldn't control herself as jabbered on about it. She stopped short and attempted to redeem herself. "Anyway, it's really interesting. I got so caught up in it."

Andy grabbed a beer, "Sounds it. What is that smell? I'm hoping it's something I'll be eating tonight."

"Yes, it is. Great detective work. Speaking of, how's your investigation going?" She casually asked.

"Pretty good so far. We've talked to a bunch of people. Got some preliminaries out of the way. How long til dinner?"

"Um, give me about a half hour to finish up the potatoes and asparagus."

"Perfect, I'm gonna go shower."

After he left the room, she could have kicked herself. Stiff Person's Syndrome? Really? Yes, it existed, but she could have come up with something more believable. Pushing those thoughts aside, she put the casserole dish containing the partially cooked potatoes into the oven.

During dinner, Suzanne tried to fish some information from Andy. She assumed that since she was part of the investigation, he'd be willing to talk about it with her. She was mistaken, when he told her he was only able to discuss the parts that involved her. She didn't press, but she was determined to find out more. For her own peace of mind, she needed to know what was going on.

They sat in the living room. Andy worked on his laptop; Suzanne pretended she was watching TV. She stole undetected glances at him while he worked. Finally, they decided to go to bed. Suzanne had to get up early to make it look like she was going to work. Andy didn't need to leave until seven.

Suzanne lay in bed with her stomach in knots. She dozed on and off. But her anxiety prevented her from rest. Her mind was working overtime and she wished it would shut down for just a little while. She could worry and suppose all she wanted, but until she knew what was going on, she would never relax.

She listened to Andy's breathing, praying he would settle into sleep. She heard his breathing slow, becoming shallower as the low hum of faint snoring took over. At three a.m., she quietly rolled out of bed, careful not to wake him.

Once in the kitchen, she opened his laptop. She knew he didn't use a password for access. She had told him he should since he used it for much of his work. Right now, she was relieved he hadn't listened to her.

She was acutely aware of the noises in the house. She couldn't become so engrossed in her search that she would miss the sound of the bedroom door opening. She'd be screwed if he discovered what she was doing. She knew that was not an option, but she felt compelled to take the risk anyway. She had to be fast.

She went into his Word files to read his notes. The first notes included some details of the autopsy. She was alarmed by its preciseness considering that the body was so badly decomposed. As a nurse, she should have realized that the bones would still be viable with their own story to tell.

Next, she quickly scanned his written record of the phone calls he and Shaker had made. Nothing much there. She moved on to the recap of the interview with Saint Millie Popper. Suzanne knew the saint was holding back. Eric had shared some tidbits of his childhood with her. Maybe she'd have to mention some of those things to Andy. She could say she just remembered what he had said.

Next, she read about Josh. She recalled what a low life creep he was. He would lie to make himself look better. The only difference between Josh and Eric was that Eric believed his own lies. In any event, there wasn't anything there. She continued scanning some of the other thoughts Andy had jotted down before checking the time.

She closed the Word document and took a hurried look at his recent search history in Google. She made a few hasty notes and stuck the paper in her bathrobe pocket. She made sure she closed her windows and shut down the computer just as she heard the toilet flush. She abruptly snapped the laptop shut; her heart beating wildly.

"Suzanne, what the hell are you doing?"

She paled when she saw Andy standing in the doorway.

Chapter 39

At that instant, Suzanne thought she would vomit. She knew she looked guilty. But in the nanoseconds from Andy's appearance to her response, her rational thoughts screamed self-preservation and she smiled. "Good mornin' babe."

Andy continued to stare at her, unsure of what was going on. "Suzanne, I asked you a question. What are you doing in my laptop?"

"Oh, I'm sorry, I couldn't sleep." She said, trying to buy some time. "I wanted to look at some of our vacation pictures."

He stood still in bare feet and checkered pajama bottoms, thinking. He reminded her, "They're on the desktop. You know that."

Feeling much more in control, she answered, "Yes, but it takes so long to start up and I wanted to sit in the kitchen with my coffee. I thought they were on your laptop too."

"My laptop is mostly for work, you know that." With his back to her, he poured himself a cup of coffee and looked out the kitchen window into the dark.

"I'm sorry Andy. I guess at three a.m. my brain is not very rational."

"Yeah, I guess." Andy said as his usual patience and laidback nature was being tested. His gut was telling him to let it go for now, but to analyze later. He was also feeling betrayed. She was fully aware that his laptop was off limits. He never breached hers either. It was a show of respect for one another and their privacy as well as an unspoken rule of trust.

With her stomach still upside down, Suzanne internally commanded herself to appear nonchalant. "I was thinking about toasting up a bagel. Would you like one too?" She asked.

"No thanks, I'm going to shower. I want to get down to the precinct early. I'll grab something on the way. Aren't you working today?"

Suzanne reconsidered her pretense of going off to the hospital when she said, "No, they cancelled me today." She lied.

"Nice." He said, grabbing his cup walking towards the bathroom.

Once she heard the door close, she sank into the chair. "Damn-it," she thought, throwing her stupid bagel in the garbage.

Suzanne waited impatiently for Andy to leave. She wasn't going to have much time to get ready for her meeting. She knew if she was late, he would leave and take this chance with him.

In what seemed like forever, Andy finally left. Suzanne threw on some jeans and a sweater. She put her curls in a hasty ponytail. With no time for make-up, she was out the door, arriving at Whole Foods without a minute to spare. She spotted him in an instant. He really hadn't changed. He was still paunchy with short legs and long arms. He looked like an ape with a beer belly. Although, he had grayed, his straggly hair was still unkempt. It probably still smelled too.

She saw him casually perusing the prepared foods, picking up items to examine the ingredients. She approached him and did the same.

"Hey," she said.

"Hey, right back. This chicken dish looks pretty good, don't you think?"

She played along for anyone who might be listening. "It really does. I haven't had this one before, but all of the meals are great."

She could feel his stare through his Ray Bans. "Make it fast. What's this all about?"

Suzanne gave a brief rundown of the past few month's event. "What do you think? I need help, Leo."

"Jesus Christ. Why are you dragging me into this? Just leave it alone."

Keeping her voice low and steady, she said, "But what if they find out?"

"No one's gonna find out. Eric is dead," he smirked, "and Nicky lives on. End of story."

"But shouldn't we do something?"

"Don't get involved, honey, not yet, anyway. In this story, it's better to wait and see. You don't want to create a problem that isn't there." He picked up the chicken he was looking at. "This looks great. I'm buying it. See you later."

To Suzanne, it was inconceivable that he reacted that way. She thought he'd at least offer some advice. Instead, he bought some damned chicken and told her to wait it out. Sure, she understood what he was saying, but she also knew she wasn't capable of just sitting around waiting. She decided that if she had some knowledge, she'd be prepared. To hell with him and his damned chicken, she thought as she watched him walk away, his saggy worn jeans dragging on the ground.

Chapter 40

My phone chimed with an incoming text:

Meeting went as planned. You called that one

right.

I answered:

Excellent. TY for taking care of it.

The reply:

No prob. I told her to sit tight

I thought:

Yeah, she would have made things worse

Another response:

Ttyl

My last reply:

Later

I connected my phone to the charger and smiled. I could predict her every move, always could. I just have to keep her in check until it blows over. I figured there's no sense in stirring the pot if it's not burning. I wonder if I confide in her if she'll stop snooping around. That cop boyfriend of hers is gonna start wondering what she's up to. It's been fun playing her, but, yeah, maybe I should fill her in. She's just so damn cute when flustered.

Chapter 41

Andy was at his desk, staring at his computer. He took the last bite of his Dunkin' Donuts egg and cheese bagel sandwich. He looked in the bag wishing another would materialize, but no such luck. He tossed the crumpled brown bag into the trash. He continued scanning his laptop to see if any files were compromised, but everything appeared to be the way he left it. He felt silly thinking like that, but that was his nature when he was knee deep in an investigation.

He heard Shaker's distinctive footsteps approaching. "Good morning, partner." He said without turning around.

"Damn, the shoes gave me away, right?" Shaker laughed. "Here's your coffee."

"Thanks." Andy said, taking the cup from Shaker. "It's more the way you walk in them, then the shoes themselves."

"I'll remember that, maybe I can change it up. You get here early?"

"Just a little while ago. I wanted to go over what we had so far. And so far, it all looks like a dead end."

"I know what you mean. But hey, we got that lawyer's name yesterday. Maybe Gustafson will call us back today or we could pay another visit to his office. His secretary did say he'd be back in town late morning."

"Hey, that's something to look forward to, right?" Andy agreed.

"Can't wait." Shaker pulled out his chair and plopped into it. "Oh, before I forget, Julia wanted me to invite you and Suzanne for dinner on Friday."

"What? Oh, ok, I'll ask her and let you know later, Ok?" Andy responded.

"Ok, sounds good. Hey, what are you working on over there?"

Andy really didn't want to talk about it at this point. He still had a nagging feeling but he couldn't make up his mind if it was real or imagined. He had to admit he was really bugged that Suzanne went into his laptop. So, his answer was, "Oh, I'm just reading over the notes we've been making. Seeing if anything jumps out."

Shaker did more background research on the attorney. Gustafson would be in his early sixties now. He'd been practicing family law for more than thirty years. Teaches an ethics class at Quinnipiac College and volunteers as a legal advisor for Connecticut Bar Association. He has own private practice. However, during the time of the adoption when he was a young attorney, he worked for a firm called Heinz and Manning, specializing in independent adoptions.

Shaker continued to research the stipulations of private adoptions versus using an agency. One thing common to all adoptions, he discovered, is that the name of the birth parents is replaced with the name of the adoptive parents on the birth certificate. The original birth certificate is sealed and may only be accessed through a court petition. Some states are now opening the sealed records to adoptees, bypassing the court process.

"So, if the adoption was closed, Popper and his family wouldn't know anything about the birth parents unless they petitioned the court to release the original birth certificate."

Andy looked up, "Ok, go on."

"Well, if it was an open adoption, the paperwork would be the same, but there would have been contact, so they all would have known each other during the process. Maybe even after the birth. Wow, listen to this. An adoption with an attorney can cost around 40k. I wouldn't have thought the Poppers had that kind of cash."

"Whew, that is a lot, especially thirty something years ago."

"Yeah, I mean it was a long time ago, but it's still good information to have when we see Vince Gustafson.

"So, the million dollar question is—did Eric Popper petition to open the files?" Andy asked.

"If he did, I can't find any record of it. That's one thing we'll be sure to press Gustafson about. Even if he doesn't know, maybe he can point us to someone who does."

Chapter 42

Suzanne arrived home around noon feeling more bewildered than ever. She was relieved to have the house to herself. She needed to think. The problem was she didn't know any more now, then she knew before. She thought she knew what had happened, but now she felt like her memory was becoming distorted to fit the current puzzle. She remembered learning that simple suggestions could cause false memories. Was that what was happening to her?

She sat at the kitchen table with her hands clasped around her hot coffee mug. The chill she was experiencing wasn't being warmed; it ran too deep. Maybe Leo was right. She should just let it go.

Just then, her phone chimed with a new text. She flinched when she saw the sender:

Hey, sit tight, we're good. Will call when I can

She stared at the text and started to cry.

Chapter 43

The next morning bright and early, Carly's phone began ringing. She checked the Caller ID and saw Nick's name come up. She decided not to answer it. When he continued to call incessantly, she finally silenced the ringer, because it made her heart skip every time she heard it. The texts Nicky subsequently began sending were easier to handle. She could digest them and reply if she felt like it. If she judged his tone to be non-threatening, she was more comfortable answering the phone as well.

He began to leave voicemails frequently. In one, he professed his love for her and the desire for them to work things out. In another, he had threatened to sue her. His reason was that she had unlawfully evicted him. What? He threatened her with this lawsuit unless he she paid him a few thousand dollars along with the contents of her home. He insisted the agreement be notarized. He even gave her a deadline. "He really is on drugs. And I thought he was bad when he was drinking." she thought. She couldn't believe that he thought he had this power to issue an ultimatum and that she would just go along. Who the heck does he think he is?

While she knew he was just blowing hot air, issuing threats, she still felt an uneasy. In her rational mind, she knew that he didn't have the authority undertake this. Most likely, he would have to secure an attorney to draw up the agreement and pay someone to execute it. She thought it might be wise to talk to someone just to be sure.

He had even typed up a document and emailed it to her. It seemed very well thought out and lucid; almost calculated. She wondered if he was getting some free legal advice somewhere. That was the thing about Nicky, he pretended to be everyone's friend to get what he wanted.

"Well, he's not getting it from me!" Carly said out loud.

She replied to his email, careful with what she said so he could not use it against her. Basically, she told him that since they broke up, it was reasonable for him to move from her property. She also reminded him that unlawful eviction is meant to protect tenants not former boyfriends or spouses. She went on to say, that when he moved to his apartment, she would make certain he received some of the furnishing they had acquired along with the scant items that were his to begin with. Most of the contents were purchased by Carly so in this respect, she was being generous. It was really her hope that if she offered an equitable compromise, he would just go away. When she thought her response was well-stated in a pleasant tone, she hit send and crossed her fingers.

Nick read the email from Carly about five times. He couldn't believe she had the nerve to question him. Maybe he pushed too hard, too soon. The bitch even tried to make a deal of her own. He had to find another angle—maybe soften up a little; but she was really pissing him off.

He sat at his laptop opening his yellow-lined pad to the page where he had scribbled, "Carly". He reviewed the notes of his planning, making revisions and additions. He was so angry with her for kicking him out. Did he deserve it? Probably, but that wasn't really the point. He knew he had to just keep coming at her, appearing unpredictable. It would ensure her being off-balance and unprepared for his strategic moves. It would be fun for Nick to see Carly lose control—of everything.

Chapter 44

Andy and Shaker arrived at Vince Gustafson's office just past lunchtime. They were greeted by his para-legal, Emily. They judged her to be in her early forties. She had jet black hair pulled into a loose braid that tumbled halfway down her back. She was average height with a slim but muscular build; the gym was probably her hobby. She smiled a smile at them that did not reach her deep-set jet eyes.

"Detectives, it's nice to see you again." She said in a most professional tone.

"Hi, Emily, is Attorney Gustafson in?" Shaker asked.

"Yes, he just got here. I'll check if he's available to see you. Please have a seat." She said, gesturing with her red polished nails to the leather side chairs near the window.

When she disappeared through the door to Gustafson's inner sanctum, Andy whispered, "She's a little too uppity for my taste. What do you think?"

Shaker leaned in and said, "I think she's wound a little tight."

Andy chuckled just as Emily emerged into the waiting area. "Detectives, although, you don't have an appointment, Attorney Gustafson agreed to see you. Please follow me."

The two men stood and walked two paces behind Emily to Vince Gustafson's office. They were expecting to see the male version of Emily sitting on a throne, however, they were pleasantly surprised to be greeted by an easy-going man with genuine smile.

Vince had a full head of gray wavy hair which he wore pushed back. He had strong prominent features on a large face.

"Gentlemen, hello, I'm Vince Gustafson," he said with an outstretched hand. "Please sit and tell me what I can do for you."

Andy and Shaker sat in the leather chairs which matched the pair in the reception area.

Andy began, "Thank you for seeing us without an appointment. We appreciate that."

Vince sat back in his high-backed leather desk chair, templed his fingers as he waited for Andy to proceed.

"Well, we're in the middle of a murder investigation, and the deceased turns out to be someone whose adoption you processed about thirty or so years ago."

He laughed an affable laugh. "Detectives, certainly, you don't expect that I would remember all the adoptions I presided over? Especially one from more than thirty years ago."

Shaker piped in, "No, we realize it was a long time ago. We were hoping that because it was one of your first, you might recall something about it."

Vince fidgeted in his chair, "Ok, that makes some sense, you always remember your first, right, boys? What's the name?"

"The child's adopted name is Eric Popper. His parents are Millie and Sam Popper. Ring any bells?"

As Vince thought, Andy and Shaker studied his reaction. There may have been a glimmer of recognition in his eyes. He shifted his substantial frame in his chair.

He cleared this throat before speaking. "Hmm, I can't say I'm hearing any bells. But I'll tell you what. Let me look over my old records, I've kept them all. You understand, this is confidential information, but if there's something I can share, I will."

"We'd appreciate that, Vince. The other piece of information we're looking for is whether any of the Poppers petitioned to have the original birth documents opened. We were hoping maybe you could point us in the direction of who to talk to about that. We've reached a dead end"

"Ok, boys, I'll look into that too."

Andy and Shaker rose to leave and thanked Vince for his time. They gave him a business card. He said he would contact them later in the day or first thing in the morning.

When the door shut, Vince sat down again, put on his glasses and opened his desk drawer. He took out a flash drive that contained his old files. He had held onto them for instances just like this.

Andy and Shaker walked in silence to their Explorer. When they were secured in the vehicle, Shaker broke the quiet, "So, what did you think?"

"I don't know. I did get the feeling for just an instant that he remembered something." Andy commented.

"You too, huh?"

"Can't wait to hear what he comes back with."

They headed back to the station sharing an ominous feeling that they had just opened Pandora's Box.

Chapter 45

Brian Bailey popped open his can of beer. He leaned back in his shabby arm chair and took a gulp. "Yep, this is the good life." He looked at his can of Bud and smiled, remembering all the designer beers he had sold in his store. Yet, here he was drinking a Bud – after all, it is the "king of beers".

Brian owned a small liquor store in Farmington. The store had a great location in a small plaza that housed a thriving pizza restaurant, a hair salon, and a convenience store. When the convenience store closed down, Brian had the foresight to buy it and expand his little shop into an upscale wine and spirit joint. He still sold what the old-timers wanted, but he also catered to the new clientele in town. When he retired at the age of fifty-five, he sold his thriving business for a substantial profit.
He lived modestly in a cabin along the Farmington River on the Canton line. His cabin was by no means rustic; it had all the amenities necessary for a comfortable retirement. Brian enjoyed his privacy, especially after returning from one of his trips.

He had been on a fishing excursion in the Florida Keys which lasted about three weeks. So, when he arrived home, he was very content to relax in his favorite chair with his favorite beer. He contemplated stepping out to the porch with a cigar later in the evening.

He turned on the TV to catch up on the local news and opened the pizza box sitting on the coffee table. The smell of cheese and pepperoni was killing him. He couldn't wait any longer to dive in.

The anchors on the local news station droned on, exaggerating every detail of what they were reporting even the weather. They seemed more like actors than journalists to Brian. One story caught his attention. It seemed the body of a man had been found down the river in Farmington a few weeks ago. The reporters merely said that the investigation is pending. They didn't name the victim or give any other details.

Brian rubbed his balding head, thinking, "wow, so close to home." A fleeting image came into his consciousness and just as quickly disappeared from his grasp. He almost had it before it was gone. "Hmm, that was strange," he thought.

Chapter 46

September

Sunday

Carly woke with a start. "What was that?" She lay still in her bed, listening; the glow of the moon peeking through the blinds. She tried to concentrate on the noise she heard that jarred her from sleep. Was it real? Was it part of a dream? No, it was probably outside. Yes, it was probably one of the neighbors coming home. Then she heard it again. It was coming from inside her house.

She glanced at her clock—three a.m.-- and reached for her phone. She forced her body to relax as she clung to the phone as if it were her life preserver. A few minutes later, she heard a car engine revving. Finally, around four, she decided to get up and check things out. She hadn't heard anything since the car started.

Apprehensively, she turned the doorknob on her bedroom door, cautiously opening it. When she stepped into the hallway, her breath caught for a moment. The lights were on in the living room. "I know I turned them off." She clutched her phone to her. She had already punched in 911 on the keypad. She was ready to hit send in an instant.

Once downstairs, she knew there was no one in the house. She fell to the floor in relief. "I'm being silly. Maybe I did forget to turn off the lights." Then she smelled the odor of coffee that had been sitting on burner too long. She got up and walked into the kitchen. The pot was on and her travel mug was missing from the dish drain where she had left it. There were cigarette ashes in the sink.

The police arrived in record time. Probably a slow night of crime in Willimantic, she figured. Carly sat motionless as they looked around. She watched them looked at each other. She figured they thought she was crazy.

One of the young cops, Officer Zelinsky, was the first to speak. He was tall and wore his uniform with pride; his buzz cut freshly whizzed. He seemed cocky like most of the young officers.

"Ms. Mancuso, we've found no sign of forced entry. I'm afraid we've found no sign of anything. Nothing is out of place and you said you didn't think anything was missing except for your cup." He looked at her with sympathetic blue eyes as he spoke.

"But what about the ashes. I don't smoke." She said, as though she were being accused of something.

"Well, I guess that might indicate something. But unfortunately, it doesn't. There's no butt for fingerprints or DNA. I'm sorry. There really isn't anything we can do."

"I know someone was here. Just like the last time."

He thought for a moment before addressing her. "Well, there was nothing the last time either. I read the report. But if you do find something missing, please call us. For now, the best advice I can give you is maybe get an alarm if you're convinced someone is getting in."

Carly was aware that he was trying to be nice while he was dismissing her. "Yes, well, thank you, Officer Zelinsky. I'll consider that." She walked them to the door and watched them talk among themselves for a few minutes before they drove away.

"Great, now I know they think I'm nuts." She stood at the sink, thinking as she poured the coffee down the drain. It was six o'clock, she realized when she started a fresh pot.

Still unnerved, she paced around the house again. Everything was in its place. She decided to head to the gym, knowing a good workout would clear her head. Then she would go to Prospect Hill. "I will turn this day around," she vowed.

The chilly early Autumn morning turned to a mild afternoon in the typical New England fashion. The bright sun shone high in the sky bringing an inner warmth to Carly that settled her spirits. She had abandoned her fleece lined jacket in the car in favor of a light sweater that she brought along. She approached the house of her friends feeling thankful that she had them in her life.

They had planned to meet this morning to go over the details of Lucy's baby shower. Sunday morning was the perfect time, because Lucy would be at church. Her normal routine was to have lunch with her mother afterwards. They knew they had a few hours.

When she walked into the kitchen, the fragrance of freshly made cinnamon buns tickled her nose, making her mouth water. "Good morning," She said, grabbing a plate.

After Irene sat at the table, they went over the details that Jenn had jotted down. Her glittered fingernails twinkled with the light as she moved her fuzzy pink pen across the paper. She was the self-proclaimed party planner who would oversee this project. As she listened to the others, she revised what was already discussed, improving upon each idea.

Her list included decorations, invitations, gift ideas, and of course food. There was some debate over the issue of party games. Gracie and DeeDee were in favor, however, they were overruled by the others. Jenn crossed that item off the list, moving on to the next.

The guest list they assembled would be small, including family and close friends. Meghan and Joanie would take care of the invitations. Since Mae had an artistic streak, she would assume the responsibility of decorations. Gracie would be her helper.

DeeDee had found some cute ideas for party favors at the local craft store. They would be easy to assemble which was good since she was not as creative as Mae. Carly volunteered to assist.

They decided the food should be set up as a buffet. It would keep things informal while also providing a variety. Of course, Irene would take over that endeavor with Jenn as her helper. The menu they decided on was diverse. Choices under discussion included chips and salsa on the tables for snacking, salad, rolls, chicken marsala with egg noodles, pulled pork, vegetarian lasagna, cole slaw, a vegetable, and some form of beef, possibly a stew.

For dessert, Carly suggested getting a tray of those ginormous crème filled cupcakes from the local bakery. They could be decorated in blue and pink since the baby's gender was unknown. She said maybe they could even be arranged so each cupcake had a letter which when put together would say, "Congratulations Lucy!"

Jenn snickered, "Carly, I had no idea you were so creative."

"Yeah, well, occasionally, I can have a great idea."

"Ok, Team Lucy, we officially have a party to plan. We have just over two months to pull this together." Jenn commanded. She stood from the table and towered over the others. "May the force be with you." Everyone laughed, including Carly.

When the group disbanded, Jenn gave Carly a hug. "You ok?" she asked.

"Yeah, I'm fine. A little tired, I've been up since about three."

"Why, what's on your mind? Nicky problems?"

"No, that's not it. I heard some noises in the house and it rattled me." Carly said avoiding Jenn's gaze.

"What kind of noises?"

"It was hard to say because it woke me up. But I guess it sort of like clanging. You know, like the sound dishes or pots make. I don't know, maybe I was dreaming." She left out the part about the lights and coffee.

"Did you call the police?"

"Yeah, I felt an idiot. They told me there was nothing to find. They said I should get an alarm."

"Not a bad idea. You could always stay here or maybe at your parents' house."

"Not an option. I'm not leaving my house." Carly said emphatically.

"Ok, gotcha." Jenn checked her gaudy Michael Kors knock-off watch. "Carly, I'm sorry, I've gotta go pick up Lucy. Hey, do you want to come for the ride?"

"Oh, I can't. But, go on, you can't leave a pregnant woman standing on the side of the road."

As Jenn left, she held the door for Jackson who was just walking in. It was unusual for Jack to be here on a Sunday. Usually, another staff member checked in on the weekends. Carly decided that this casual side of him looked great. He was wearing a well-worn pair of Levi's, that fit just right, and sneakers. His usual business casual shirt was replaced with a Yankee's hoodie. His normal bookish appearance took on a whole new meaning.

"Hey, Jack," she said. "What are you doing here this morning?"

"Hi Carly. I could ask you the same thing."

"Yeah, I guess you could. We had some party planning to do for Lucy's shower."

"Oh, right." He poured the last of the coffee and grabbed a cinnamon roll. "How did it go?"

"Oh great. You know Jenn. She's on top of everything. We've all been assigned tasks and given our timelines. So, we're in countdown mode now."

"Nice. Lucy's going to love it!"

"So, Jack, you didn't answer my question, what are you doing here?"

"Oh, Shirley couldn't make it for her check-in and I had some paperwork. I figured, I might as well take her place."

Carly didn't want to pry into his private life, but, yeah, she really did. "I would have thought you'd be watching football with the guys or something today."

"Nah, they mostly go the bar and drink too much. I don't think they even pay attention to the game. So, I try to avoid that. But I have to say that sometimes it is fun when everyone is cheering."

"Yeah, I know what you mean. As long as you're all cheering for the same team, though."

"Right." He pulled up a chair. "What are your plans for the rest of the day?"

"Me? I don't know. I was thinking about calling Sally or visiting my parents. Then, there's always shopping." She laughed. "What about you?"

"Hmm, I don't know. I plan on getting out of here by four. After that, I'm open. Hey, do you want to grab a bite later?" He casually asked.

Carly felt a faint flutter or was it indigestion from all the cinnamon rolls she had eaten. She didn't understand why she felt nervous, after all he was a good friend. A very cute good friend at that. Keeping it light, she answered, "Sure, that sounds like fun."

"Great, how about we meet at the Brewery about four thirty?"

"Oh, that's good, it'll give me a couple of hours to get some stuff done." She said, checking her watch. She picked up her tote and headed for the door, "See you later."

Chapter 47

Brian Bailey sat on his porch on Sunday, tying flies. He wasn't usually an angler when he fished, but he enjoyed making the flies just the same. He usually gave them away.

While he tied, he was rocking to the music of The Band. "Man, I can't get enough of this," he thought. He was finishing his coffee, thinking how the leaves were starting to change. His cabin was enveloped by woods; he chose the trees and the cloak they provided over the exposed wide-open that his neighbors had preferred. But soon, the leaves would fall, making him visible.

He was still bothered by the report of the body found not too far from him. He couldn't pinpoint the niggling feeling he had about it. He tried to focus his thoughts on the fleeting images he couldn't quite grasp. Since it was well over a year ago, he knew his memory might not have anything to do with the body. That is if he could remember at all.

Brian grabbed his gear and headed into the cabin. Time for a beer and some football. He knew the Patriots would be starting around four. He heated up some chili to snack on while he watched. He'd make dinner later. As he stood by his kitchen window, he began grating some cheddar to top the chili. In an instant, an image danced into his head. This time it was different. He was able to reach out and grab it.

"Well, I'll be," he thought as he fully remembered. "I wonder if it means anything. "I'll have to call the police first thing in the morning." He wrote down his thoughts to be sure he wouldn't forget again.

Chapter 48

Carly decided to visit with her parents before going to meet Jack. Although, she spoke with them daily, she hadn't been to see them in about a week. On the way, she called Sally too, to check in. She was working the weekend, so she didn't have time to talk.

Carly pulled into the driveway and as usual, her father was working in the garage. "Hey little girl!" Sal said as he walked towards her, holding a screwdriver.

"Hi Dad," She said as she kissed him. "What are you doing?" She asked, pointing at the wrench.

"Oh this? I'm putting together a bookcase for your mother." He pointed to a four-tier light oak unit.

"Wow, that's beautiful, Dad! Did you make it from scratch?"

"Oh, I'm just assembling it. But I gotta tell you that I probably could have made it. It's a pretty simple design."

"You probably could. I don't doubt you for a minute." They laughed and headed into the house. "Hey Gi, look who I found."

Her mom hugged her, "I'm so happy you had time to come over."

"I know mom, I missed my weekly dinner, last Wednesday."

"Are you staying for dinner tonight? I'm making sauce, meatballs, and spaghetti. Nothing too fancy. I can put some chicken in the oven if you want."

Carly knew she'd disappoint her parents, but she told them, "Oh that sounds great, but I'm meeting a friend for an early dinner."

Before her father could say anything, Carly's mother interceded. "Are you meeting Sally?"

"No, she's working. I'm meeting Jackson Foley. He's the manager at the shelter where I volunteer. I think you met him once."

Her mother's smile broadened. "A date? You have a date? That's wonderful! I mean, it's about time you met someone nice after all you've been through with Nicky."

"Mom, hold on. First off, you make it sound like a miracle that I'd have a date. I could have a date if I found someone worth dating. I'm just a little gun-shy. And yes, Jack seems nice."

Her dad piped in, "Gi, I keep telling her to try those online computer dating things that we see on TV. People are always meeting and getting married."

"That's a good idea, Sal. I think your father's right. They always look so happy. What do you think about that, Carly?"

"Yeah, why don't you try it, Sweetie?"

"Ok, you both are way off topic. For now, let's drop the online stuff. I'm not ready to put myself out there like that. Remember, I only just broke up with Nicky a few months ago."

Her mother grinned at her father who said, "So, tell us about your date. Where are you going?"

"Well, I was about to tell you that Jack and I are just friends. We're just meeting for dinner. It's not a date."

"Whatever you say, honey." Her mother smiled.

They sat at the kitchen table while Gi stirred the sauce. Carly helped her mother ease the giant meatballs into the pot where they would simmer for a few hours. Her father had disappeared into the garage to finish the bookcase.

Carly and her mom had an easy relationship. They chatted about silly things. Carly told her about the baby shower. However, Carly didn't mention any of the other stuff that was going on. At this point, there was really nothing to tell. She didn't see the point of worrying her parents unnecessarily.

She kissed them both about three and headed home to get ready for her... her what? Her dinner with a friend.

Chapter 49

Carly arrived home and changed into a pair of black jeans. She wanted to look pretty but at the same time she wanted to appear casual. She chose a pair of black suede boots with a chunky block heel. The top she decided on was a purple and black print V-neck in a short tunic style. She fixed her short hair to give it that appropriately messed up look. After applying some fresh make-up, she grabbed her purse and headed out the door.

When she arrived at the brewery, she found Jack had already secured a corner table in the bar. He stood to greet her and helped her with her jacket.

When they sat again, he said, "You look great, but you always do."

"Oh, thank you. So do you. This is nice."

"Yeah it is. Oh, I already ordered a beer, hope you don't mind. What would you like? I'll go grab it since it's so crowded. Our waitress is probably really busy"

"It is! I forgot it would still be busy with the late games. I'd love a Malbec."

"You got it. Be right back."

Carly watched Jack walk to the bar to order her drink and smiled. Interesting stuff here. He had abandoned his sweatshirt and worn jeans in favor of a dark washed pair and a button-down shirt. He was wearing dark framed glasses which brought out the green in his eyes. When he brought her wine to the table, she forgot that she had been staring.

"Are you ok?" He asked, placing a napkin on the table before setting her glass down.

"Oh yeah, I'm good." She smiled and continued, "I think this is the first time we've ever gotten together outside of the house."

"Yeah, I guess it is. Cheers." He said, raising his glass to hers.

"You 'cheers' too?" She laughed and clinked his glass with hers. "That's so funny. People always think that's weird that I do that. It's one of my rules."

"That is funny. It's one of mine too."

Now that the ice was broken, they settled into comfortable conversation that had nothing to do with work. They shared appetizers and ordered a flatbread pizza for dinner.

When their second drink arrived, Carly finally asked, "So, Jack, I've never asked if you're married or otherwise attached. All I know is that you had a stalker girlfriend."

"Hmmm, so, I'm mysterious. I kind of like that." He sat back and let her curiosity build.

"Oh, that's not fair. You know all about the 'Nick' thing." She kidded.

"Ok, ok. I'm divorced. I was married for about six years. Her name was Leah. One morning, she handed me my coffee and divorce papers. Said, she didn't want to be married anymore. She picked up the suitcase that was by the door and left. I haven't seen or heard from her in four years."

"Oh, Jack, I'm so sorry. That's horrible. What did you do?"

"Well, after I got over the shock, I realized it was really ok. I thought long and hard about things and realized that for a few years we were just going through the motions. The hardest part was my daughter. Rosie was three when Leah left us. I guess she didn't want to be a mother anymore either."

"Oh wow. I didn't know." Carly said, suddenly feeling so sad for Jackson.

"It's ok, really. I don't like to tell my clients about my private life unless it has bearing on what they're dealing with. But anyway, Rosie and I are very happy. So, I guess you could say I am attached—to an amazing seven-year old."

Carly thought for a few minutes, not really knowing what to say. "You're incredible, Jack. I bet you're a great father."

"Haha, well I try. She's really a good kid so she makes it easy." Jack pulled out his phone and showed Carly a picture of the most adorable little girl she had ever seen.

Rosie was thin and wiry wearing a tee-shirt and leggings. She had soft-looking long brown hair with natural red highlights. The kind that only children are blessed with. Carly could see in the photo that she had the same sparkle in her hazel eyes that Jack had.

"She's beautiful, Jack." Carly had so many questions but didn't know where to start. She figured it was probably best not to ask them right now. That could wait for another time.

"Thanks, I think so." Jack sipped his beer and slipped his phone back in his pocket as he beamed with pride.

Their conversation turned to Nick, as expected. Carly brushed over the topic. She didn't want to spoil the fun they were having. She didn't want the sparks she felt to fade.

Jack reached across the table, putting his hand on Carly's. "You know, I've been wanting to ask you out for a long time. But I knew the timing wasn't right. I hope this was ok."

She looked at him and said, "Yes, this was perfect. I didn't know what to think at first. You know, was it just two friends getting together or was it a date? But, yeah, I'm definitely happy you asked."

"Me too."

When they finished the most amazing chocolate mousse in the world, Jack checked the time. "Wow, it's seven-thirty already. I should probably get going. My mom and dad are watching Rosie."

"I bet they love that. But you're right."

Jack paid the bill. He wouldn't allow Carly to even leave the tip when she offered. He walked her to her car as they held hands. When she opened the door, she thanked him. He searched her eyes, finding what he was looking for and bent down to kiss her. Magic.

Chapter 50

September

Monday

During her weekend off, Suzanne and Andy drove to Mystic where they enjoyed a walk along the crowded streets, shopping. The sun was warm, blanketing them in soothing coziness. It was just what they needed. Andy was beginning to let go of his uneasiness over Suzanne and his laptop. Bright and early Monday morning, Suzanne was at work. She felt like herself again; the anxiety of the last few weeks had evaporated into the mist.

Carly awoke early to a peaceful calm in her home. She found herself smiling with thoughts of her impromptu "date" with Jackson. She rolled out of bed, grabbed her robe, and glided to the kitchen. As usual, the coffee had brewed, releasing that enticing aroma that beckoned "good morning" to her. She poured her first cup, wondering what it would be like to see Jack today. Especially after that kiss.

Andy arrived at the station to find Shaker was already there. As usual, he had picked up a Starbucks coffee for him on the way. Andy could see that Shaker was on edge about something. He put his jacket over the chair, waiting for Shaker to spill the beans. Shaker told Andy that there had been a message from Vince Gustafson. It seemed he had some information for them. They decided to drive to his office without warning of a return call. Andy grabbed his jacket and coffee and they left.

Brian Bailey sipped his coffee and read his morning paper. Online, he checked his investments. When he finished his morning ritual, he read the notes he had jotted the day before. He didn't know if they meant anything or even if the timing was right, but he figured he should call it in and let the police sort it out. He picked up his phone and punched in the numbers. When the dispatcher answered, he asked to speak with the detectives in charge of the investigation. He was told they were out. He left a voicemail.

Nicky wasn't an early riser. The only reason he was awake so early was because his breakfast tray had been delivered and he didn't want to miss it. He looked at his meal, realizing he would eat it and enjoy the slop, no matter how much he protested otherwise. After all, there really weren't any other options. He took the extra apple and orange he usually ordered and put them on the windowsill with all the others he had been hoarding during his stay. With bits of scrambled egg stuck to his chin, he grabbed his yellow pad with his greasy fingers glazed from bacon fat. He flipped it open and crossed off an item on the list.

The car was parked in the church lot just down the street. The driver had a good view of Carly's house. He watched her step onto the porch with her coffee in hand. He smiled as he studied her face when she noticed the half empty beer can sitting on the table. She looked around with a puzzled expression, then tossed it into the recycle bin. He would keep these reminders coming.

Chapter 51

In almost two months that Nick had been in rehab, he had shown significant improvement. He was given the ok for discharge as soon as Kendall secured his apartment and disability benefits. She had been working with a state program called "Money Follows the Person" which provides patients with housing, funding, and care so they could move back into the community. The other benefits of the program were that it was cheaper for the state then paying for a prolonged hospital stay; it also freed up hospital beds.

When Nick had finished his breakfast, Kendall knocked on his door. "Good morning," she said as she poked her head into his room. Her burgundy hair now streaked with what looked like the Crayola color of purple pizazz, flopped around her small face.

"Oh, hey, Kendall. What's up?" He asked, looking up from his tray.

"Well, I've got good news. That apartment you liked was approved by MFP. We can start the discharge process."

"Really? That's amazing. How long til I can move?"

"I'm thinking possibly November first. We have to get the lease together with the property manager. So, it will still hinge on that. I think it will go pretty smoothly."

"Thanks, Kendall. I really appreciate how hard you worked on that."

As Kendall turned to leave, her nose ring caught a ray of sun and twinkled. Nick thought she was an angel at that moment, or was it an elf. It didn't really matter, he was on his way.

He had a new list to make. As he started to think, he started to feel a little nervous. He wondered how he was going to make it on his own. He usually had charmed someone else into the task. But now, he'd be alone in his apartment. What would he do with his time? How would he make money?

He knew he had options; he'd been planning for this day. He was also aware he still had an account under a false name. There was plenty of money there. It was just never enough. He thought about Kendall, then quickly dismissed it. "She makes shit besides she's way too young and stupid." he thought.

Chapter 52

Andy and Shaker arrived at Vince Gustafson's office shortly after ten that morning. Emily objected, but showed them in after some convincing. "Vince, those two detectives are here to see you." She said in a somewhat contemptuous tone.

Vince rose from his desk and told her to have them come in. "Gentlemen, what a nice surprise. Although, to be honest, I was expecting you. I understand your rulebook. Better to show up unannounced, right?" He laughed. "Please, have a seat." He gestured to chairs facing his desk.

"Good morning Vince. Thank you for seeing us." Shaker replied. "So, to get to the point, in your message, you said you might have some information. Is that correct?"

Andy took out his notebook, and added, "We're all ears."

Vince sat down and a serious expression passed over his face. "Well, I reviewed some of my notes from the adoption. I really don't know if any of this will be helpful, but I thought I should share what I can. You realize most of the facts are confidential."

"Yes, of course." The detectives answered in unison.

"Ok, good. Well, after reading my notes, some memories were triggered. At the time I was a fresh faced young attorney. I was eager to make a difference. I wanted to help people. So, I went into family law. I was aware that so many people were getting screwed by the legal system in family matters, simply because they were unaware how to navigate it. I joined Heinz and Manning.

"So one day, this couple, the Popper's come to see me. They tell me their story of how desperately they want to adopt a child. They explain how the agencies had turned them down because they were in their forties. In those days, thirty-odd years ago, age mattered. Anyway, I was moved and saddened by their tale. I could see they had been struggling with this for a long time.

"I explained the process of locating a candidate. At that point, they told me they knew someone who needed to give up their baby. I told them, that was usually the best way to proceed with this type of private adoption."

Shaker jotted a note---Millie said it was a closed adoption; she didn't know the parents.

Vince continued, "We went over the details of how things would work along with the documents that needed to be filed. I explained that my usual fee in this type of situation was approximately $52,000. I said if they wished to move forward, I would need a retainer of $20,000 to start the proceedings. They didn't flinch. Sam Popper took out a checkbook right on the spot.

"Normally, I wouldn't have wondered, but the Poppers were working class people. I couldn't imagine that this fee would be so easily accessible. I hoped they weren't draining their life savings. But, again, they didn't even bat an eye.

"So, we started the process and moved forward from that point. That, detectives, is all I can tell you. The rest is confidential." Vince sat back, hoping Andy and Shaker wouldn't press him for more information.

Andy was the first to speak. "Ok, Vince, thanks, that's great. Did you ask about the money? Like how they could afford it?"

"I do remember saying something along the lines that I didn't want them to go bankrupt over this." He added, "although, I could have handled that too." He laughed and continued. "Anyway, they assured me, they were financially stable and money was not a problem. Gentlemen, before you even ask, as long as a client has the means to pay the fees, I normally don't ask where it came from."

"I have a couple of questions." Shaker piped in. "What was your impression of the Poppers? How did they act?"

"Hmm," he thought. "I guess I'd say they were confident. They seemed relieved when I said I would take their case."

"Ok, why do you think they came to you, a green attorney with only about six months of practicing under your belt? I mean no offense." Andy wondered.

"None taken. I suppose the other partners and associates were busy. This probably seemed cut and dried. So they assigned it to me. I should add however, that because I was new, I was probably more diligent to make sure all the 'i's' were dotted, so to be speak."

Andy and Shaker knew this was about all they were going to get out of Vince. They thanked him for his time and his efforts. When they left, Vince knew that the records could be subpoenaed if they required more information. He wondered if he should call Millie Popper.

Andy and Shaker decided to stop at Plan B Burgers for lunch before heading back to the station. Shaker order his usual Baja burger with jalapenos and avocado, while Andy preferred a more traditional cheeseburger with lettuce and tomato. As they waited for their food, they took out their notes to compare what they had, along with their thoughts about it.

Shaker began, "So, I heard a few discrepancies. Maybe it has to do with memories fading and changing over thirty years. I don't know. What are you thinking?"

"I'm thinking the same thing. I have to say that some of those inconsistencies wouldn't really change. Like, Millie saying they didn't know the birth parents. You know, either she did or she didn't. You just don't forget stuff like that."

"Yeah, true. I'm also bugged by the money." Shaker added. "I think we should visit Millie again. I mean, I don't know what it's gonna get us as far as Popper's death is concerned, but I think it's something we ought to finish."

"I agree. Leave no stone unturned." Andy took a bite of his burger, thinking about how this next interview would pan out.

Chapter 53

Carly was meeting Sally for lunch at the hospital where she worked. UCONN-John Dempsey hospital had an upscale food court with a wonderful reputation so Carly enjoyed meeting there. It gave them a chance to catch up when time would not otherwise permit.

Route 6 was a country road that intersected many small towns east of the river. As Carly drove, she was awestruck by the amazing color display she was experiencing. The leaves were in vivid shades of reds, golds, and oranges. She couldn't help but be distracted by the beauty.

When her phone rang, she pressed the answer key on her steering wheel. "Hello?" she said as she glanced at the caller display. Her heart sank. Shit.

"Hey, Carly, it's Nick. How are you?" He said from the other end.

He sounded ok, she thought. Keeping it light, she answered, "Hi Nick, how are you?"

"Oh, I'm great. I got some good news today. Looks like I'll be getting out of here in a couple of weeks."

"Oh, Nick, that's fabulous!" She answered, meaning it.

"Yeah, it is pretty cool. They approved the apartment I liked so I'll be moving there. The state is paying for it all through that program I told you about. At least until I can get back to work."

"That sounds great. I bet you're excited."

"Yeah, I really am. So, hey, I'm gonna need the rest of my things. I'll get another list together.

She thought, "what else could he need?" She said, "Ok, let me know."

"And Carly, just so you know, this isn't over. If you don't give me what I want or do what I tell you, I'll finish what I started before I got sick." The line went dead.

As those words sunk in, she tightened her grip on the wheel, knowing she had to focus on driving, although she felt like vomiting. While she merged onto I-84, she kept thinking, "What just happened? Everything was going well, then he says that. Was that a threat?"

Nicky was grinning when he clicked off the call. "Gotcha," he thought. He was so pleased with himself at that moment. He knew he could work her like a marionette. He could be the puppet-master. His mind began to wander as he tried to think which sitcom used that story line. Was it Seinfeld? No, that's not right. Frazier, yes, that was it. Wait, no it wasn't. Which one was it, he thought feeling his anxiety rise. Then he remembered, it was Wings. Yea, of course it was. Nick felt better that he remembered. He agreed that, yes, he would be the puppet-master.

Carly was still flustered when she arrived at the hospital. She text Sally to let her know she was there. They had agreed to meet in the cafeteria. Carly secured a table and waited for her friend to join her.

Sally walked in and Carly smiled when she spotted her. She was wearing her white lab coat with her name embroidered above the breast pocket; her glasses hung from a beaded chain around her neck. With her tawny hair held in place by a thin stretchy headband, she approached Carly with her bright smile.

"Look at you," Carly laughed, suddenly feeling more relaxed. "You look like a real doctor!"

Sally giggled along, "Well, I think that's probably a good thing." She put her jacket on the chair. "Let's go grab some food."

After they made their selections, they returned to the table. Carly took a bite of her lobster taco. "Oh my god, I am always amazed how good the food is here."

"It really is. I love the chicken and provolone pesto panini. I always get it when they have it." Sally nibbled at first, watching the steam come off her sandwich.

While they ate, they talked and laughed. Carly told Sally about her date with Jackson. She tried not to let the phone call from Nick spoil their time together. She would handle this herself.

"It sounds like you two hit it off. You seem really excited. I'm so happy you met someone normal."

"Oh Sally, it was such a nice night. I think because we started off being comfortable with each other. And of course, the sparks were always there I guess." She blushed.

"That's cool he has a daughter. You never knew that?"

"No, I was surprised. But he just lights up when he talks about Rosie. She's a real doll. I hope I can meet her someday."

"Oh, I'm sure you will. But probably not until he's comfortable with the relationship. That's a hard thing for single parents. You know introducing someone to their kids."

"Hmm, I never thought of it that way." Carly said thoughtfully.

Their conversation moved onto Sally's daughter Alyssa. She started taking dance lessons and was now tapping all over the house. Carly smiled. She could just picture her goddaughter dancing around. She was always in motion.

Sally checked her watch. "Damn, that hour went fast. I've got an appointment in a half hour. I should head back to prep."

With a feigned frown, Carly said, "Oh, ok. I guess if you have to go."

Sally walked Carly to the lobby and they hugged good-bye.

Chapter 54

On the drive home, Carly felt happy. It was always great to see Sally. She was proud of herself for not bringing up Nicky. She was sick of him always cropping up in conversation. It made her feel whiny and wishy washy to talk about the way he made her feel.

As she drove, her mind drifted to what he had said. The part about finishing what he started. As she recalled, the day before he went to the hospital, she gathered her courage and asked him to move out. It was probably not a good time since he was pretty drunk, but he was always drunk, so there would never be a good time.

He reacted worse than she anticipated. First, there was the expected yelling, name calling, and accusations. Next, he started slamming doors and throwing things; he smashed her mug against the wall. Then without warning, he came at her. He grabbed her arm and wrenched it behind her back nearly pulling it out of the socket. Then he put the knife to her throat.

In a reflexive move, she kicked him in the groin. The pain was dulled by the alcohol, but he was stunned for a minute. He loosened his grip and she got out of his grasp. Stinking of booze, he came at her again, but she grabbed the phone to call the police. He suddenly backed off and started to laugh.

"You stupid whore. I'm going to bed." He just walked away and shut the bedroom door. Within seconds, she could hear the rumble of his snoring.

She shuddered from the memory. Did he mean he would kill her? No, it couldn't be. That was just too insane.

Chapter 55

Instead of going back to the office, Andy and Shaker drove to Millie Popper's apartment, unannounced. They walked down the long hall leading to her door. Andy knocked. Within a few minutes, Millie opened the door.

"Oh, Detective Shaker," she said. She shifted her glance to Andy, unsure of who this stranger was.

"Hi, Millie. This is my partner, Andy Gallagher. Is this a bad time? May we come in?"

"Hello Detective Gallagher. Yes, of course, you can come in, I've got some time before my hair appointment." She stood back and gestured for them to enter. "Do you have some new information about my son?"

They entered and Andy said, "Nothing really, but we do have a couple of questions for you that might help with our investigation."

"Please, sit down. Would you like some coffee?" She offered.

"No thank you," Shaker answered. "Hopefully, we won't take up too much of your time."

As they sat, Andy pulled out his little notebook. "I'm just going to take some notes, if that's ok with you, Millie."

"Oh yes, that's fine. Now tell me what this is all about."

Shaker began, "Well, first, is there anything else you remembered about Eric that might be useful? She shook her head and he continued. "Ok, well we were able to find the attorney you used for the adoption. His name was Vince Gustafson. Does that ring a bell?"

"Yes, yes, it does. I knew it was something like that. Go on." She said.

"Well, it seems that Vince kept some personal notes which didn't breach any confidentiality. He shared with us that you might have known Eric's birth parents. He told us you already had a baby in mind to adopt. Is that true?"

She fiddled with the buttons on her cardigan. "Hmm, let me think."

"Millie, when I spoke with you, I believe you told me it was a closed adoption. Naturally, this new information confused me, so I thought I should talk to you again." Shaker asked in a non-confrontational manner.

"Yes, of course, you'd want to double check." She thought for a moment. "Now that you nudged my memory, I do recall being referred to an expectant mother who needed to give up her baby."

"Did you meet this mother? Do you know her name?" Andy added.

"No, I'm sorry I don't. I didn't meet her either. You're asking me to remember something that happened more than thirty years ago." She answered.

Andy then said, "Millie, most mothers remember every detail about their children's birth no matter how old they are. I just thought since you wanted a baby for so long, you would too."

She frowned. "I'm sorry, maybe I filed the name away because I felt Eric was mine."

They let it go because they could see they were upsetting her. Shaker spoke up. "I understand, Millie. I do have another question. Vince told us the cost of the private adoption. I was wondering how you and your husband were able to afford it."

Millie glared at them for a nanosecond, then looked down. "We borrowed the money from Sam's parents. It's embarrassing for me to say we didn't have that kind of money."

The detectives nodded and Andy spoke next. "I understand. Thank you, Millie, I think that clears it all up." Shaker agreed and they stood to leave.

She walked them to the door. When she closed it, they walked down the hall without a word or glance to each other, in case she was watching through the peephole.

Once in their car, they agreed, that Millie Popper was not being upfront with them.

"She's holding something back. Either the identity of the birth mother or how they got the money. Andy lit a cigarette and blew out the smoke. "This whole thing is starting to be like that onion cliché."

Shaker opened his window. "Yep, you got that right. Let the peeling continue."

Chapter 56

Millie peered through the tiny hole in her door and watched the distorted images of the detectives enter the elevator. She pulled a tattered business card from her wallet that had yellowed from time. There were some faded handwritten notes on the back. She picked one of the numbers she had written and dialed her phone.

"Attorney Gustafson's office." A businesslike female voice answered.

"Hello, I would like to speak with him please."

"Whom may I say is calling?" The woman said.

"This is Millicent Popper."

"Please hold a moment, Mrs. Popper. I'll see if he's available.

Millie became impatient as she listened to the "hold" music playing something that resembled an orchestrated version of a Journey song. Finally, the woman picked up again.

"I'm sorry to have kept you waiting. Attorney Gustafson can speak with you now briefly."

Before Millie realized she was on hold again, a jovial man's voice picked up, "Millie Popper, what a pleasure to hear from you."

"Vince, what's going on?" She asked him.

"Well, Millie, I can't say your call surprises me. I was actually going to call you."

"When Vince? When were you going to call me? It's too late now. Those two detectives just left. Why did you have to tell them I knew Eric's birth parents. Now they think I'm a liar!"

"Because my dear, if I didn't and they subpoenaed any of the records or documents, they would have found it themselves. I cannot afford to have my good name compromised either. So, the million dollar question is, what did you tell them?"

"I told them that I was referred to the birth mother but couldn't recall the name."

"And did they believe you?" Vince asked.

"I think so. I told them that after thirty years, it was hard to remember the details."

"Well, that's wonderful. What's the problem then?"

"I don't want trouble and I don't want them snooping. Can't you do anything?"

"I'm afraid not. Even though I've got copies of some things, the official records are sealed with the court. Millie, you know, you can always tell the truth about the adoption." Vince advised her.

"Yeah, I can, but I won't. Thanks for nothing, Vince. Please call me if you hear anything else.

"I will, and you do the same. It's always a pleasure Millie." He said and heard her hang up the phone.

Chapter 57

By the time Carly got home, it was too late to go to Prospect Hill. She felt badly about missing a day there. But she also was sorry she'd missed seeing Jackson. She hoped he didn't think she was avoiding him. But at the same time, she didn't want to seem like she was obsessed with him. She wondered if she should text him. But, he hadn't text her either. Oh, the rules of dating, she thought. Perhaps, she was over-thinking things.

Suzanne had enjoyed her weekend off. She felt the tension with Andy dissolving. Hopefully, he would forget that she had been looking in his laptop and they could get back to the way they were. It was just perfect.

Happy to have a day off all to herself, she planned what she would do. No drama today. Nick had told her to sit tight. She supposed he knew what he was doing. She felt a wave of relief when he contacted her a few days ago.

By noon, she accomplished almost all of the tasks on her list. She was invigorated by the energy this freedom had released. She cleaned and straightened, putting the house back in order. Suzanne was inspired to make a fabulous dinner for her and Andy; complete with candlelight and wine. She sat to make a grocery list for the ingredients she would need as well as the normal items they were low on.

While she wrote, her phone chimed signaling an incoming text. She glanced to see the sender's identification. It was Nick:

Hey there sunshine. Wanted to let you know I'm getting out in a couple of weeks. Hoping I can count on you if I need anything. Don't worry, all is well and will be.

She thought for a moment and responded:

Ok, yes of course. Just be careful. We've come too far.

His response:

Careful is my middle name. lol. Will be in touch. ☐ xoxo

She put her phone in her purse, grabbed her reusable grocery bags, and headed off to the store.

Brian Bailey had left four messages at the police station for Andy and Shaker. When he got no callback, he figured what he had to say wasn't important to them. He had things to do and couldn't sit around waiting any longer. He grabbed his keys and left the cabin. His phone was on the kitchen counter.

By the time the detectives had returned to the station, it was close to three p.m. They knew Millie's answers were evasive, so there was some extra digging to do. But where to start? Shaker brought up the idea of getting a court order for the adoption records and just being done with it. Andy agreed it might be the wise thing to do at this point since they were at a dead end. Everyone involved seemed to have issues with memory loss. They wrote up their reports so they could present a clear concise argument to the DA to secure an order for the documents.

Andy picked up a pile of pink message memos and waved them at Shaker who sat facing him. "Why do they write these things when they're using voicemail? What a waste. Unbelievable."

He put the messages aside and listened to the voicemail. He discovered four were from the same caller and corresponded to the pink memos. Brian Bailey. They all said the same thing. "I might have information about the body you found. Not sure about the time frame though."

"Dammit," Andy said. "Listen to this." He handed the phone to Shaker. "Why the hell didn't dispatch put this through to us when it first came in?"

Andy dialed the phone number left with the message. No Answer. He looked up the address belonging to Brian Bailey, Canton. "Come on, let's go."

They grabbed their jackets and raced to the door.

Chapter 58

Andy and Shaker slowly navigated the winding road that ran parallel to the Farmington River. From their GPS, they knew the street they were looking for would be a quick turn off down a dirt road. The other side of street rose steeply uphill to large developments with expansive homes.

Once they found the location, Andy took the turn, driving down the narrow pseudo street. The houses were sparse in this section, providing complete privacy to the residents. They were nearly down to the river, when they arrived at the upscale log cabin. It was modest and cozy in comparison to some of the other homes, but well maintained.

Andy parked the car and they walked up the path to the wrap-around porch. After knocking for a few minutes, they knew Bailey wasn't home. As they were about to admit defeat, a white Pathfinder pulled in behind them. They watched as a man of average size slowly got out of the vehicle. He pushed his ray-bans on top of his head, keeping his eyes on the two men staring at him from his porch.

"Can I help you, gentlemen?   He called, staying near his vehicle to provide a cautious distance.

"Brian Bailey?" Shaker answered.

"Who wants to know?" Bailey hollered back.

"We're detectives Gallagher and Shaker. I believe you called us today." Shaker said.

"Jeez, why didn't you say so in the first place?" Brian exhaled with relief. "Can I see some badges, before I come closer?" They flashed their shields, but from a distance, Brian still couldn't be sure. He would have to take a chance. "Ok, boys, give me a minute. I've got to grab some stuff to bring in."

Andy and Shaker waited while Brian unloaded his car. He carried a couple of bags of groceries up the path. When he reached the porch, he asked to see their ID again, admitting that he didn't get a good look from the distance. When he was satisfied, he invited them in.

They followed him into the cabin, noting the feel of comfort it afforded. For a bachelor's home, it was surprisingly tidy and uncluttered. The overstuffed sofa and club chairs were well used but not shabby. It appeared to be the perfect hideaway.

As Brian led them into his modern kitchen, he put the bags on the counter and asked them to sit. "You guys want some coffee? I'm gonna make some." They both nodded. "Great, so I suppose you got my messages, it that right?"

Andy answered, "Yes, we tried to call but didn't get an answer."

Brian picked up the phone lying on the counter, "And this would be why. I left it home when I went out. I didn't hear from you and I had things to do. I couldn't wait around all day. Figured you didn't care what I had to say."

"On the contrary, Brian, we do want to hear what you know. I apologize that our dispatcher didn't send your message to us while we were in the field. So, why don't you tell us what you know. And why did it take you so long to come forward?"

Bailey poured the coffee and handed each one a mug. He sat at the table with them, collecting his thoughts. "Ok, I was away for a few weeks. Fishing trip in Florida. Anyway, I got back a couple of days ago. I was catching up on mail and news when I saw this report on TV about a body that was found. It freaked me out a little because it was so close to home. I mean, stuff like that doesn't happen here.

"Something popped into my head and I wasn't sure what I was remembering. Then last night, it all came back. I wrote it down to be sure I had it all right. Now, I'm not sure if this was the right time, but I think what I saw happened a year or so ago. It stuck out because it was cold and the water was running fast. I thought it was strange that someone would want to go swimming under those conditions."

Andy continued to take notes. "Go on," he said.

"Ok, so I was sitting on the porch tying flies. It's a hobby, relaxes me, you know. Anyway, across the river, over there," he pointed to a spot on the other side where the river had cut a high bank. Tree roots and the sharp edges of rocks could be seen jutting out. He continued, "I see three people. I think one of them was a woman. They didn't see me because the trees were fuller then.   I don't know if they're talking or arguing. But I can see one of the guys pointing his finger in the chest of the other guy. The girl is pacing back and forth with her hands shoved in her jacket pockets. Every once in a while, she stops and says something. The two guys keep talking, then another guy comes along. He was bigger than other two. He starts talking or whatever too. Again, I can't hear if they're talking or yelling, because the river is moving fast so it washes out the sound. I went in the house for a second because my phone was ringing. When I came out, I see one of the guys take a dive into the water. I thought, Christ, he's a crazy bastard.   That's it."

Shaker thought for a moment, then asked, "You didn't see anything else?" He didn't want to let on about the broken bones or skull fracture.

Bailey shook his head. "No, that was it. But, I don't know, it seemed important. It just looked like a weird situation—the three of them all talking at the one guy who dove in the water."

Andy asked, "Can you described any of them?"

"No, I'm sorry. They were on the other side. I couldn't see their faces. I can tell you, they had jackets on. The big guy was wearing a Red Sox hoodie, he was sort of stocky too. The other two guys were about the same size and had on zip ups like North Face stuff. The girl had a jacket that came to her knees and a baseball cap on her head. I knew it was a girl because the coat was more like something a girl would wear."

After hearing Brian's account of what he saw that day, Andy and Shaker thought he just might be an eyewitness to everything leading up to the homicide. The missing part was actually the witnessing of the blows that Eric Popper took before he went into the water.

"Ok, Brian, thank you. This is really helpful. We're gonna look into it. Probably do another search in that area. If you think of anything else, call us." Andy handed Brian a card with his cell phone number to make sure that next time he received the call in a timely manner.

"Glad to help." Brian offered and walked them to the door.

The two detectives decided to drive to other side of the river to take a look around the area Brian Bailey had pointed to. It was a long shot, for sure, but maybe something had been left behind that wouldn't have been altered by nature. When they arrived, they hiked down to the bank, finding the location. They could see Bailey's cabin on the other side which was not camouflaged by the trees at this time of year. They supposed that he could see them from his vantage point but they wouldn't have been able to spot him, especially if they were not aware of his presence.

They took pictures of the area before they began their work. With gloves on and evidence bags that they unrealistically hoped to fill, they poked around. The sound of the river rushing below them amidst the quiet of the gentle breeze of the trees produced a hypnotic tranquility. Adapting to the peaceful silence, they separately went about their search. The pair found an assortment of cigarette butts, empty beer cans, and even a condom. They each wondered out loud, how people could be so careless with their trash when surrounded by such an awe-inspiring slice of nature.

Something shiny caught Phil Shaker's attention. It was embedded in the earth where webbed tree roots were exposed. He examined it closely before extracting it. To his disappointment, he realized it was only a penny. He left it in its resting place, not wanting to disturb the soil.

As Shaker continued to look around, Andy called to him, breaking the silent spell. "Hey, I think I found something."

Shaker carefully stepped over some loose rocks and approached his partner. "What do you have?"

After Andy had taken a few photos of the item, he gingerly removed the tiny bit from the shredded area where grass met rock. It was a small diamond stud earring. "What do you think? Could it be something?"

Shaker looked at the jewelry and commented, "I think, judging by how stuck it was, it could have been there a while."

"Yeah, I thought the same thing. Problem is after so much time, we're not likely to get any DNA off it. Still, let's take it. Could be something." Andy bagged the earring.

After about an hour, their search yielded no further results. The sun was setting so light was not on their side. They decided to pack it in and head back to the station.

Chapter 59

Nick's obsession with Carly was growing. He had no concrete reason for wanting revenge. In his twisted mind, she was responsible for his current situation. He couldn't comprehend that he, ultimately, had done this to himself. His anger had blinded him to that fact. Nothing was ever his fault; there was always someone to blame. In this case, it was Carly. Because, after all, she had kicked him out on his ass just because he got sick. He did not like rejection. He refused to believe that his volatile abusive temper amplified by his drinking may have been the catalyst.

As his discharge plans moved forward, he continued to strategize his payback plan. Yes, she would pay for her blatant disregard of his well-being. He was superior to everyone, including perfect little Carly Mancuso, in every way.

Sylvia, his nurse, intruded upon his thoughts, when she knocked on his door. "Time for your meds, Nick." She said.

Looking forward to his Percocet fix, he smiled and told her to come in. He took the small cup containing about ten pills for different reasons and swallowed them in one gulp.

"Won't be long now, Nick." She added. "You've come such a long way in just a few months."

"I know, I'm feeling pretty good." He answered. "It'll be nice to get back to normal life again."

Sylvia agreed, but wondered how much of a "normal" life he would have. She knew how close to death he had been. His body and mind would always have some deficits because of that.

He needed the multitude of medications to regulate and maintain his "normalcy".

"Well, let me know if you need anything." She said as she walked out of his room.

Chapter 60

A chicken was roasting in the oven. The smells of honey, lemon, and herb DE 'Provence wafted through the house. Suzanne had also added some white wine to the mixture. She would roast some red bliss potatoes with garlic and onion, then toss a simple Caesar salad. This was one of Andy's favorite meals.

She set the table and opened a bottle of an Oberon cab to give it enough time to breathe. Of course, she poured herself a small amount to sample—who wouldn't, she thought to herself. As she sipped, she prepared a small plate of warm peppered shrimp with a cool pesto dip. Suzanne enjoyed the nights they snacked in the kitchen while they waited for dinner. It was just after six, Andy would be home soon.

At seven, Suzanne took the chicken out of the oven and covered it with foil, to keep it moist. It looked perfect. She did the same with the potatoes. She poured another sip of wine and sampled a few more shrimp. At seven-thirty, she received a text from Andy, saying that he'd been held up and he probably wouldn't be home for an hour or two. Her reply was colored with understanding. She told him she'd keep dinner warm for him as well. She put her phone on the table and poured what was more than a sip of wine. She finished the shrimp.

During the night, Suzanne and Andy exchanged a few more texts which concerned his ETA. Finally, at 8:45, Andy walked through the door.

"Hey, Suzie Q, I'm so sorry I'm late. We were in the middle of something and needed to wrap it up before we left." He kissed her on the cheek.

"I know, I get it. I should be used to it by now. It's just that I made us this fabulous dinner."

"I can smell it. Amazing as always." He picked up the bottle of wine and poured—Just about a glass left. He rinsed out the bottle and saw the shrimp shells in the sink. "Well, I'm happy you ate a little."

"Yeah, I got hungry. I opened another bottle of wine in case there wasn't enough left. It's over there," she pointed. She added. "Are you ready to eat?"

"Oh, I had a grinder a little earlier."

"Of course you did." She slurred. "Well, I'm going to have some, the smell has been driving me crazy." With fumbling fingers, she ripped back the foil and a tore off a hunk of the breast meat. She spooned a few potatoes and some soggy salad onto her plate. Before sitting at the table, she refilled her glass from the fresh bottle.

Andy watched her eat as if she hadn't eaten in days. She was loading one forkful after another into her mouth. He was relieved he was certified in advanced life support in case he need to administer a Heimlich to her. He decided to put a few pieces of chicken on his plate to appease her and maybe slow her down. He wasn't really hungry, but it did smell pretty good. "This is great, Suzanne."

Surprised, she looked up at him with her fork in her hand. She had been so consumed in the food that she didn't know he was sitting with her. "Oh, yeah, it is. Hungry, after all?" She asked.

"I guess I am." He answered.

Being conscious of her slurred speech, she over-enunciated her words as she spoke. "So, what kept you so late? Still working on Eric's case?"

"Well, I can't really get into details, but yeah, we had a couple of interesting developments. We just needed to do some follow-up and get the reports in."

Losing her patience with this case and the fact that he didn't even care he was so late she blurted, "Well, why can't you tell me anything about it, Andy? It's not like I'm gonna go broadcasting it."

"Suzanne, you know I don't like to talk about my cases at home. I know some cops talk things over with their spouses, but I just can't. Especially since this involves you to a degree."

"Shit, Andy, how does it involve me? Just because I knew the guy? How about maybe because I knew him, I could help you make sense of your new 'interesting developments'. Did you ever think of that?" She spoke in a tone that was approaching something pretty close to shouting. Her face was red and she felt anger rising in her that made her want to explode. She took a deep breath in an attempt to calm herself before she did.

Stunned by her outburst, Andy just looked at her with his mouth full of chicken. "Ok, ok, calm down. There's no....."

"Don't tell me to calm down." She interrupted. "I made a nice romantic dinner then you come home two hours late. I'm sick of this investigation and your secrecy. I'm sick of your damn job and I'm sick of you too. If it involves Eric, it involves me." She was now at a full shouting volume.

He knew she'd drank a lot of wine, but it wasn't a good excuse. He struck back. "Well, you can always hack my laptop again if you really have to know." He threw down his napkin and brought his plate to the sink. He re-covered the food and stored it in the fridge.

The tension had grown so thick, he couldn't see through it. If he had, he would have noticed the tear leaking from the corner of her eye as she remained immobile at the table. Instead, he just left the room.

Chapter 61

Late September

Tuesday

Bright and early, Carly was sipping her coffee. She wanted to get an early start on things today. She had a few things to do around the house before heading out to Prospect Hill. She looked forward to seeing her friends, especially Jackson.

She had not spoken with him since their date two days ago, so she was feeling a little apprehensive. Whatever happened, she could handle it. It had been a lovely evening and if that was all that came from it, she could be content. It had been a long time since she let herself feel that way. It was wonderful to realize that she still could.

When she finished her morning chores, she showered and dressed. She fixed her short hair, separating the layers with her fingers to give it just the right amount of messiness. As she put on her new Frye boots, her heart skipped with an involuntary flutter. She smiled to herself when realized that she felt just a little nervous about seeing Jack.

At nine, she was ready to go. She walked up the steep hill leading to the house. No matter how many times she took this walk, she was always enchanted by the house. She imagined what it must have been like back in the day when the town was brimming with industry and wealth. She envisioned men wearing suits with skinny ties and top-hats; women with corseted dresses in rich jeweled colors that flowed when they walked.

She wondered if the family that once lived there sat on the spindled porch waiting for the embellished carriage to arrive in the circular driveway. Did fair-haired children sprint off the porch to meet their father when he arrived from his factory? She pictured the scene of dad scooping them up in his arms and twirling them around with a hearty deep laugh of joy. The kind of joy that only the love of children could bring.

She walked up the path to the house, suddenly feeling a twinge of sadness. She wondered if she would ever feel that joy. She made herself shake it off. Her life was full of people who she loved and loved her in return. For now, that was enough It had to be.

She pushed open the front door and as usual, the smell of Irene's breakfast preparation assaulted her senses. Instant hunger. Carly strolled into the kitchen, finding it bustling with activity. Everyone had a specific job each morning before they left for their various obligations.

"Good morning," she called. "I was hoping I'd be on time for breakfast."

Jenn was the first to speak, "Carly, yeah! You made it." Jenn put down the plates she was carrying and squeezed Carly in her typical way of saying hello.

The others also expressed their pleasure when they saw Carly. Although, it had only been two days, they still missed her. She was part of their family.

"Yes, I did." She laughed. "Irene, is there time for me to run up to say hello to Jack?" she asked.

"Yes, but be quick." Irene answered. She insisted on eating while the food was hot and fresh.

"Ok, be right back." Carly climbed the stairs to the third floor office, knowing she'd find Jack there going over his daily paperwork. He preferred to get it out of the way early so it wouldn't interfere with his other duties. With some apprehension, she poked her head in the door.

"Good morning," she called to him.

When he heard her voice, he rose from his desk and approached her. Then he surprised her when he wrapped her in his arms. "I'm so happy to see you." He whispered. "I worried when I didn't hear from you yesterday."

When he let her go, she studied his face and said, "I'm happy to see you too. I think I also worried."

He didn't realize he was holding his breath when he exhaled. "I guess since it's been so long for both us, we're acting like high-schoolers."

She laughed, recognizing that for her, her feelings had been bottled for a few years now. She never thought she feel them again. "Is that your clinical judgment?" she asked.

"I guess it is." They stood for a moment, facing each other, just holding hands.

"So, um, can we get together again sometime?" Carly asked. "I mean if you're busy, I get it."

"I'd like that. But something bothers me." He said with his face scrunched in puzzlement.

"What is it?" She asked, fearing the worst.

"Well, what do people do when they start dating? I mean, we could go out to eat, that's always good and of course, a necessity. But seriously, do we plan activities? Remember, I haven't dated in a long time."

"Oh my god, you're right," she laughed. "I don't know. I guess we find things that we like to do and do them together. We could always take a ride somewhere."

"I guess that's true. It's probably more important that whatever we do, we talk and get to know each other in this new way."

"I would agree." She stood on her tip-toes and kissed him on the cheek. "I do like you, Jackson Foley."

Together, they descended the stair and headed toward the kitchen.

After breakfast and clean-up, Jack disappeared to his office to finish some work. Carly sat with Jenn and Irene to assess the progress for Lucy's baby shower. They had one week to complete the final preparation.   Jenn reported that the others were on task. Irene's menu was ready to go as well. The problem looming now was how to keep Lucy out of the house so they could decorate and set-up.

Carly suggested that Lucy's mother could help with that. "I was thinking that after her usual Sunday church with her mom, her mom could have all sorts of errands to do. They could be busy for a couple of hours. What do you think?"

"I think that's a great plan. So obvious, I wish I thought of it." Jenn laughed.

"Yeah, I figure it would give us about three hours or so for the cooking and decorating. Is that enough time for you Irene?"

Irene thought for a minute. "That should be perfect. I can start on Saturday too. Since I'm usually cooking something, I don't think Lucy would think anything of it."

"Perfect! Operation Lucy is now in fully activated." Jenn chuckled as the three high-fived.

Suzanne sat at her laptop monitoring her patient. Her head throbbed from the large volume of wine she had consumed the night before. Her stomach felt queasy even though she had chugged some Pepto before she left. She hoped her breath didn't wreak of that stale alcohol smell that lingers the next day.

She thought of Andy, pretending to sleep when she snuck out of bed. She couldn't be sure if he had slept during the night because she had pretty much passed out. She had polished off the second bottle after he left her in the kitchen.

She was so angry with him, although her reasons weren't as rational this morning as they had been last night. Then he made the crack about his laptop. She knew her outburst was the catalyst, but still he didn't have to bring it up. She assumed they were over that. "What's that rule?" she thought. "Oh yeah, never assume anything."

She kept watch on her patient who had been improving over the past few days. Her history was similar to Nick's; however, she didn't suffer as much damage as he had. She was lucky. She hung another bag of medication, checking to be sure of the dosage. "Ativan, man, could I use some of that right now." She restarted the drip.

Chapter 62

Staring at the whiteboard, he thought out loud, "So, I guess the big question is-- what now? I mean we've got bits and pieces of a lot of interesting things. But do they make a whole?"

Phil Shaker glanced up from his desk. "Oh, nice job, man, you're referring to Gestalt."

"What the heck are you talking about, oh master of all things trivial?" Andy said shaking his head at Shaker and not for the first time today.

"Come on, tell me you know what Gestalt is. You amaze me sometimes, Andy. For a smart guy, well, I don't have to say the rest."

"Alright, I've heard of it, but I guess I'm not as schooled as you. Why don't you fill me in."

"Well it's really a pretty simple concept. See, you can have all these random parts that don't mean a thing. But when you put them together as a whole, they form something. Like, for example, if you saw a flat piece of wood and a few random wooden bars, you wouldn't think much of it. But if you put them together, you would have a table. The whole is greater than its parts." Andy nodded. "So, my friend, when you said we've got all these bits of information, you hit the nail on the head. We have to figure out how they make a whole. And my gut tells me that they do."

Andy laughed, "Does your gut also tell you, you're a pain in the ass?"

"Actually, I was complimenting you on your observational skills. It made me realize what we're doing."

"Thanks buddy, but you don't have to suck up."

Continuing to smile, Andy said, "So, I guess we should finish getting the adoption papers, then move from there."

"Yeah, makes sense. Any progress about that yet?"

"The DA said we'd have a better chance getting Gustafson's records then unsealing the birth certificate. I guess we start there."

Chapter 63

Carly arrived home later that afternoon, feeling exhilarated after her walk down the hill. However, she smiled to herself knowing that wasn't the only reason. Her encounter with Jack had eliminated the doubt she had been experiencing. She knew he felt the same and that just made her plain happy.

She opened her front door and inhaled the sweet smell of freshly brewed coffee. Then, she felt sick. "I know I didn't set up the pot. I would never do that in the afternoon." Cautiously, she entered the kitchen and turned off the coffee maker. Her previously missing go-cup sat on the counter waiting to be filled.

"What the heck is going on?" She thought. She scanned the room for anything else out of place. Before leaving the kitchen, Carly grabbed the baseball bat she kept in the pantry. Taking baby steps, she walked from room to room, praying that no one would jump out at her.

She stood at the bottom of the staircase, knowing she would have to go up. In the back of her mind, she heard a voice saying, "don't go up." She thought of those movies where the helpless girl always goes up and gets trapped. But she was not helpless and she would not get trapped.

She began her slow ascent, step by step. She listened intently for any foreign sound. The only thing she heard was her own breathing. She prayed the intruder couldn't. When she reached the top, she warily entered three of the four bedrooms. She was close to exhaling in relief when she took a step into the fourth bedroom- hers. Then she saw it, there on the bed. The note had her name on it. In a childish scrawl it said, "I'll be seeing you soon."

She dropped the bat and dialed 911.

Sitting in his favorite spot, he watched from the church lot across the street. Lighting another cigarette, he smiled when he thought of how juicy this was getting. He was really enjoying the game. The best part was that no one could tie him to any of it. No one knew who he was.

When the police arrived, the young officers hesitated before getting out of the cruiser. Officer Zelinsky had been here before. He explained to his partner that this woman was convinced someone was getting into her house and messing with her stuff. He muttered that he thought she was just forgetful or maybe she wanted attention. Either way, they had a job to do. They exited their car and walked to the door.

When Carly saw them approach, she immediately threw open the door. She couldn't help but notice the exasperated looks on their face. Her immediate response was frustration with their attitude. Instead, she apologized for bothering them, perhaps somewhat sarcastically.

"Oh no problem, Ms. Mancuso." Zelinsky said. "So, what was it this time? A grilled cheese sandwich left on the counter?"

She composed herself and spoke in a confident but flat pointed tone of voice. "That was not called for Officer. The missing cup made a reappearance and was left sitting on the counter next the fresh coffee that I did not make. In addition, officers, a note was left on my bed. I did not touch it, so you can see for yourself." She looked at their faces, noting a lack of acknowledgement. She asked, "what would you like to see first?"

Officer Zelinsky glanced at his partner, "Well, let's have a look at the coffee pot first." They followed her into the kitchen doing a quick scan of the rooms along the way. Upon arriving in the kitchen, they performed an obligatory inspection of the area. "And you're sure you didn't make it earlier?"

"Officer, I am sure. The pot has a two hour shut off timer. I have been away for three hours. I am certain you can do the math. And if your next response is to point out that I may have set the time to have it brewed upon my return, you can check it to see that I have not changed it from its original time of six a.m." It was all she could do to keep her cool.

"Ok, thank you, I see. May we see the note?"

"Yes, please follow me." Carly led them upstairs and pointed to the note on the bed. "I think that proves that someone was in my home."

Zelinsky lost some of his smugness and retrieved the note with a gloved hand. He placed it in a bag. "Do you have any idea who might be doing this? He asked, taking the situation more seriously.

"I would say it's my former boyfriend. However, he's in a rehab hospital right now so I doubt it's him. And if it's not him, I just don't know who it could be."

The young policemen took her statement and asked a few more questions. They decided to check out Nick Pellegrino after hearing some of the history. It was a long shot since he was still in the hospital.

"Ms. Mancuso, I don't think you're in any danger. But we will speak with Mr. Pellegrino to assess him."

Carly still wasn't sure about these two, but she thanked them all the same. They assured her, they would get back to her with any additional information.

He watched the cops leave, thinking this was better than the movies. But then, real life always was. He made a quick call, then drove away.

Chapter 64

When the police left, Carly dumped the coffee and threw away the cup that had reappeared. She was annoyed with herself for not doing something sooner. She knew she couldn't depend on that Zelinsky guy. He was a green cop on a power trip. She realized he wasn't going to lift a finger; he was probably laughing at her right now. Yes, he might run the scenario by his superior, but most likely, it wouldn't go much farther than that because he would paint the picture with his subjective point of view.

Knowing that her investment in the situation meant more to her than Zelinsky, she thought, Rule of the day---don't count on others to do the job for you. Do it yourself. Do it right.

Carly dialed her phone which was answered on the first ring. "You, ok?" Jenn asked when she saw Carly's name on caller ID.

"Yes, I'm fine. But I've got a little problem and I think I need your help."

"I'm all ears," Jenn replied.

Carly remembered that Jenn's father, Orlando Diaz, had a small home security business which lent itself to many connections. When Jenn left her husband, Marty, her dad had him followed. Marty had been an abusive and vengeful husband pounding Jenn into the ground both psychologically and physically. The night Jenn finally mustered the courage to leave him, she lay in the emergency room with three cracked ribs, a black eye, and a pretty bad concussion. The charges against Marty never stuck and Orlando knew when someone was this determined, a restraining order would not be enough. It was at that moment, her father called in favors because he needed to know his daughter would be safe.

After explaining the situation to Jenn in greater detail, Jenn assured Carly that she would call her father. "I wish you had told me all of this sooner, Carly." She said. From her own experience she knew things were escalating. Carly said she would wait to hear from Orlando.

Carly thought of calling Sally next but decided against it. Although, her advice was sound and intuitive, Sally was always practical. She didn't want to be talked out of taking action. Practical was not an option.

Orlando called Carly within a few minutes. They discussed the events of the past few weeks. Orlando offered some idea, "Carly, let me install a system for you. That's the first step at this point. We need to keep whoever this is out of your home. I can put up a few hidden cameras too inside and outside."

"I agree, Mr. Diaz. At this point, I know I'm not imagining things."

"Ok, I'll send someone over first thing in the morning. Next, I've got a couple of associates who work in the investigation part of the business. Mostly domestic stuff. You know, unfaithful husbands, stuff like that. I'll make a call and we watch Nicky, you know keep tabs on him. I'd love to put some monitoring device in his room, but I think that's a long shot. So far, so good, Carly?"

"So far, very good."

"Ok, I'm gonna make some calls and put the wheels in motion. I'll call you tomorrow, but in the meantime, expect Gary Cardwell to be at your house for setup at seven a.m. Check his ID, you don't want to let someone in, assuming it's him."

"Got it. Thank you so much, Mr. Diaz. I appreciate your advice and your help."

"No problem at all, Carly. I'm happy to help"

When the call was ended, Carly felt a great sense of relief.

As predicted, Zelinsky recapped the incident at Carly's house with his superior. He colored the facts with a distorted point of view. The note, they decided, did not sound threatening. However, it needed to be logged in with the rest of the documentation. Case closed.

Chapter 65

Suzanne arrived home from work following what she considered to be the longest eight hour shift of her life. Note to self, do not drink a bottle and a half of wine on a work night. She felt exhausted from the sheer effort of maintaining her professional focus.

She inhaled the mystical elixir of the gods called coffee. As some of the fog lifted, she wondered what would happen when Andy came home. She couldn't stand the thick silence. She knew she should apologize, but then so should he. They needed to talk or this mess would only fester until it exploded in her face.

After a long exhausting day, Phil Shaker walked to Andy's desk with triumph on his face and paper in hand. "We got it. The subpoena for Gustafson's records. The judge signed it. The DA said if we get something useful from him, we still may be able to get the official documents unsealed."

Andy had been distracted most of the day, trying to keep his tryst with Suzanne compartmentalized. It just made him wonder what was up with her. He brought himself back to the present and this case, when he answered, "That's great. When can we go see him?"

Shaker checked the time. "Well, buddy, it almost five. My guess is ol' Vinnie is long gone for the day."

"You're probably right. I didn't realize it was so late already."

"Time flies and all that, you know. I guess we wait til the morning. Think you'll be able to sleep with the anticipation?" He laughed.

His spirits lifting, Andy said, "Don't you worry about me, I'll sleep like a baby and be up bright and early."

"So, I have to ask. What's up? You haven't been your usual sarcastic self." Shaker noticed.

"I guess I hid it well, if the omnipotent Phil Shaker just noticed." Andy smiled.

"Nah, I picked up on it early today. Thought you might shake it off. So, what gives?"

"Oh, Suzanne and I had a fight last night. She was all drunk and pissy when I got home. Going on about the case. I finally snapped and told her if she wanted information, she could always snoop my laptop again. Not sure what to expect when I get home."

"Oh man, that sucks." For once, Shaker had no tid-bit of advice to offer his best friend and partner.

"Yeah it does. Anyway, I thought maybe, if I told her something, she'd back off and feel better about the case. Aside from the fact she dated the guy and he tried to kill her, I just can't figure why she's interested in the investigation."

"Hell, I don't know, maybe that's why. She still has some fear of him and needs to know he's really gone?" Shaker added.

"Hmmm," Andy thought. "you know, I guess that makes some sense. The almighty Shaker has spoken. No other pearls of wisdom to impart?"

Shaker smiled and thought for a minute. "Yeah, give her something. Something small and inconsequential. Something that won't affect the investigation or the facts we have so far."

"You know, I think that might be a good idea." Andy suddenly felt some freedom from the burden he'd been carrying all day. "I think I'll head out early today. Maybe I can get things back on track."

"Sounds good to me. Anyway, there's not much more we can do today. Let's head over to Gustafson's about nine tomorrow."

"Ok, I'll see you early." Andy grabbed his jacket and left for home.

Suzanne was still sitting at the kitchen table when Andy walked in the door. She was almost afraid to look at him when she heard his gentle voice say,

"Hey Suzie Q, I'm sorry." He sat down next to her, eyeing her wearied expression.

"Andy, I'm the one who should be apologizing to you. I had too much to drink which is no excuse, but I'm sorry for that and the things I said."

"Listen," he went on, "I understand now why you need to know about the case."

Her expression changed with a flash of alarm in her eyes. "You do?" She answered, keeping her voice steady.

"Yeah, I do. You need to be sure it was Eric's body, so he can never hurt you again."

With a quick shift in her emotions, she agreed. "Yes, I guess that's it."

"I'm sorry I didn't understand that sooner. Well, I did tell you that the DNA proved it was Eric. I can also tell you we got an order to look at the adoption attorney's documents. That's a good thing because if we can find his birth parents we can figure out if he was doing something shady with them. Like blackmail."

"I know about the DNA thing and that's good. But how can the adoption records help?" She asked attempting to sound interested instead of concerned.

"We'll know when we see them. Like I said, blackmail is a powerful thing."

Her heart was beating hard. She composed herself and said. "I guess you're right. Listen, I'm hungry and tired. Can we just order a pizza tonight?"

With a smile, Andy said, "Of course, that sounds great. I'm going to shower. Order whatever you want." He kissed her on top of her head.

Suzanne thought for a moment and immediately shot off a text:

They're opening the adoption records. ?????

Immediately she received a response:

Shit   I'm getting out of here. We need to talk.

She wrote back:

I'll try to get free.

She called in a large pepper and tomato pizza and sat at the table waiting for it to arrive.

Chapter 66

They say karma is a bitch. Well, I don't know about that. Yeah, I survived, but I really don't believe I crashed and burned because of karma. I didn't do anything wrong, well, not really. If everyone along the way, just did what I told them, things would have been just fine. I'm so much smarter than they are. If they'd have just shut up and listened to me, there wouldn't have been any problems. I still think about that.

So, here I sit in a nursing-rehab facility after a very long stint at the hospital. I'm finally ready to move into my own place. I'm pretty healthy now, relatively speaking; yeah, I still need some care and a lot of medical follow-up. But I've gotten strong, I'm packed, and I'm ready to go. The nurses will miss me because of course they like me very much. I'm important here. I give them advice on better ways to do things. You see from my vantage point as a patient, I know how to make things better in this hell-hole of a rehab center.

Finally, Nurse Ratchett, as I affectionately refer to Sylvia, my day nurse, comes to tell me my ride is here. I'm heading out to my new apartment. I'm a little excited because it's all paid for by the state. You see, I'm technically disabled now. I was able to get into this program so I could go "home". I guess it's cheaper for them than paying for my hospital stay.

I take a last look around the little hovel of a room that has been my home for the past few months. Shaking my head, I think, "good riddance. No sentimentality here." I pick up the crumpled paper bag and cardboard box that hold all my possessions and I slam the door shut behind me. "Look out world, I'm really back."

Chapter 67

Late September

Wednesday

As Nick settled into his new digs, he surveyed the room. He was pleased with his furniture selections. He was also loving his new bed. His cable and internet had been installed the previous day, so he was ready to go. He had his yellow-lined pad in front of him where he sat at his new desk with his new laptop. All bought and paid for, compliments of the state and this wonderful patient program. "Thank you, Connecticut," he said out loud.

Before he got down to the business of making contacts in the real estate field, he had one more important call to make. He punched in the numbers on his phone. The recipient answered immediately, but with impatience looming in his tone. He listened intently to what Nick had to say. Hesitantly, he agreed, and the call was disconnected.

He finished his work and checked the time. He admitted to himself he was feeling exhausted after his first afternoon home. He had a very productive day. It was time turn in.

Chapter 68

Thursday

Carly was awake bright and early, waiting for the security installer to arrive. Gary Cardwell, appeared at her door with his identification in hand. He walked in, surveying her house along the way. He made recommendations for placement of motion detectors and door sensors. He thought a small discreet camera outside would be a nice addition to the system.

The installation was quick and painless. Carly was happy Mr. Diaz's company preferred a wireless approach. It went much more smoothly than if drilling and wiring were involved. Once finished, Gary went over the system with Carly. She was impressed by its simplicity.

Promptly at eight, she was dressed and left for Prospect Hill. The shower was only three days away and they needed to regroup while Lucy was at her doctor's appointment.

She arrived about the same time as Jack. "Hey you." She said.

"Hey back. Listen Carley, I was thinking that it might be nice if we went out to dinner tonight. It's short notice, but what do you think?"

She laughed. "Well, it's not like I have so much going on that I have to plan too much. But yeah, I think that sounds great. What time and where?"

"I was thinking a real date. You know, I'll pick you up at six and take you somewhere amazing."

"Oh wow, how fun. So, where is this amazing place? I need to dress accordingly.

"How about Bobby Flay's at the Mohegan Sun Casino?" He asked, hoping she'd like his choice.

"What a great place. That sound like fun. We can shop too or gamble if we want."

"Yeah, that's what I thought too. Plus, I think there's a band in the Wolf's Den tonight. Lots to do besides just dinner. Then, it's a date?" He asked.

"It's a date."

As usual, they walked into the house to be greeted by the smell of Irene's breakfast. Everyone sat and ate together. Family. Jackson excused himself after patting his full belly and headed to his office. Lucy left shortly thereafter, when her ride arrived to take her to her appointment in Hartford.

During the cleanup, the remaining women, reviewed their assigned tasks for the upcoming shower. They had all made progress and so far, everything was moving forward as planned. Jenn checked items off her list, feeling satisfied, that they would pull this off.

Nicky received the text he was waiting for. He smiled and plugged the charger into his phone. He could put that behind him and move forward towards his money-making scheme. He still had "operation Carly" on his mind, so every so often, he would scribble a note on his yellow pad.

Luckily for Suzanne, it was her scheduled day off. She had many things on her "to-do list", but meeting Nick was becoming a priority. She was tentative about talking to him again, despite the fact that she needed to know what was going on. Everything was so confusing to her.

Brian Bailey woke from a vivid dream. "I wonder," he thought and jotted down what he remembered from it. He turned over and fell back into sleep.

Andy arrived at the station early. He smiled when he saw that Shaker had beat him. His ritual coffee sat on his desk waiting for him.

He took a lingering sip and thanked his partner, "So, what brings you in so early?'

"The anticipation is killing me. I can't wait to get my hands on those documents."

Andy laughed and agreed that this was going to be good day. They were hopeful that the adoption records would tell them something they didn't know before.

Shaker closed his laptop and checked the time. "Nine o'clock. Showtime." Off they went.

Chapter 69

The two detectives arrived at the office of Attorney Vince Gustafson shortly after nine; subpoena in hand. His secretary was not present to greet them. They walked to Vince's office and found him engrossed in something on his computer.

"Morning, Vince." Andy called through the open door.

"Oh, detectives. To what do I owe the honor of such an early morning visit?" He asked in his jovial manner. He rose to greet them, extending his meaty hand in their direction.

"Nice to see you too, Vince." Shaker said. "So, Vince, we got the subpoena for you records. Can you get things together for us?"

Vince plopped in his chair with a thump of defeat. "Sure. May I see it?" He read it carefully, trying to buy some time as he did. "I guess it's all in order. I suppose there's no dissuading you to drop this search?" He finally said.

"Sorry, Vince." Andy answered.

"Ok, well, I put the old docs on flash drives to save storage space. Let me just look for it. I keep them all labeled in the file cabinet." He unlocked the cabinet and began looking for the file marked "Popper adoption".

Andy and Shaker observed Vince methodically go through the thumb-drives in the cabinet. Each was in an individual case and filed alphabetically by year.

"Hmm. Strange." He said.

They saw him becoming somewhat frazzled as he searched a second time.

"Is there a problem?" Andy asked.

Vince looked up with concern knitting his brows. "It's not here."

"Didn't you just have it the other day?" Shaker reminded him.

"No, that one contained my personal notes. The one I'm looking for has the preliminary court documents. I'm afraid, it's just not here." Vince held up his hands in defeat. Inside, he felt relief.

"Hey Vince, let's go through all the years. Maybe it was filed in the wrong period."

"Do you know how many years and cases I've handled. This could take days."

"We'll each take a drawer. Maybe that'll make it move faster." Andy offered. "And where's your secretary? She could help."

"Yes, but Emily's off today, as luck would have it." He frowned. "Alright, but we're only looking for the Popper drive. If you see any other name that peaks your interest, don't even think about asking about it."

"Understood." The two nodded.

It took most of the morning searching through four drawers containing the small plastic cases that protected each drive. The search yielded no results. The case in question was definitely not there. What they did find, however, was a minute scratch in the wood near the lock.

Vince admitted he had not noticed the defect previously. He also stated that he was sure if it was there, he would have.

"Ok, so are we all thinking someone picked the lock and took the drive?" Shaker finally said.

Vince wiped the faint beads of sweat that was forming on his forehead. "I will concede that. I just can't imagine why."

"So, now what? Let's get the techs here. Maybe there are some prints or something they can find." Andy made the call from his cell phone. As they waited, they asked Vince for his personal flash-drive.

"Sorry, boys, but the subpoena was for court records. Nothing personal, I hope you understand."

Chapter 70

He noticed the camera the minute he got out of the car. Interesting development, he thought. Dressed in his usual gas company uniform, he got back in the car and buckled up. No sense in taking any chances. This might call for a different approach.

It was mid-afternoon when Suzanne arrived to meet Nick at his apartment. When she walked in wearing sunglasses, he had to laugh.

"Is that a disguise? Little dramatic, don't you think? You're not a spy, you know. Should have put up your hair instead."

"Well, I feel like I'm being strung along. You have got to level with me. I've built a nice little life for myself. You know that. Then here you are and all hell breaks loose. I won't have whatever you're doing ruin it."

"Calm down. Nothing concerns you. Just relax and stay out of it."

After an hour, Suzanne felt the meeting with Nick went well. He convinced her that all was just fine and dandy. She still couldn't shake the feeling that Nicky's idea of "fine and dandy" differed from her own. She decided to lie low but to keep her ears and eyes opened.

Chapter 71

Carly was dressed and ready when Jackson arrived, promptly at six p.m. She was wearing a pair of black palazzo pants with a fitted black top that hit her at the waist. She wore a short pink cardigan and black ankle-strap pumps. She checked herself in the mirror on the way to answer the door.

Jack was smiling at her as she opened it. From behind his back, he handed her a bunch of multi-colored gerbera daisies and gave her a kiss.

"Oh, Jack, these are beautiful. You're so sweet. I guess this is a real date, after all."

"It definitely is." He told her. "All set for our big adventure? I made reservations for six forty-five."

"Ok, let's go." Carly grabbed her purse, set the alarm, and pulled the door closed behind her.

They arrived in plenty of time and were seated right away. They started with a bottle of wine while they studied the menu. They decided to share an appetizer of the lobster avocado cocktail. Jack ordered a filet mignon; Carly chose the salmon. It was a fabulous dinner that included laughter along with comfortable conversation and an indescribable chocolate mousse cake for dessert.

When they finished, they grabbed a couple of coffees and strolled around the casino. Jack indulged Carly's need to peruse the shops. They lost a few dollars on the slot machines. When they heard the band playing, they found themselves drawn to the

Wolf Den, which was a free area for musical acts. They were both excited to see Eddie Money performing.

They weren't able to grab seats, so they stood just outside the circular area. As they listened, Carly was swaying to the music, singing along. Jack took Carly by the hand, spinning her around as they started to dance in the perimeter. Jack was naturally a great dancer, but since he didn't take himself seriously, he had Carly laughing at some of his exaggerated moves. She, of course, went right along with him, dips and all. They sang along with Eddie to "Take me Home Tonight". They sang to each other complete with animation and imaginary mics and all.

When the evening came to an end, they walked to the car with their Godiva dark chocolate soft serve cones. Jack looked at his watch. "You know, this is the first time I've checked all night. It's after midnight. Can you believe it?"

"Really? Where did the time go?" She pulled her sweater closer to her. "It's a little chilly tonight."

He put his arm around her. "I'll keep you warm. Here, why don't you take my jacket." He offered.

"Oh no, thanks we're almost to the car anyway. Man, this ice cream is amazing!" After a few more steps she said, "Jack, this was a fabulous night. It's the best date I've ever been on. But you know, I think it's because of the company. Thank you."

He opened the car door for her. "Thank you too. I had an amazing time too. Boy, for two people who weren't sure what to do on a date, we really rocked it, huh?"

"I guess we did!"

Jack pulled the car into Carly's driveway and walked her to the door. Their conversation had briefly touched upon the events surrounding her need for an alarm system. She opened the door and disarmed it, feeling safe. Jack took her in his arms and kissed her good-night. The kiss was an explosion for them. The sparks that flew caused them to be lost in each other, in this moment that seemed to last forever. They gazed deeply at each other with heavy eyes.

"I think I should go." Jack said. "For tonight, anyway.

Carly searched his face and knew he was right. It was too soon.

When she shut the door, she drifted through her living room, still caught in the haze of romance and the kiss. She realized she was smiling while she set up her coffee pot. "What a night." She said and headed up to bed.

As she lay in bed, anxiety began to build in her. A memory was surfacing that she tried to bury. "Why am I thinking of that, right now?"

It was after a night out with Nick about a few months before he crashed and burned, ending up in the hospital. The evening had started out nicely enough. But then he had one too many shots as usual. He became belligerent, accusing her of flirting with the waiter, who by the way was only twenty-one. He had become so offensive, that a man from the next table stepped in and asked him to keep it down. Instead of lashing out at the man, Nick composed himself and complied with his usual charm.

When they arrived home, all Carly wanted was to go to bed to get away from him. Instead, Nick grabbed her in an attempt to kiss her. He had other things in mind. She pulled away unable to tolerate the stench of his liquored breath. He lunged at her again and pushed her to the ground. He forced himself on top of her tearing at her clothes. Wildly, with all the strength she could muster, she shoved him off her.

She stood over him, "Leave me the hell alone, you bastard."

She tried to shake those thoughts with some deep breaths. When did he become that monster? Was she too smitten to recognize the signs? Had he always been that way? He seemed to transform into the beast without notice. She then, realized the memory of that night was triggered by Jack's kiss at the door. She cursed Nick Pellegrino and his ability to slither into her life without warning.

When she finally relaxed enough to sleep, it was fitful at best. Giving in to the restlessness of the night, she rose early. The coffee started brewing and soon the world would be a better place. She had to admit that as tired as she was, her spirits were no longer dragged down. She would not allow Nick to ruin the wonderful night she had.

While she waited for her coffee, she checked her phone. She hadn't looked at it all last night. How interesting was that? She discovered there was a voicemail from Orlando Diaz.

"Hi, Carly, it's Orlando. Something came up. Give me a call."

Somewhat apprehensive from the cryptic message, she decided to get it over with. She dialed the number without realizing the time. It was five-thirty a.m.

"Oh dear," she thought, and was about to hang up when a cheerful Orlando Diaz answered.

"Hey Carly, you're up early."

"I might say the same about you. I hope I didn't wake you. I didn't realize the time when I called."

"No worries, I've been up for a while now. I'm actually on my third coffee." He laughed.

She laughed along with him, commenting that she had just poured her first. "So, Mr. Diaz, I'm almost afraid to ask, but what was your voicemail all about?"

Getting right to the point, he said, "The guy who's following Pellegrino, saw him meet with a woman yesterday. She was average size, wearing sunglasses. She had blonde hair, kind of curly. Anyway, we ran her plates. Name is Suzanne McGregor. Ring any bells?"

Carly thought for a few minutes and decided the information meant nothing to her. "No, I don't think so."

"Ok, I just thought you should know. If you do think of something, let me know. We can always follow the woman too."

"Thank you, I'll let you know if anything comes to mind."

They disconnected the call. She sipped her coffee, checked her emails, then decided to shower. As the hot water washed over her, something clicked. Nick's nurse was Suzanne and she was a blonde. "What the heck?" she said. She had to think this one through first. Mulling it over, she wondered if she should call Orlando back. He could always do a background check on that nurse.

Or maybe Nick charmed his way into her life as he had done with so many others. "Yep, something to think about for sure."

Chapter 72

Friday

Early Friday morning, Andy and Shaker discussed what they had so far. After the crime scene techs inspected Vince Gustafson's office, they were able to determine that there had been a break-in. The exterior door lock had been manipulated in the same way of the file cabinet. There were no finger prints left, as expected.

"Who would want that file? And who knew we were interested in them?" Andy said out loud.

"I've been thinking about that too. Millie Popper is really the only other person that I can think of."

"But she wouldn't have the resources to do this. Yeah, true, she wouldn't want those records exposed, but still, I can't see her thinking of a plan like this."

Shaker put down his pen and conceded, "I guess we're back at square one. Maybe we should go back to the DA and the judge to open the adoption files after all."

"Man, this whole case is taking way too long. We should have been beyond this step weeks ago."

"Agreed." Shaker said. "Let's hit the road, maybe we can get something done today."

While they were getting ready to leave, The ME, Dr. Oates, sauntered over to them, grinning. "Hey boys, glad I caught you in."

"Hey Doc," Shaker said, "what brings to our neck of the woods?"

"I'm glad you asked, Phil, my boy. I'm going to tell you a little story."

Andy and Shaker sat down, hoping this tale wouldn't take too long.

"Go on," Andy replied, hoping to hurry things along.

"Well, remember our body from the river?" They both nodded; how could they not? The doc went on, "Well, after I got identification from the DNA sample, you boys were talking about those genealogy sites. You know you send in some spit or a check swab and find out where you're from. So, I took the liberty of submitting my sample to one of those sites on the off-chance that another person, perhaps a relative, may have done the same." They perked up. "It seems, I got a hit. I was notified by the server that my DNA sample matches that of someone who may be a close relative."

Both detectives were speaking at once, but Andy won. "You submitted the sample and got a match? Well, who is it? Go on."

"Well, it seems if you are the actual party, you can get the information if permission is granted on both sides. However, in this case, we need a warrant to access the data."

"Is this even legal?" Shaker asked in mild defeat.

"Yes, my boy, it is. I looked into it extensively, before even sending the sample. There have been quite a few criminal cases, old and new, where this has been done with astonishing results."

"This is incredible, Doc. Amazing work." Andy glanced over at Shaker, "I think when we see the DA, we get a warrant for this too."

"Here you go." Dr. Oates said as he handed them a copy of the report.

The detectives slapped a high-five and raced out of the station as the ME watched, smiling proudly.

Chapter 73

Carly called Jack to thank him once again, but also to let him know something had come up, so she would not be able to make it to the house. She didn't want him to think she might be avoiding him. So silly, she admitted to herself, but she could imagine thinking those same thoughts if the tables were turned.

She couldn't rid herself of the thoughts about Nick and that nurse. She called the hospital to confirm that Suzanne McGregor was working. She decided to pay her a visit.

Arriving at the hospital, Carly shuddered when she stepped onto the elevator. What an awful couple of months she had spent here. However, she had to admit, the outcome was positive. Nicky survived and he was out of her house.

As she stepped off the elevator, she realized she may not be allowed to enter the ICU since she had no business there. She sat in the lounge for a moment to collect her thoughts. That was the problem with impulsivity; she should have thought this through first. She decided that if she said she was there to thank the team, maybe they'd let her in. Quickly, she dismissed that idea; it was just weird to pop into an ICU to say thanks. She should have brought cookies or a pizza. Something that gave her a better reason to be there.

She decided to walk to the bakery across the street. It would only take a few minutes, and then she'd have a token gift that they'd let her in with. She grabbed her tote and walked towards the elevator. From behind her, she heard voices. When she turned around, she saw two nurses. One of whom was Suzanne. Of course, lunchtime—what a break.

They entered the elevator with Carly. On the way to cafeteria, Carly glanced at Suzanne, pretending to just now recognize her. "Suzanne?"

"Yes." She answered.

"Hi, I'm Carly. You probably don't remember me. You took care of my boyfriend, Nick, a few months ago."

With instant acknowledgment, Suzanne paled. "Oh yes, I do remember. How are you? And how is he doing?"

"Well, I was hoping to talk to you in private." Carly said, giving the other nurse a sideways look.

The elevator door opened and as they stepped out, Suzanne told her friend, she'd join her in a few minutes. "Ok, Carly. What's going on? Is everything alright?"

"Well, I think so. But I have to know why you were with Nick yesterday?" Carly cut to the point.

Stunned and almost speechless, Suzanne muttered, "I thought you broke up."

"That's not what I asked and that doesn't matter right now. I just want to know why you were with Nick. How do you know him?"

Trying to buy time, Suzanne glanced around, as if to summon a savior. She answered, "Well, the reason I asked if you broke up is because I might want to see him." She knew her voice sounded weak and unconvincing, but she'd have to continue with that line.

"What? You stayed in touch with him after he left the ICU? That doesn't sound right or ethical, especially since you really didn't know our situation."

"Well, it's really not like that." She backpedaled. "He called here looking for his, uh, phone charger. I found it and brought it to him. We talked and that was it." Suzanne lied.

Carly studied her. "A phone charger? Seriously? You know he could have bought one at the gas station for like ten bucks. Or you could have mailed it to him. And why did you take on this task?"

Cutting her off, Suzanne said, "Listen, Carly, this is my lunch and I don't want to be rude, but I'm hungry. This is a little ridiculous of you to be here anyway. That's what happened, take it or leave it. Good luck with everything."

Suzanne couldn't walk away fast enough. She quickly melded with the lunch crowd, hoping Carly wouldn't detect the dread on her face. She turned back but saw Carly was gone. With some relief, she pulled a Xanax from her pocket and swallowed it dry.

Carly watched Suzanne scurry away. She was definitely frazzled. She was also definitely lying. About what though? Maybe Orlando could help with those questions. She punched his number in her phone. When he answered, she explained what transpired.

Orlando smiled to himself. "Oh Carly, you should let the professionals handle this. But really, excellent job. You probably did get a reaction that we wouldn't have. The problem is now she knows she's been caught, so we may not catch them together again. I'll talk to one of my guys and see where we should go from here with her."

"Thanks, Mr. Diaz." Carly disconnected the call.

On the ride home, she contemplated her encounter with Suzanne. How did this fit in with Nick? How did it fit with whomever was getting into her house? Did it fit at all? Maybe she was just being paranoid. She decided to write down her thoughts about this once she was home. Perhaps that would organize things, enabling her to see some sort of connection more clearly. Or maybe not.

Chapter 74

"What the heck, Nick?" Suzanne screamed into the phone. "That old girlfriend of yours is following me. She came to the hospital today to ask me why I was with you yesterday."

Nicky sat up straight when he heard this. "What? Are you kidding? Why would she...no, no, she's following me. She'd have no reason to follow you."

"Well, it really doesn't matter who she's after, the point is she saw me with you and then she shows up at my job."

Trying to be calm to get details out of a hysterical Suzanne took work, but eventually he said, "Ok, relax and tell me what you said."

Suzanne reiterated the conversation. Nicky laughed. "A Charger? And you told her you're interested in me?"

"I know, I know. Stupid, but it was the first thing that popped into my head. It wasn't like I had time to think."

"Do you think she bought it?"

"Of course, she didn't buy it! Would you?"

He thought again and said, "Who knows? Sometimes the truth is stranger than a lie, so maybe she did. But in any case, we need to be careful from now on if we need to talk. Unless you want a date, that is."

"You're an ass." Suzanne said, hanging up, wishing for an old fashioned phone that she could slam down hard to make the point.

Nicky made a quick call. "Hey, listen. She's following me, so don't come here. If we have to get together, we'll take some precautions"

"Got it. Thanks for the heads-up. She's also got an alarm system with cameras. I may have some other ideas, time to step it up, I think? Maybe, I'll wait a little bit."

"Sounds good. Just keep me posted." Nick said and hung up. "Man, I'm missing all the fun."

Chapter 75

Brian Bailey was on his knees beside his bed attempting to make a trade with his dog. The chicken treat in exchange for the feather he needed for his fly. The dog seemed to be winning the negotiation; it was clear that there would be no compromise. Brian sweetened the pot and threw in a tennis ball. When the swap was reluctantly agreed upon by said dog, Brian snatched up the feather before he lost it again. When he did, however, he noticed a crumpled piece of paper lying where the dog had been. He reached for it and read it.

"Damn-it, I forgot all about that. I went into such a deep sleep after I wrote it. Hey, thanks buddy." He said to his dog Buster. He got up and looked for the detectives' card in the kitchen.

He finally located it in the basket with the other cards he had in his collection. In his otherwise meticulously tidy home, it was one place where he deposited clutter. It was after five. There had been no recent news about the body, so he decided it could wait until Monday. He put the card on his fridge with a magnet so he would remember.

Brian had some other things to do before the sun set. He was contemplating another trip. He wasn't sure where he wanted to go this time, so he had some research to do. For him, the planning was the best part.

Chapter 76

The warrant was secured for the genealogy site to obtain the identity of the match for Eric Popper's DNA sample. The DA's office contacted the site's legal department and faxed the warrant to the number that was provided. Since it was late Friday afternoon, he was told that the results would arrive on Monday.

The petition for the original birth certificate was another story. The DA was advised that the only parties allowed to open the documents were the adoptive parents or the child in question. He was further informed, that because the knowledge in this instance was only needed for information gathering, it was not considered a valid request. If there was an urgency for medical treatment that might be aided by uncovering the biological parents' identity and history, the DA might have had a chance.

The conclusion was they would have to wait until Monday. The DA assisting Andy and Shaker was Bernie Falcone. Although, he was making a name for himself in the office, he was one of the good guys. He wasn't after the glory or the headlines. He was after the "right thing". When he first started working with the detectives, it was all very routine. However, now it was getting interesting. He told them he'd be in their corner if they needed anything else.

Chapter 77

Saturday

Early Saturday morning, Carly met Jenn at a local coffee shop. They needed to firm up the plans for the Lucy's shower. As they walked back to the house, sipping from their steaming go-cups, they went over the plans.

Jenn told her that Mae and Gracie were all set with the decorations. Of course, there would be balloons, but Mae wanted the colors to vary from the standard pastels of blue, pink, and green. Instead she opted for vibrant jewel tones to signify strength and strong spirit. She would carry that theme to the table linens and centerpieces.

Carly said that she and DeeDee had finished the party favors as well. They decided on small colorfully embroidered sachets in the shape of the butterflies. They were filled with lavender and vanilla. A purple ribbon fastened a bag of Munson's chocolate to each one. Munson's was a local chocolate company which was well-known in Connecticut. It rivaled Godiva. Carly would pick up the cupcakes in the morning.

When they reached the house, they knew Irene had begun the cooking. Lucy wouldn't think anything of it because Irene was always cooking something. The smell coming from the house was intoxicating.

"Wow, that is heavenly." Carly said, taking a lingering breath to absorb it all.

"It sure is." Jenn agreed just as the door opened. "Hey, Lucy."

"Hey back." She said and waddled to the chair on the porch.

Carly smiled at her and her belly. "You look so cute. I can't believe it's October first; only a month away already. It went so fast."

Lucy shook her head and looked at Carly, smiling. "Fast for you, but not me. But yeah, this little darling is gonna be here soon. I can't wait to meet him or her."

"Have you settled on names yet?" Carly asked.

"Oh my god, that's such a big responsibility. If I pick the wrong name, it could alter or even ruin his or her life."

"Well, I don't know about that." Jenn laughed.

"Seriously, if I pick William but his name should have been Andrew, it could be life-changing."

Carly offered a suggestion. "Why don't you have two boy and girl names ready. Then when you see him or her, you'll know what name they look like."

"Yeah, I guess I could do that. I also read that I should say the name with the last name and say it out loud."

"So what are the choices?" Jenn asked.

"Alex or Charlie Owens for a boy. Then Maria or Olivia Owens for a girl." Lucy looked at both women, anticipating a response.

Carly spoke first. "I love them! They're strong beautiful names."

"I agree, really great choices." Jenn said.

"Thanks, I thought so too. My mom likes them too. She didn't even mind that I didn't use my dad's name, which by the way is Dallas."

"Dallas, I like that too."

"Yeah, me too, but I want my child to have his or her own identity, you know, no comparisons, a brand new name for a brand new life."

Carly gave Lucy a hug and went inside to see Jack. Although it was Saturday, she knew he would be there for a couple of hours in the morning. She hoped she hadn't missed him. She realized she almost did when she saw him on his way down the stairs wearing his jacket.

"Oh hi, Carly, I was just heading out."

"Hi Jack. I'm being bold here, but are you doing anything today?"

"Well, I promised Rosie we'd go ice skating today."

"Oh, that's fun."

"Yeah, it is. Hey, why don't you come?"

"Oh Jack, I don't know. We only just started dating, do you think that's a good idea? Plus, I don't want to intrude on your time with Rosie."

"Listen, I know this is all new for us, but it would be fun. I think it would be a good way to meet Rosie too. A no pressure situation and no intrusion. As far as it being soon in our relationship, I think that's ok too. I have a good feeling about us."

Nervously, she answered. "Ok, but I'll meet you there. It'll be less awkward. And as far as the no pressure goes, you haven't seen me skate yet. Actually, slide would probably be a better way to describe my skills."

Jack laughed and said they'd be at the rink about eleven. They would grab a quick lunch afterwards as they usually did. Apparently, Rosie loved the Shady Glen cheeseburgers and fountain milkshakes, but then, who didn't?

Carly walked home trying to decide what one wears when ice skating with a seven-year old. Along the way, she decided to make a quick stop at the Willimantic Food co-op. It was around the corner from her house near the big church with the stained glass windows and tall spires that danced in the reflection of the sun.

Every time she walked in the store, she took a deep breath to savor that first scent of its earthiness. Here, she could buy organic produce, grown mostly by local farms. There were bins of grains and staples such as flours, coffees, teas, and spices; most of which were fair trade products. However, today, all she needed were some apples, local feta cheese and fresh olives. While she picked out her Galas, a round man with scraggly grey hair, stood next to her, putting some Red Delicious in his basket.

"The fruit here is amazing. Organic really does make a difference".

She turned to him and nodded in agreement. "It really does. I only buy my fruit and veggies here."

She continued on her way to pick out the other items she needed. Once she made her way through the store on this crowded Saturday morning, she walked up the hill to her house. She needed to change and head out to the ice rink in Bolton which was about twenty minutes from her. She didn't want to be late.

Chapter 78

Suzanne's phone sat on the counter charging. It was her weekend off and she was enjoying a peaceful moment in the shower. She was trying to be normal around Andy when she suggested they go to the bookstore then out to lunch. He thought it sounded like a nice way to spend the day. He needed some downtime from work too.

Andy sat at the table, going over some of his notes, when he heard her phone buzzing. He stood up to look in case it was a call from work that she might need to take. Caller ID indicated that the caller was "pop".

"Who is that? He thought. He replaced the phone on the counter, waiting for Suzanne to come back to the kitchen.

When she strolled in, coffee cup in hand, she appeared relaxed. She had straightened her hair allowing it fall softly around her face. She was wearing comfortable jeans with a long sweater and tall black suede boots. She gave Andy a kiss on the forehead and put her cup in the sink. Unplugging her fully charged phone, she looked at the alert that notified her of a recent missed call. When she saw the name, she quickly put the phone in her purse. Her heart was beating a little faster, but she told herself Andy had not seen it. Everything would be alright.

"I'm all set to go, babe. You ready?" Andy asked.

"I am." She told him and grabbed her purse.

They drove to West Farms Mall to check out Barnes and Noble. Suzanne was eager to check out the discounted books in hopes of discovering a new author or a mystery she hadn't read before from one of her favorites. Andy's preference leaned toward books with historical topics. He like the non-fiction stories that took him through real events in the form of a story.

He parked the car, excited that on a Saturday, he had a scored a primo parking spot close to the entrance. They held hands and he held the door open for her.

"Hey, Suzanne, who's pop?" He asked casually, walking in behind her.

He couldn't see her face from his vantage point, but if he had, he would have been shocked by the sudden bloodless pallor that left her white and clammy.

"What?" she asked, attempting to delay her response.

"Pop, who is it? I saw the name come up on your phone while you were in the shower."

Quickly, she cleared her throat and answered with the obvious. "Oh, that's dad."

Searching his recollection of her estranged relationship with her father, he said, "That's funny, you haven't talked to him in what?—a year or so?"

"I suppose. I probably should call him back. I'm just not ready. Maybe later."

"Yeah, I guess." he said. "Mull it over first."

They went their separate ways in the bookstore. Andy filed the conversation away in the compartment marked "Suzanne". Meanwhile, Suzanne took a few deep breaths, deciding she had handled the questions well.

Chapter 79

Carly arrived at the rink first. She nervously sat on one of the benches tying the laces of her rented skates. Common sense told her she had nothing to fear. After all, children were so accepting of others; they came with no pre-conceived notions or prejudices, unlike those who had experiences which colored their point of view. But she also knew that with all their innocence, children had the power to spot a phony or someone with unsavory intentions. She needed to get a grip.

As she stood unsteadily on her skates, her ankles wobbling back and forth in a feeble attempt to keep her upright, she saw Jackson walk in holding the hand of a beautiful little girl. She was chattering away with animation in her face as well as her movements. Jack was beaming as he nodded in acknowledgement to his daughter.

"Rosie," he said, "this is my friend, Carly."

"Hi, Carly. Daddy told me you were gonna meet us here."

Carly bent down, struggling not to tip over in her skates. "Hi Rosie. I am so happy to meet you. Your dad has told me so much about you." Rosie smiled and looked at her father. "I have a huge favor to ask"

"A favor? What kind of favor?" Rosie asked curiously.

"Well, I am not a very good skater. But I hear that you are. I might need your help. Would that be ok?"

"Oh yes, Carly. I would love to help you. Daddy can help too. He taught me. He used to play hockey. Did you know that? He's a really, really good skater. He said the most important rule of skating is not to be afraid of falling because everyone does. His second most important rule is that you have to know how to stop." She started giggling when she said that because it always seemed funny to her.

Carly laughed too. "I guess stopping is pretty important."

"Come on Carly, let's go." Rosie said after she put on her skates. She grabbed Carly's hand to help steady her as they walked toward the ice.

As Carly, skated close to the boards for security, Jackson and Rosie stayed nearby. Every once in a while, they would speed off together. This was a good thing because it allowed Carly to focus and become more confident. By the end of two hours, her feet were aching, but she was comfortable enough to leave the refuge of the railings. She was proudly able to join Jack and Rosie in center ice to watch Rosie practice her Olympic spins.

Later, at lunch, Jack could see that his little Rosie and Carly had become good friends. They ate the famous cheeseburgers that had crispy cheese fanned out around them. They shared a vanilla shake, which it seemed was a favorite to both. When lunch ended, they said good-bye at their cars. No one was more surprised than Carly, when Rosie threw her arms around her and kissed her sweetly on the cheek. Carly squeezed her in return, welling with emotions she was surprised to learn she felt.

"Thank you, Rosie, for letting me spend the afternoon with you and your dad. I had so much fun. And thank you for teaching me to skate."

"Oh, you are very welcome. Are you gonna come to our house?"

Jack answered for Carly, "Yes, sweetie-pie, Carly will be coming to our house sometime." He winked at Carly. "But right now, we've got to get going." He looked at Carly again and said, "So, I'll pick you up about six? Dinner?"

Caught off guard, she said, "Yes, sure, dinner." She drove off with her head spinning in the aftermath of the simple joy she was feeling.

Chapter 80

Orlando Diaz had done a background check on Suzanne McGregor. Nothing really jumped out at him. He found the old case records referring an incident she had with a guy name Eric Popper. He noted that she had moved from Stonington to Farmington after that incident. He also followed her nursing career, which was impressive. Then when he searched for records about Eric Popper, he unearthed a brief news story that said his body was recently found washed up on the banks of the Farmington River. It seemed he'd been dead for well over a year at the time of discovery. Investigation pending.

Orlando wondered why was this woman hanging around someone like Nicky Pellegrino? Her background had revealed nothing unsavory. But, then again, nothing jumped out at him about Nick either, except of course his obsession with Carly.

Orlando just couldn't figure out who was doing the stalking. When it first started, Nick had been in the hospital. However, since he'd been on his own, he didn't have a car. Obviously, he wasn't using a taxi to do it. He supposed there was yet another link in the chain that needed to be connected.

Once they had left the bookstore, Andy and Suzanne went to Moe's for lunch. While Suzanne picked at her rice and avocado salad in the tortilla shell, Andy dug into his pulled pork burrito.

"So, are you going to call your father?" He asked out of the blue.

Being caught off guard, Suzanne stumbled, "What? Oh, I don't know, maybe. Probably. I have to think about it."

"Aren't you curious why he's calling after all this time?" he pressed. Andy really didn't know why it was bothering him so much. But something about it just didn't sit right with him.

"I really don't care why he called, Andy. You know as well as I do, he always wants something. He thinks he can just pick up the phone once every year or so and all will be forgiven." She pushed her food away. "I'm done. Are you ready to go?"

He wasn't and quite frankly, he was starting to get annoyed at her moods lately. "Actually, no, I'm not ready. I'd like to finish my lunch."

"Well, I'll be outside waiting." She took a cigarette from the pack in his pocket and marched outside.

He took another bite, wiped the cheese off his chin, thinking that something was definitely up with her.

When Carly arrived home, she was already getting excited to spend more time with Jack. She had had such a wonderful time with him and Rosie ice skating. She just didn't want this day to end.

She hung her quilted jacket next to the one she had worn this morning and noticed something peeking out from the pocket. "What's that?" she wondered. She pulled it out, realizing it was a note. She read it quickly, then read it again. It said:

Look how close I can get to you and you didn't even realize it. I'm always there. I'm a master. But, Carly, my dear, the opposite is true of you. I know you've been snooping around me.

And I'm warning you, Don't. You'll be very sorry. Next time, you'll know I'm there.

She quickly dropped it as if it were on fire. She couldn't call the police. They wouldn't take her seriously. Nick probably knew that too. She called Orlando instead.

"Diaz Home Security." He answered in his upbeat voice. Then seeing the caller ID, he added, "Hey Carly, what's up?"

After her brief update, he said, "Well, I don't think is good. I'm being honest with you. From my experience, when someone is as obsessed as Nick, there is a process and many times it escalates. His stalking is becoming serious. He's not just playing games with your stuff anymore."

"So, what do we do?"

"I think you have to go to the police again. I know, they've been assholes to you, but this could be a real threat. You told me he made some vague verbal threats, but you have this in writing. You might have a good chance of getting a restraining order now."

"But Mr. Diaz, why is he doing this? I haven't done anything to him, I just broke it off."

"That's the thing Carly, it doesn't matter. From what I've read about obsessions, once he gets it stuck in his twisted head, he can't rationalize it. Do you think you might have seen him today?"

"No, I mean, he would have had to be pretty close to me to slip that note in my pocket, right?

Orlando, was stumped too. "Carly, listen, think through your day. Tell me about where you went while you were wearing that jacket, who you talked to."

She recounted her day to him. When she talked about the food co-op, he stopped her. "Wait, rewind. The guy with the apples. He was talking to you and standing close. Could he be the one?"

"I don't know. I don't remember any contact. Oh, wait a minute, he did drop the bag he was carrying. When he bent down to pick it up, I think he brushed against me."

"Ok, I wonder if that's the guy. We know Nick couldn't have done some of those things because he was in the hospital. "Focus Carly, what did he look like?"

Again, she replayed the scene in her head and said. "Round, beer belly round, kind of big. Greasy grey hair, round puffy face."

"That's good. I wonder if my guys have seen anyone like that near Nick's apartment. I'll check the video from the camera we put outside too. I bet he saw it and that's why he approached you in the store."

"Wow, you're good at this, Mr. Diaz. You should have been a detective."

He smiled, "Yeah, I should have, but that's a conversation for another time. For now, I'm going to make some calls. I'll check what we have on the camera too. I think I'll have one of the guys do a drive-by to just to be sure no one's hanging around your house. But in the meantime, please be careful."

"I will, I promise. And thank you." Feeling better but still not at ease, she ended the call. "How am I going to be able to be normal at dinner? I guess I'm going to tell Jack about this." She wondered if he'd want a girlfriend who was being stalked and threatened by a sociopath. Probably not. She figured it was better to end it now. She wanted to protect Jack and Rosie from whatever was happening to her. She also needed to protect herself from falling in love if Jack decided her current situation was more than he bargained for. With stubborn resolve, she made a hard decision.

Chapter 81

"Hey Joey, it's Orlando."

"Hey buddy, hold on a sec." Joey Artuna put his roast beef grinder on the table and wiped his hands. "What's up?"

"Well, you know that guy we've been following?"

"Yeah, not much new on this end."

"Well, some other stuff has come up." Orlando continued to lay out the details he had so far for Joey. Joey had been one of Orlando's friends from his shady days; before he went straight. Joey and some of the others had eventually followed Orlando, putting the skills they had learned on the streets to legitimate use. They also kept some of the contacts from the old neighborhood who often would be able to go places they couldn't. Following his account, Orlando said, "so, what do you think?"

"I think it sounds like trouble. Should we keep doing what we're doing or is it time to bring in the police?"

"I did tell her she should, but she didn't want to, not yet anyway. There's a few things that bother me about this whole thing."

Joey agreed, "I feel the same. I can't help but think there's something familiar about this Nicky guy. I feel like I've seen him before, but I can't pinpoint it."

"You too, huh? I'm wondering if we can find this other guy, the pieces might fall into place."

When they hung up, it had been decided that Orlando would monitor Carly's neighborhood to check if someone's hanging around. Joey would continue to keep tabs on Nicky. Orlando admitted he was concerned that Nicky was becoming too fixated on Carly. Each point of contact seemed to be getting more brazen. Definitely troubling.

He picked up his notes about Suzanne and Nicky, hoping something would pop out and say, "Here I am". He supposed that only happened on TV. He decided he should dig deeper into the backgrounds. Again, there was really nothing on Nick.

He decided to check the on-line yearbooks and public records for Suzanne's college days at Central Connecticut State University where she attended nursing school. He was disappointed to discover that CCSU did not allow access on-line. This meant Orlando would have to wait until Monday and go to the college library in person. He much preferred doing his research under the cover of the internet.

Without much conversation, Andy and Suzanne drove home. What should have been an easy day out turned south rather quickly. Andy was aware he had instigated the change in direction because he couldn't let that missed call go, unaddressed. It irked him. He knew Suzanne well enough to understand there was something she wasn't telling him. Her reaction to his questions validated that. He was thinking as he drove that maybe he wouldn't push anymore, not so soon, anyway. Instead, he would observe and be aware. Obviously, he was missing something and she had no intention of sharing whatever it was.

Chapter 82

Carly was ready when Jackson arrived at six. She smiled. "Always on time," she thought. When she opened the door, he pulled her close and kissed her. The moment lingered forever.

"I've been wanting to do that all day." He said when they parted.

"Me too." She sighed and took his hand. They decided to drive to Brewery because the chill of early November was settling in.

Carly and Jack settled into their seats at a table in the bar. Tonight they sat side by side, speaking in low tones; lost in each other's eyes. Carly was amazed at the complexity of emotions she was feeling. She felt as though she were tumbling head first into the love her head told her she must end. She needed to savor every moment until the time was right to bear her soul to Jack.

Smiling back at her, Jack reached for her hand after they order a few apps to share. Neither of them felt hungry after the big lunch they had.

"Carly, I've been wanting to ask you this, and if you don't want to talk about it, I'll understand."

"This sounds serious."

"Well, not really. But I know you said/gave up your singing career because it wasn't really what you wanted from life. You said you wanted to give back. Did something happen?"

She thought for a moment, then said, "Yeah, something happened."

Carly told Jack about one of her best friends. It seemed that Jill had been abused by her husband for years and never let on to anyone about it. She was embarrassed and ashamed, believing it was her fault. Early on, Jill had sought counseling for her and husband. Then he beat her with more wrath because she dared to air their dirty laundry. Of course, he always apologized as if those words made everything better.

Carly explained that one morning, she stopped at Jill's house because she was worried. It seemed that Jill had cancelled lunch three days in a row claiming she had the flu. Carly wanted to check on her and see if she needed anything. When Jill answered the door, Carly saw fading sickly yellow bruises around her swollen eyes.

At first, Jill said it was from her sinuses and runny nose. Carly pushed, realizing that this was not right. She didn't want to believe that all this time Jill was living in this hellish cycle. After Jill admitted the truth, they sat and cried, planning a way for Jill to escape.

A few days later, Jill had packed, ready to slip away with Carly who was leaving for a tour, when her husband had come early. He pummeled her until she was unconscious. She lay bleeding with shallow breaths at the foot of the stairs when Carly arrived.

Carly screamed and pushed the madman out of the way. He stood with tears streaming down his face, mumbling something that sounded like "I'm sorry." When the ambulance brought Jill to the hospital, she lived in a coma for a week before she died.

Carly looked at Jack, who was staring at her in shock. "If only I got there a few minutes earlier. If only I had known from the beginning. My career just didn't seem to matter anymore. Yeah, it was great for me, but there are so many people who don't have it so great. My heart wasn't in it anymore. I don't think it ever really was. I knew I had help to other women before they ended up like Jill."

"Wow, I'm so sorry, Carly." He glanced blankly at his plate.

"It took a while to get over. That was another reason I travelled and lived life like woman possessed when I quit."

Jack said softly, "Is that why you bought Prospect Hill?"

She abruptly stopped. "You know? No one was supposed to know."

"I only found out recently. It came up at one of the legal meetings. I had no idea our benefactor was you."

She searched his face and squeezed his hand tightly in hers. "Please, Jack, don't tell anyone."

"I won't, I promise."

After yet another deep breath, Carly finally said, "There's more, Jack. Since the mood is already spoiled, I have to tell you some things about Nick." She recounted some of the details of their relationship, using the abridged version. Jack said he had suspected as much. Then Carly described the recent events.

She ended by saying, "I think we should stop seeing each other. I'm falling too hard for you. I can't let him hurt you or Rosie." He started to say something and she raised her hand to stop him. "No, my mind is made up. We can't start a relationship while this is happening around me. I don't want you to be brave and feel I need protection. You don't need the drama either. You deserve a normal relationship, so do I."

"Carly, maybe I can help. Maybe a little drama is ok." He joked.

"No, Jack, not this kind of drama."

They walked to the car and when they reached her front door, they held each other for what seemed like an eternity. Jack spoke first, "Carly, I can't let you go. You don't need to be all noble. You deserve to be happy. I can help with that too. Sometimes, you have to let people help you."

"Oh Jack, my mother said the same thing not too long ago. I'm so used to taking care of things on my own. I just don't know how to lean on others. I'd like to lean on you, but.."

He kissed her again, "but nothing. We've got something amazing going on here. Sleep on it, OK? Come over after the shower tomorrow. We'll have Sunday dinner at my house. By the way, you mom sounds like a smart lady."

"Oh, the shower, I almost forgot. I mean, I did forget. I have so much to do." Before she went in the house she turned and said, "Yes, I'd love to have Sunday dinner with you and your family."

Chapter 83

Sunday

Carly had stayed up late Saturday night, reviewing her list for Sunday. When she was satisfied, she hadn't left anything undone, she went to bed. Sunday morning, she was awake, bright and early, feeling refreshed. She supposed that some of it had to do with her confession to Jack about everything. It was probably better that some of those things were now out in the open.

His reaction was what she had expected, however, she couldn't hold to her decision to let him go. He was right, they would see this through together. A new rule, she should accept the fact that it's ok lean on others who care.

Following her ritual of coffee and contemplation, she dressed in a black tea length knit dress. It had some splashy geometric appliques that added a pretty pop of color. She wore light grey suede boots for contrast as well. When she applied her scarlet red lipstick, she decided she was ready.

Carly arrived at the house shortly after Lucy left for church. Jenn had told her they had about three hours before she would return. The other women were rocking and rolling with activity to the music that played in the background. They were a marvelous sight in their party clothes as each one attended to the task they had undertaken. As usual, the smells coming from the kitchen were overwhelming.

Carly delivered six dozen humongous cupcakes to the kitchen. The bakery had arranged them precisely as ordered. The center ones each held a green letter that when put together read,

"Congratulations Lucy." All the cupcakes were positioned to alternate their pink and blue frosting. The cakes themselves were yellow or chocolate. The yellow cakes were filled with chocolate mousse; the chocolate had a cappuccino crème inside. When she was satisfied, she joined the others to assist in the final phase of decorating. Irene, of course, needed no help in the kitchen.

In the large dining room, that had once been a place of formal family gatherings, tables were set with vivid purple tablecloths. On top of each sat a bouquet of balloons in the jewel tones that had been chosen by Mae. At the base of each in upside down miniature umbrellas, sat sprigs of lavender and sage. The sachet favors were placed at each one of the forty seats for the expected guests. Wearing her glittered sweater and stretchy black pants, Jenn was directing the scene to make certain the details were executed according to the plans.

Promptly at eleven-thirty, the guests began arriving. Lucy was expected an hour later. Each guest, held a glass of champagne punch, standing silently facing the door, when Jenn gave the signal that Lucy had arrived. As she strolled through the living room with her mother, her nose was her guide. She drifted on the scents towards what she thought she soon would be eating.

She wondered where everyone was. The house was too quiet. When she waddled into the dining room, all of a sudden and all at once, she was greeted by an overwhelming chorus of "SURPRISE!". In a moment of uncertainty, she scanned the faces of forty people who stood before her, cheering and clapping. When she saw the banner that bore her name hung above a stack of wrapped gifts, were piled high, she quickly processed what was happening.

"Oh my god!" she exclaimed. "I can't believe it. For me?"

Everyone in attendance gathered around Lucy to congratulate her. Jenn handed her a glass of non-alcoholic punch, enveloping Lucy in a bear hug, and patted her belly that neared the bursting point—one month to go.

Irene had set the food out buffet style, which allowed her to eat with everyone and enjoy the party as well. They feasted on pulled pork, chicken marsala, and Italian beef stew, which meant it had cheese and wine in it and was served over pasta.

The shower was the *an* enormous success. During dessert, Lucy opened the gifts. She received everything a new mother would need for her baby, including gift cards for those unforeseen extras. She told her guests that he or she will love it all.

At three-thirty, the last of guests left. The clean-up began. It was swift and efficient. With everyone, except Lucy pitching in, the job was done in no time. At approximately four-thirty, Lucy strolled into the kitchen to calmly announce that her water had broken. She also decided that the twinges she had been experiencing on and off during the day were in fact contractions. Irene and Jenn were her designated coaches.

Irene called the doctor, who advised them to go to the hospital. Because it was four weeks early, Lucy had not packed a bag yet. Jenn quickly put together pajamas, some toiletries and makeup; anything else that might be needed could always be sent for. She also notified Lucy's mom.

It was quite a sight to see these eight women of diverse backgrounds usher the very pregnant but smiling Lucy Owens to the car. The ones who remained at the house would finish the clean-up and wait for news of the birth of him or her. What a perfectly appropriate ending to a perfect baby shower.

Carly shot off a quick text to Jack so he would know. She also told him, she would arrive at his house shortly after five. She was too excited to be nervous about going to his house for the first time and meeting his parents. Jack had explained that Sunday dinners had become an important tradition, though sometimes they occurred on Saturday.

She parked her car in the driveway of the small cape style home where Jack and Rosie live. She observed how well-maintained it was, noting that Jack attended to detail at home as well as work.

Jackson greeted her at the door with a kiss. "I'm so happy to see you."

"Me too," she said.

He led her in, taking her hand. She felt the warmth from the crackling fire in the living room. His parents, both tall and lean like Jack, rose to meet her. However, they were all ambushed by Rosie, who at that instant bounded from her bedroom and pounced on Carly with her seven-year old hug.

"You came!! I knew you would. Carly, do you want to see my bedroom?"

Smiling at Jack, Carly answered, "Of course I do."

Jack intervened and said, "Whoa, Rosie, let's give Carly a chance to take off her coat. She hasn't been properly introduced to Grandma and Grandpa yet either."

Sullenly, Rosie agreed—first things first she supposed.

Jack's parents were in their sixties like her own. His mother was stylish but down-to earth. Although, she was smiling and welcoming, Carly detected her scrutinizing glance. After all a mother's first instinct would be to protect her son from a broken heart among other things. His father, however, like most men, accepted her immediately. Men never considered those issues.

Following the introductions, Carly joined Rosie in her very purple and pink bedroom. "I'm loving this, Rosie! It's so you."

Rosie beamed as her hazel eyes twinkled with delight. "Thank you. Daddy and I did it together. I picked out the colors and he painted. She plopped on the fluffy flowery comforter on her bed. Hugging one of the purple fuzzy throw pillows, she motioned Carly to sit next to her. They talked and laughed for a few minutes, conspiring as new best friends do. Rosie showed Carly her photo album that had pictures of she and Jack. Carly's heart melted with each one. The love and life they shared was abundant and full. Her only hope was that she might fit in and be part of it someday.

Jack stood in the doorway, taking in the scene with pleasure. He was beyond thrilled at the bond he saw forming. His wish was being granted before his eyes. He was falling in love with this woman and so was his daughter.

"You two ready to eat?" He finally asked.

"Oh yes, Daddy." Rosie answered, hopping of the bed.

"I will do my best too." Carly winked at him.

Carly jumped right in to help Jack's mom put the food on the table. Mrs. Foley, nodded with approval. Before sitting at the table, Carly and Jack put their phones on the counter. They didn't want to miss any update from Jenn or Irene about Lucy.

They ate pot roast with gravy and mashed potatoes and broccoli. Mrs. Foley had also prepared some homemade biscuits. It was a hearty meal full of comfort. To Carly, it felt like being at her own parent's table. Good conversation, nothing too heavy, and lots of laughing.

When the meal had ended, Carly helped Mrs. Foley with the clean-up. Rosie pitched in as well. Jack put on a pot of coffee, noticing his phone had a text alert. Carly looked at him, smiling, then saw she had a text as well. Both were from Jenn. It was an update that said:

8 cm dilated. Lucy's doing well. She's in good spirits and has not threatened anyone yet. Lol. We hope to meet him or her very soon.

Jack and Carly simultaneously laughed and hugged. "Yeah," Carly squealed. His parents and Rosie watched, wondering what they missed.

Jack laughed. "It's Lucy, she's in labor. The baby should be here anytime."

At the end of the evening, Jack walked Carly to her car. "You sure you can't stay until we hear about the baby?"

"No, I should go. It's been a long day. But thank you, Jack. Tonight was wonderful.   Do you think your parents liked me?"

"I think they did, especially my dad. I think once my mom got over being the mama bear, she fell for you too."

"I hope so. I liked them too. It's easy to see where you get it from."

As he held her and kissed her good-night, he whispered that one of these days, they might not have to say goodnight. They would spend it together. She could have melted on the spot.

Carly whispered back, "I would like that very much, Jackson Foley."

She arrived at home and after straightening up, she settled into the comfort of her bed about ten. Within minutes, she was sound asleep with contentment on her face and in her dreams. At five minutes to midnight, she was startled awake by the chime of her phone. She read the text:

Alexander Owens has entered the world. He weighed in at 7lb 2oz, 21 inches. He's perfect in every way. Mamma Lucy is great too.

Jenn had attached a picture of Lucy snuggling her baby. He really was perfect. A beautiful baby boy. She text back:

He is beautiful! I can't believe we have a baby boy! Please kiss Alex and Lucy for me. I'll be there tomorrow.

She turned off her light and drifted off again as the peace and joy washed over her.

Chapter 84

Monday

Inevitably, Monday follows Sunday. People everywhere drag themselves out of bed to start the new week. Some haven't slept much, lying awake all night with the anticipation of going back to work while others endure hangovers from too much celebration over their favorite teams scoring that big win. But still, Monday comes and the beat goes on.

Orlando Diaz was up early as usual. He had organized his day with the many things he needed to accomplish. He grabbed his coffee to go and did a drive around Carly's house. Nothing out of the ordinary. His next stop was his office. He needed to gather some of the reports that Joey had left for him. His final stop would be at the CCSU library. He knew he would spend a long day there perusing all available documents for some background on Suzanne McGregor pre-dating what he already knew about her.

Suzanne tip-toed around Andy as they got ready for work. They hadn't spoken much since the incident on Saturday. Uncomfortably, she sipped her coffee. She wished she knew what to say, but there was nothing. Anything she said would only make it worse.

When he entered the kitchen, he walked past her as if she was invisible. It was so unlike Andy. He was usually so carefree and eager to fix everything. Now, however, his face was taut with concern. She muttered something about a shower and exited the kitchen.

When she left, Andy picked up her cell phone. Thinking that two can play this game, he scrolled through her call log. Noting four calls from pop in the last week, he checked further and discovered that they were not missed calls. In fact, some of the calls had lasted for close to ten minutes. "What the hell is going on?" He began to check her texts but heard her coming down the stairs. He put her phone where he found it and stirred his coffee. He'd look into that tonight.

She told him she was leaving and he replied, "I'll be home a little later than usual. You can eat without me."

She tried to make a joke. "I hope you don't have a date."

He brushed off her attempt at humor and flatly said, "No, expecting some information that might need follow-up." He grabbed his cup and left before her, without kissing her good-by.

Raring to go, bright and early, Brian Bailey grabbed the can of dog food for Buster. When he closed the refrigerator door, he saw his note. "Damn, I forgot all about that. Don't worry Buster, you get to eat before I make the call."

Carly met Jack at the hospital. They found Jenn napping in the waiting room; Irene had gone home around one. Carly touched her lightly on the shoulder. "Hey, sleepy head, why didn't you go home?"

Shaking off the cobwebs, Jenn studied Carly and Jack. "I couldn't leave her here alone. What if she needed something? I'll stay until her mom comes back."

Carly sat down next to Jenn on the orange vinyl sofa. "That's what I love about you." The two friends hugged each other. "I can't believe it, he or she is a he. I'm so excited."

Jenn said, "It was the most amazing thing. Yeah, a little gross, I guess, but seeing our little Alex enter the world with all his bravado was incredible. He's a very special little guy. And Lucy is pretty amazing herself."

Jack sat on the other side of Jenn, beaming along with the two women.

Andy arrived at the station to find Shaker was already there. "Wow, this is like what twice? Three times that you're here before me? I hope there's still a coffee with my name on it."

"Hey partner, of course there is." He continued. "I'm a little anxious to get those results today. Any idea how long we have to wait?"

"No clue. Do we have anything we need to do in the meantime?" Andy asked.

"I was thinking about calling Gustafson. I thought it would be fun to rattle him. You know, tell him about the DNA thing. How does that saying go? Oh yeah, shake the tree and see what falls out."

Andy scratched his head, "What the heck are you talking about now?"

Incredulously, Shaker stared at Andy. "You're kidding, right? It's an old saying. In our case, it means, that if we get Gustafson riled up, hinting about this valuable information, he might start talking and say something he shouldn't. Man, for a smart guy, you are dense sometimes, Andy."

"Ok, ok, I get it. No need for insults." He laughed. However, Shaker's last words got him thinking. "Hmm for a smart guy, I'm dense. What else have I missed because of that?" He thought.

Nicky popped a couple of Percocets. They cleared his head more than caffeine. They also dulled the pains he still experienced in his belly. No matter, it was going to be a good day. He knew he shouldn't meet Leo, but they had some face-to-face business to attend to. He would leave by the back entrance to his building covered up in a scarf and a hoodie. Maybe he'd throw on his reading glasses just for fun. At least, he could conceal himself for a little while.

After leaving the hospital, Carly impulsively took a drive to Farmington. She located Nicky's apartment with the help of her GPS. She knew he'd see her if she was on foot, so she decided park her vehicle down the road a bit. "Surveillance," she smiled. "I'm like a real spy." However, she knew this was no joke.

As she sat with her phone on her lap, she saw two men walking down the street. The one who induced instant nausea, she knew to be Nick. She'd recognize him anywhere, even in that stupid get-up. He wasn't fooling anyone. She recoiled when she glanced at the other man's face. "Oh my god, he's the guy from co-op." She took a few pictures with her phone and sent them off to Orlando.

She observed the two for a few more minutes. Something was exchanged as they shook hands and parted ways. Once Nick was tucked back in his building, she drove away.

Orlando sat at a table in the library with a hoard of yearbooks spread out around him. He was only interested in the Suzanne's graduation year, but he decided look at some of the other years as well. It might lead him to some friends she had had at the time.

His phone vibrated with a text alert. Carly was the sender. He opened the message and saw the photo. First, he smiled at her tenacity, the he frowned at her recklessness. She could have put herself in danger, if Nick thought he was cornered in some way. From his experience, Orlando knew that's how guys like Nicky Pellegrino operated.

He looked at the photo, intently, and shook his head. "Well, I'll be." He quickly shot off a text to Joey.

Once settled in for the morning, Brian Bailey, placed a call to Detective Andrew Gallagher according the card he was given. Andy looked over at Shaker and answered, remembering who Bailey was.

"Gallagher." He said.

"Hi, detective Gallagher, this is Brian Bailey. We spoke a couple of weeks ago about that body."

"Yes, Brian, I remember. What can I do for you?" Andy questioned in a professional tone of voice.

"Well, I remembered something else about the three people I saw. Do you want me to come down?"

Andy thought for a minute. "Yeah, that would probably be better than taking the statement over the phone. Then I could get you to sign off on it."

"Ok, I'll be there in an hour or so. Does that work?"

"Yeah, sure, Brian. I'll be here."

Shaker had been listening to Andy's end of the conversation. "So, what gives?"

"Seems like Bailey remembered something else about the scene he saw. He's coming in about an hour to amend his statement."

"Interesting." Phil Shaker commented.

On her way to work, Suzanne made a brief call to Nick. She shared the events of her weekend that started with Andy seeing the missed call. The only thing Nick had to say about that was, "So why don't you change the contact name? Do I have to think of everything?"

She was usually a smart woman, but the underlying panic within her was interfering with her thought process. Nothing seemed clear. She felt stupid. Of course, she should change the contact name. What an idiot!

Chapter 85

Shaker had placed numerous calls to Bernie Falcone, the DA. Bernie knew they were impatiently awaiting the information from the genealogy site. He was waiting too. He, himself, had placed numerous calls to the site's legal department. He had been advised that due to the time difference he would have to be patient. Not only was he anxious to get the results, but the fact that this was even possible for evidence gathering in investigations, well, it opened a new world for law enforcement.

"Three hours, we have to wait at least three hours." Shaker said with defeat in his voice.

"Well, Bailey will be a distraction. Then you can always call Vince and shake that tree." Andy pointed out with optimism.

"True, true."

The phone on Andy's desk rang. He picked it up and was notified that Brian Bailey had arrived. To his partner, he said, "I'll go out and take his statement if it's short. I won't bring him in here unless there's more we both need to hear."

"Good idea." Shaker noted.

Bailey rose when Andy walked through the locked doors that separated the cramped waiting area from the rest of the station. "Detective, good to see you again."

"Same here Brian. Have a seat, we can talk out here."

Brian chuckled to himself. "Nice room," he said with notable sarcasm, "I suppose it's this way on purpose. You want to keep your visitor's nerves on edge, right? Plus, you don't want them so comfortable that they'll stay too long."

Andy tried to hide his smile when he said, "Yeah, I guess that's it. So, what's this all about Brian?" he said, attempting to redirect the conversation.

"Well, I remembered something. Actually, I remembered it last week, wrote it down when it came to me during the night. Then I completely forgot until I found the note I wrote to myself. That was Friday—knew I'd have to wait until today."

Pushing him along, Andy said, "go on." He took out his pad.

"Well, it was about the one I thought was a girl. Like I said, I couldn't see any faces or what-have-you, but at one point she took off the ball cap. That's what I remembered. She had blonde hair tucked up in it and definitely a girl. Don't know if that helps, but at least it's more than you had before."

"That's great, Brian. It could help once we start putting the pieces together. Can you just write that on the bottom of your statement and sign it with today's date?"

"Sure thing." Brian Bailey signed the document with the faceless dispatcher who sat behind the tinted glass acting as a witness. They shook hands and he left.

Joey had spoken with Orlando about the photo. Although it had been a few years, he knew exactly where to track this guy down; or at least where to start. He couldn't believe that after all this time Leo reappeared. He also wondered, as did Orlando, how the heck he knew Nicky.

Joey drove to the neighboring town of Bristol, where he knew Leo had resided. He approached the run-down apartment building which was located behind one of the grocery stores on the main drag. Leo's name was still on the resident list. He rang the accompanying buzzer to gain entry. Of course, it wasn't working.

He'd just have to do what everyone does—wait it out for someone who was coming or going and follow them through the doors.

When he finally had his shot, he walked through with an elderly gentleman feigning to search for his keys. He thanked the man and pressed the button on the elevator for the fifth floor. The doors opened, he smiled at the man, and exited into the long dreary hallway. His footsteps were muffled by the worn and stained wall-to-wall carpeting. He thought that maybe once it had been blue, hard to tell now, he thought. He arrived at the door and put his thumb over the peep hole prior to knocking. He could hear the radio sound being lowered as footsteps neared the door.

It took a few minutes, but finally, Leo asked, "Who is it?"

Joey supposed Leo had checked the peep hole before asking. He answered, "It's the super. Need to check the gas."

Since gas was nothing to take lightly and it didn't even register with Leo that being the "gas man" was his cover; he opened the door. "Oh jeez, Joey! What the fuck? Why didn't you just say it was you?"

"Hey Leo, didn't think you'd want to see me. How you doing? See you're in the same shithole."

Leo loosened up and gave a laugh. "Yeah, you know, I'm comfortable here. It suits me. Plus, the rent is pretty good. Leaves me with disposable cash for my other interests. Hey, come on in." he gestured widely and opened the door fully. "So, what gives, Joey? To what do I owe this pleasure?"

Joey surveyed the room quickly, noting that it was clean and furnished well. "Hey, nice place. Looks like you're doing alright. Lost a few pounds too?"

"Yeah, you know I eat well, hit the gym, don't drink as much." Then Leo became serious. "So, Joey, why are you here? I know you weren't just in the neighborhood."

Joey pulled out a picture of Nick. "Know this guy?"

Leo looked at it, then handed it back to Joey. "No, can't say I do. Why? What's the sap done?"

"Can't really say, he's just someone we're looking at. One of the guys thought you might be working with him."

"I don't know who gave you that idea, but nope, isn't me. Never saw him before."

Joey pulled out his phone and pulled up the photo Carly had taken of Leo and Nick together. He showed it to Leo, "Well Leo, pictures don't lie. What about this one"

Leo swallowed and tried to back his way out of it. "Oh, it's that guy? Didn't recognize him in the first picture. He was all bundled up when I talked to him today. Anyway, he asked me for a couple of bucks to grab some food. Said he was out of work. Ya know, I felt sorry for him. I slipped him a ten. That was it."

Joey wasn't buying it. The story was too pat and Leo was talking too much and too fast. A sure sign of someone making up a tale on the spot. "Oh ok, Leo. I just had to check it out. You know, part of the job. Anyway, let me know if you think of something else."

Ushering Joey towards the door, Leo said, "Sure thing buddy, really great to see you again. We gotta go out for a beer sometime, catch up, right?"

"Yeah, sounds good. Hey, see you around Leo." The door shut behind Joey before he finished his sentence. He thought to himself how interesting that encounter had been. He was itching to find out more. He wrote down his notes, send a text to Orlando, and pulled out of the driveway.

Chapter 86

Orlando had gone over the yearbooks, page by page. He made it a rule to be thorough. He figured if he found something later, he'd have to do this anyway. Why not do it the right way from the start? Since he only had an approximate idea of when Suzanne graduated, there were a few books that he needed to check out. He was on the third one when he finally hit pay dirt.

He stared at the photo in front of him. He examined it close-up and from a distance. He all but turned it upside-down but the image didn't change. He pulled up the picture of Suzanne he had on his phone. Comparing the two, he declared to himself, "This can't be her. Unless she changed everything about herself."

The Suzanne McGregor in the yearbook was a nursing graduate. Her face was round and freckled. She still wore the curly locks, but here it was red. He also noted that she had graduated with honors. There was also a list of activities and clubs she was involved in. He'd start there. Excitedly, he flipped the pages to the club section.

He located the yearbook committee, scanned the group shot, and found her again. He looked at the other students but didn't recognize any. He next found the page with swim team. "Ok, there she is." Again, he scoured the other faces, but no one jumped out at him. After checking two more clubs, his last effort was the drama club. He found her smiling for the camera with Nick standing next to her, his arm around her waist.

He read the names in the photo, scanning for the name next to Suzanne McGregor. "Now this is just getting weird. The name says Eric Popper but the photo is a younger Nicky Pellegrino. Damn." He took more snapshots with his phone. The more photos he saw of Eric as a young man, the more he tried to recall if he had ever come in contact with him. He looked so damned familiar.

Orlando wasn't sure exactly what he had stepped into. This all started because he needed to find Suzanne's link to everything. Knowing more of her background and her link to Nick, would have helped with Carly's protection. But now, he found himself the bearer of some very interesting information. He was able to connect Suzanne with both Eric and Nicky. He'd have to do some searching on his own using the data bases he subscribed to.

Nicky's phone was ringing off the hook. "Can't these people do anything without him? First it was Leo, then Suzanne. If they just kept to the plan, using only the phone, and stayed the hell away from him, no one would have known that they knew each other. But the damn fools kept wanting to see him.

Carly met Sally for a quick lunch to catch up on things in person. Before she drove back to Willimantic, she decided to drive by Nick's apartment again. She pulled into Starbucks to grab a coffee on the way when she received a call from Orlando. He told her about Joey's visit to Leo. He hinted at having a prior relationship with Leo back in the day. He also told her to be careful if she saw him again.

The next tidbit he said he would text, however, he wanted her on the phone when she received it. Immediately, her phone chimed and she opened the text. There were a few photos. There was one of Suzanne before her apparent make-over. And there was one of Suzanne sans make-over with Nicky. From college?

"So, Nick and Suzanne knew each other back in college?" Orlando told her to look at the next picture. The final photo was the list of names. Carly read them twice, then asked Orlando, "What is this?"

"Carly, I think in our attempt to look into Nick and Suzanne, we stumbled onto something else."

"But the guy's name is Eric Popper. Who the heck is Eric Popper?"

"And that, is the 'sixty-four thousand dollar' question, my dear. Eric Popper is dead."

This time she followed Orlando's advice. She turned her car around and got the hell out of there. Her watch would have to wait until they knew more.

Chapter 87

The phone started ringing and Andy picked it up. Shaker eyed him with a question mark. Andy nodded, it was Bernie Falcone, the DA. Andy jotted a few things down as he listened. His only comments were yes, you're kidding, and got it. He said thank you and hung up the phone.

"Well?" Shaker asked.

"Ok, here goes. Eric Popper's DNA matched a woman named Ann Pellegrino-Martin. It was a close match like that of a sibling."

"Yeah, so who is she?"

"Well, here's the thing. We know that name. Remember, Suzanne had that patient a while ago named Nicky Pellegrino—she thought he was Popper at first?" He thought for a minute. "No shit, I can't believe this"

"Hold on, are we talking like soap opera evil twins here?" Shaker asked.

"Yeah, I think we are."

"Wow, cool. I love the whole evil twin story line."

Andy looked at his partner incredulously, "Seriously? This is some crazy shit. But you know what? We got a bigger problem."

"Like?" His partner wanted to know.

"Like, who's the evil twin in our story? The dead guy or the guy from the hospital. Who, by the way, is now walking the streets."

Chapter 88

Andy and Shaker found it hard to believe the news they had just received. The investigation had just taken an unexpected twist, forcing them to regroup with the bits and pieces of information they had previously gathered. The evil twin cliché---who would have thought it could happen in real life?

"We have to keep this quiet, buddy." Shaker said.

"No kidding. So where do we start?"

"I'm thinking we start with this Nicky. He seems to have the biggest connection to Popper. Or maybe the sister." Shaker offered.

"What about Millie Popper? We need to know how she went about the adoption. Like who else knew, how she came to adopt the twin." Andy thought out loud.

They decided to use the white board to list everything they had so far. Shaker organized the list which included the approximate time of death—twelve to eighteen months ago. He wrote the names of the players which included, Nicky, Eric, Millie, Gustafson, and now Ann Pellegrino-Martin. He apologized to Andy as he added Suzanne to the list.

He then added the information they had gotten from Brian Bailey. Now they were certain two of the people present that afternoon on the river bank were Nicky Pellegrino and Eric Popper. There was a woman and bigger guy as well. They had an earring that could have belonged to any of them.

They knew Eric would have had a scar in the temple area, but since most of his skin had disintegrated from his face, that was a dead end. No pun intended. Andy recalled that Suzanne thought she had seen a scar on her patient, then decided it was more of a scratch. They still didn't know which one of them was the dead guy.

They had more than they had before, but less than they needed. Time to get down to business. They had a few people to interview.

In the early afternoon, Andy and Shaker picked up grinders from George's in the Unionville section of Farmington. Their food was second to none and the diverse menu never disappointed. The owners were a generous Greek couple who knew most of the patrons by name. They had the unique ability to welcome customers to the restaurant and make them feel like they had come home. It also happened to be located on the other side of the metal bridge from the Pellegrino hardware store.

They parked the SUV in the small lot behind the store. "You ready?" Shaker asked Andy.

"Hang on a sec, just want to make sure I don't have lettuce in my teeth." He checked the mirror and said, "Ready to roll."

"You never cease to amaze me. Let's do it."

Wearing jeans and light winter jackets, they strolled to the counter and asked to speak with Ann. The clerk excused herself and returned moments later followed by a thin woman of average height. Her sleek brown hair was shoulder length and angled to frame her face. She wore jeans with a crisp white shirt tucked in the front but hanging loose in the back.

She approached the detectives smiling, "Hi, what can I do for you?" She asked.

Shaker took the floor, "Hi Ann, We're detectives Shaker and Gallagher." They showed her their shields. "Is there someplace private we can talk."

Her smile slowly melted into a frown. Her twinkling blue eyes lost their luster. "Sure, let's go to my office, it's just up those stairs." She said, leading the way.

It was a cluttered space with a small desk and an old computer. They sat on the weathered mismatched chairs she had pulled closer to the desk. "Ok, so what is this all about?"

Andy spoke first. "Well, Ann, we'd like to ask a few questions about your brother."

She let out a breath. "My brother? What's he done now?"

"Well, we need some information because there's some confusion about him. For now, we're just trying to clear some things up."

Looking puzzled, she decided to answer frankly. Gentlemen, my brother is a shit."

Andy was unusually speechless, so Shaker asked, "Ok, tell us about that."

"Nicky was great guy. I mean, everyone loved him. He was that guy that everyone wanted to be around; he was very charismatic. He could talk to anyone about anything. He loved to laugh and have fun. He was great in this business too. The customers trusted him and so did I. Even though I was half owner with him after our parents died, I let him handle things because he was a natural. I had my own career.

"He knew numbers too; had a knack for them. We were always way ahead in the black. Then he started changing. I attribute that to his increase in drinking. Then he moves away and ends up in the hospital. His drinking made him crash, but he won't admit it."

"How did he change?" Andy asked.

"He thought he could be a big shot in real estate. Thought he knew everything. He even convinced his girlfriend of it too. He always had a bit of a temper, but his fuse had gotten shorter at that time too." She wasn't holding back, so after another breath, she continued. "When he ended up in the hospital, I discovered that the store was going in the complete opposite direction-- in the red. He had pretty much lost it all. My husband and I paid off everything with our own savings."

Not commenting on anything, Andy asked. "You said he had a girlfriend. What's her name?"

"Carly. Carly Mancuso. Very sweet girl with a heart of gold. Even though things were strained between them, she took responsibility for his care when he was in the hospital. I had already washed my hands of my brother."   "Where is he living now?

Ann told them that to the best of her knowledge, he resided in an apartment in Farmington. She added that Carly still lived in Willimantic.

During the few moments of silence, Ann thought about anything else she might offer them. She was still puzzled about the real reason for the visit.

It was then that Shaker continued the dialogue by asking about the genealogy site. "So, here's the thing, Ann. It looks like the DNA sample you submitted to the genealogy site came up with a match that indicated a sibling."

"Well, that's pretty obvious because I have a brother. But I'm thinking there's more, am I right?"

"Yes. So, it appears that the person your sample matched up with was not Nicky, but a guy named Eric Popper. It was his DNA that was submitted. Do you know him?"

She shook her head. "What does that mean?"

Andy informed her that it most likely meant Eric and Nick were twins since their DNA would be identical.

Flabbergasted at the news, she sank back in her chair. "How can this be?"

"That's what we're trying to find out, Ann. Oh, one more question. This girlfriend, Carly, is she by any chance a blonde?" Andy asked.

"Carly? No. She's got short chestnut hair."

They thanked her for her time and decided they should pay Millie Popper another visit.

Andy and Shaker walked down the long hallway leading to Millie's apartment. They had discussed what they would ask on the short drive over. When they knocked, they heard approaching footsteps, then nothing.

They looked at each other, then Phil Shaker said, "Millie, we know you're there. Can you open the door, please?"

Slowly the door opened, and Millie looked back and forth between them, eyeing them suspiciously. In a cheerful voice, that she mustered from deep inside her, she asked, "Hello detectives, what can I do for you?"

Shaker politely asked if they could come in for minute. He told her they had a few things to clarify and they would not take much of time. Feeling a small bit of relief, Millie gestured for them to enter.

"Have a seat, gentlemen. Can I get you some coffee or a snack? I just took an apple coffee cake out of the oven."

"Oh, that's what that wonderful smell is." Andy noted. "But no thank you, Millie. We really don't want to tie you up too long."

"Ok then." Shae sat across from them on the sofa.

Shaker began. "So, Millie, we were wondering how you knew the Pellegrinos and came to adopt one of their twins?"

It was pure luck that Millie was not holding a cup of coffee for if she had one in her hand, she surely would have dropped it at that moment. She cleared her throat and asked, "I'm sorry? I don't understand."

"I asked about the Pellegrinos. We were curious how you knew them." Shaker added, "You might as well tell us Millie. We have DNA proof that Eric had a twin."

"Ok, alright. Terry Pellegrino, Eric's mother, was my half-sister."

"So, why did you adopt one of her twins?" Andy asked out of curiosity.

"Well, my lovely half-sister had one child already, Ann. When she found out she was going to have twins, she couldn't handle that. She had enough trouble with the one that she already had. Terry was not cut out to be a mother. It interfered with her social life. She knew that we were looking to adopt and offered us this chance."

Andy wrote a few notes. "So, I take it she paid all the adoption costs?"

"Well, of course she did. Sam and I could never have afforded it, otherwise."

Shaker piped in. "Now, I'm curious. How come they never ran into each other in town or family gatherings? I mean, did they know about each other?"

"No, of course not. That would have been hard to explain, now wouldn't it? Identical half-cousins? Really, detectives. Part of our arrangement, was that Sam and I would move to another part of the state. We would be sure that our paths never crossed.

So, after we had our baby, we moved. Terry and I kept in touch privately. Terry started a trust which deposited to our account regularly. It would ensure that Eric never wanted for anything; he would be allowed the same opportunities that the other children had." Millie dabbed at her eyes with the tissue she had tucked in her sleeve. "Detectives, we loved Eric and raised him the best we could. Sure, he was a difficult child and needed discipline. I guess he was destined not to be perfect like Nick and Ann."

Trying to keep her on track, Andy redirected her. "It sounds like Mr. Pellegrino wasn't aware of the arrangement. Is that true?"

"Ted Pellegrino loved Terry and did whatever he could to make her happy."

"Millie, I'm confused. Why all the secrecy? This adoption wasn't illegal. Maybe cold on the parent's part."

"Because I promised that I would never tell anyone. After Ted and Terry died, the trust continued, so I was still bound to it."

I see," Andy commented. "Are you still receiving money?"

Millie nodded and looked down.

"But he's was a grown man. And now that he's deceased?"

"Terry provided for my future as well."

Shaker thought it was time to shift gears. "Millie, do you know if Eric found out about Nick?"

"Eric knew he was adopted. We never kept that from him. But as I told you once before, I had not spoken to him in a few years. So, I really don't have a clue if he knew or not."

Andy figured at this point, there was nothing more to gain by talking to Millie Popper. They confirmed what they needed to know. "Well, thank you, Millie. We appreciate your time."

Once again, they walked down the long hallway away from Millie Popper's apartment when Shaker said, "Man, this is some screwed up shit."

Andy glanced at this partner, saying, "Yep, it sure is."

Chapter 89

"This is getting ridiculous now. What the fuck are those two detectives doing here?" he thought, peering through the peephole. "Ok, showtime."

Nick opened the door a crack, feigning cautiousness. Smiling he asked, "Hello, can I help you?"

Although he couldn't see his full face through the slit in the opening, Andy was already astounded by the likeness to Eric Popper as he remembered him. Same wavy brown hair, same tall lanky build. However, this man appeared disheveled, his eyes were flat and glossed over. They didn't possess that glint of life that he remembered from all those years ago.

He said, "Nick, Nick Pellegrino?"

"Yes, I'm Nicky. And you are?"

Shaker and Andy held out their badges and introduced themselves to Nick. They told him they had a few questions and were hoping he would help them.

Nicky opened the door and allowed them entry into his control center. When he saw the detectives approaching, he had quickly thrown his notes and data into the hall closet.

As they entered, Andy took note of the cluttered space in which Nick lived. There were McDonald's bags and empty pizza boxes scattered throughout the walk-through kitchenette. The Chinese food containers were overflowing from the trash. The room smelled of rancid food, stale smoke, and burnt coffee.

Nick, himself, was drawn and not as fit as he had been. He wore a tee-shirt with some sport team's logo, but it was so faded, Andy could not recognize which team it was. The armpits bore stains from his sweat and had holes that showed when he moved his arms, gesturing for them to sit.

Andy sat on the arm of the goodwill sofa, while Shaker opted for the folding chair next to it. Nick shuffled some newspapers to the other side of the couch and plopped himself into it.

Shaker began. "Nick, we don't want to take much of your time, so we'll get right to it." He continued, "Did you know you had a twin?"

Nick manufactured a stunned look of disbelief coupled with some shock and answered, "I'm sorry, but could repeat that? I thought I heard you ask if I had a twin."

Shaker acknowledged that it was indeed what he had said. Andy, sat silently observing.

Nicky pushed his grimy hair out of his eyes and stared back at Shaker. With his most sincere voice, he made complete eye contact. "I'm absolutely speechless. Are you sure about this?"

Shaker nodded and explained only that they had DNA from a man that matched his. They never mentioned any names or linked it with a homicide victim.

Nicky sadly said, "I had no idea. I wish I knew." In a soft voice, he added sadly, "Not just a brother, but a twin. My god, this is just amazing." Fishing for exactly what Shaker was after, Nicky then said, "Can I meet him? Or is there more to the story and the reason you're both here?"

Andy spoke up. "We can't give any more information just now."

Shaker interrupted and asked, "Do you know someone named Carly Mancuso?"

For a second, Andy detected a flash of red eclipse over Nick's face. He answered, "Well, yeah, she used to be my girlfriend. We broke up after my accident. Haven't seen her in a long time."

"How about the name Eric Popper? Any bells?"

"Look detectives, I don't mean to be rude, but I don't know why you're asking me these questions. You come in here and tell me I've got a twin out there and don't tell me why." He teared up on cue and continued. "I'm recovering from a serious illness. I'm really not up to this."

"Ok, Nick, we get it. But here's my card. Please call if you're feeling up to another chat." Shaker told him.

"Thank you, thank you. Yes, I will, I need to lie down now. This news has my head spinning." He took the card and stared at it. He remained on the couch rubbing his temples in confusion as the detective let themselves out.

Once back in their car, Andy and Shaker compared notes. They agreed there was something "off" about Nicky Pellegrino. It wasn't just from his accident or illness as he had referred to either. He seemed almost too cliché in his response and reactions. In their gut, they knew he warranted further attention.

Through a crack in the curtains, Nicky watched them drive away and smiled. "Good riddance. Well, at least I know my acting is still in the Oscar league." He shot off a text to Suzanne and told her to call off her boyfriend. He also said he didn't care what she had to say in order to do it.

Suzanne threw her phone across the car seat after she read his text. She wondered how to broach the subject with Andy. It posed a dilemma especially because he wasn't exactly speaking to her right now. Well, she had to think of something; it would benefit all of them. She punched a response to Nick. She told him she'd figure something out. She ended her message by saying, "Go to hell."

Chapter 90

Carly arrived home feeling unsettled from the information she and Orlando had exchanged earlier in the day. She needed to call Orlando so they could talk more; maybe figure something out. She felt the need to write it down and have organization of the jumbled thoughts running around in her head.

She grabbed her mail on the way in and tossed it on the counter. Setting the alarm, she prepared her coffee. Her afternoon cup was something she looked forward to. After changing into a comfy pair of yoga pants, she poured the single cup that had just finished brewing.

She began sorting through the mail; most of it ended up in the trash anyway. A plain envelope with only her name on it caught her eye. Tentatively, she opened it and found a note inside. It said:

I warned you. Stop nosing around me. I don't want any more visits from   your friends either. You better do more than have an alarm because it's not gonna help you, honey.

Carly picked up the phone and called Orlando. After hearing what she told him, he said they would meet first thing in the morning and go to the police station with all the information they had. His instincts were waving red flags all over the place. Orlando never ignored a red flag. Carly didn't have to think twice. She agreed.

She calmed herself by texting Jack. She wanted to call him all day after their visit to see Lucy and the baby. The timing just hadn't clicked. He immediately answered her. He explained that Rosie was having a girl's night with his mother. They were shopping and going to have dinner. He asked Carly if she wanted to grab a quick bite with him. Of course, she agreed to that too. It was the perfect remedy to settle her nerves. It would also be better to tell Jack about the day's events in person.

He was just leaving work, so he said he'd pick her up on the way. She quickly changed back into her jeans and was ready when he arrived. Just the sight of his boyish smile made her heart flutter. All her worried thoughts drifted away; they just didn't seem quite as important anymore.

He took her hand and they walked to his car. "Look at us," he said, "being spontaneous. I think we're getting good at this dating thing."

Carly giggled. "I think you are right about that."

"Hungry?" he asked.

"All of a sudden, I'm starving."

They took their usual spot in the bar at one of the high-top tables. Carly ordered her wine; Jack a craft brew. They toasted and ordered. While they waited, Carly told Jack about her day. He listened with the intuition of a counselor and the heart of a man who wanted to protect her.

"Carly, I think Orlando is right. Aside from the fact that this guy is sick, his stalking is escalating. I think you also have enough convincing evidence to get a restraining order and make it stick. But I suspect, he'll find a way around that too, like he did with the video and the mailbox.

"But this other stuff worries me too. Like who are these people? What is going on? I think you're doing the right thing going to the police."

She sighed, "I thought you were going to think I was the crazy one. Anyway, thanks, I needed to hear myself talk about it out loud. You know, when it was just Nicky being an ass, it was unnerving, but I could handle it. Then he started getting a little too close for comfort and the police acted like I was a nut. Until I started getting the notes. That made me feel like I had a reason to apply for a restraining order. I knew I wasn't imagining things. I was happy to have Orlando check things out too. But I never expected all this other stuff to come up. It's all just so strange."

When their food arrived, Jack said, "Do you feel safe being alone tonight?"

Carly put her fork down. "I hadn't thought about it, but yeah, I think I'll be fine. I'll set the alarm and keep my phone with me."

"I could stay if you have any doubts. I'll be the perfect gentleman too. I'll sleep on the couch." He offered, although he really didn't want to be a gentleman.

She laughed, "That's so sweet, Jack. But I think I'll be fine. And by the way, if you do ever stay over, you don't have to sleep on the couch."

He looked at her, suggestively. "Oh no? I was hoping you'd say that. I like that idea."

She teased him and said, "I have two spare bedrooms."

Suzanne had been home long enough to start dinner before Andy walked in. Although, she was exhausted from a stressful day at work, she knew she had to make things right with Andy for many reasons. When she saw him, without a word, she went to him and wrapped her arms around him.

"I'm so sorry. I don't know what's wrong with me. Please forgive me." The tears that welled I her eyes were real. He had no idea how truly heartfelt they were. Neither did she until that moment.

He relaxed into her embrace, feeling a similar rush of emotion. "Oh, Suzanne, we have to get past this." He whispered through the curls that fells across her face. "I do love you, you know."

With a catch in her voice, she said, "I know. I love you too."

They stood inches apart staring at each other. "Do we need to talk about anything?" He asked her.

"No, I was just being irrational and stupid. Can we let it go?"

"For now. But at some point, you're going to have to trust me. I won't bring up your father again until you're ready." He said, even though he still had a nagging feeling that there was something off about the whole thing, remembering the calls that she had taken.

As they went through the dance of dinner preparation, the vibe in the kitchen had changed. There was no anger, there was no joy. Instead it was replaced by melancholy, exhaustion, and comfort. It saddened each of them to know something so small was capable of creating a divide. It was also a comfort to know how deep their feelings ran. They must move forward.

As they ate, they tried to be normal. Andy's attempt at his usual humor was slowly breaking the ice. They talked about everything except the elephant in the room---his case and her phone call.

When they had finished, Suzanne went into the bedroom to change into her sweats, while Andy cleared the table. He heard her phone buzz on the counter nearby. He glanced at the home screen and saw a text from someone named EN. The preview line to the text said:

"What'd you say to your idiot boyfriend?"

Andy's heart sunk. "Whoever you are, I'm thinking I'm not the idiot here." He didn't have time to open the text to read the rest. He would wait until Suzanne had gone to sleep.

Monday had been an interesting day: good for some; not so good for others. All in all, it came and went, as Mondays usually do.

Chapter 91

Tuesday

Early in the morning, Andy crawled out of bed. Suzanne was sleeping soundly and not due to get up for at least an hour. Cautiously, he slipped downstairs and picked up her phone. With his nerves on edge and his senses on high alert, he began scrolling through her text history.

The first two names were his, and this EN person. When he opened the texts, he couldn't believe how many entries were there. He quickly read through some. Although, they were cryptic in nature, he knew there was no innocent explanation. He snapped a few pictures of the texts. He would read them later.

He then went to her call log, and soon discovered many calls to and from the same person. One of those calls coincided with the date and time of the call from "pop". He realized she had changed the contact name. At this point, he had seen enough. He decided to head out earlier than usual to go to the station and try to sort out what this meant.

After he showered, he heard Suzanne moving in the kitchen. The coffee smelled great, but he wanted to get out there before he blew his cool. He'd take a cup to go instead. He realized that maybe he had been dense, but not anymore.

"Good morning," she said. "You're up early."

"Yeah, I had a text from Shaker. We're meeting early." Changing the subject, he said casually, "Coffee smells amazing. I'll take a cup to drink on the way." He poured it, snapped on the lid, and pecked her quickly on the cheek. He couldn't get out fast enough.

Carly was awake early. She sent a text to Orlando telling him she would be leaving shortly. He replied that he would be waiting.

It was still dark when she pulled out of her driveway. She sipped her coffee in new her go-cup. She decided she liked this cup better than the one she had tossed a few days ago. She had also sent Jack a text to let him know she was on her way and that she would stop at the Prospect Hill later in the day if there was time.

She made good time, considering the time of day. Rush hour traffic hadn't begun yet. As she pulled into his parking lot, she could see the red and purple colors illuminating the sky as sunrise began its brilliant display. Smiling, she exited her car and locked the door.

Orlando's security business was housed in an old home that had been converted to offices. It had a beautiful front door with frosted glass that squeaked when she opened it. Inside, the glossy dark woodwork enhanced the warm sage of the walls. The staircase leading to Orlando's office creaked with age and character.

She poked her head through the door, "Mr. Diaz?"

He came around the corner and gave her a hug. He was about five-seven, with dark wiry hair like his daughter. He wore a mustache and wire rimmed glasses. Orlando Diaz was confident by nature, but practical in thought. When he had fled the gang life, he found himself working in the security field. Once he took over the business, he procured a private investigator license and added that to the services provided.

"Come on in, Carly. Have a seat." He said pointing to the round table near the window.

They sat at the table for an hour, organizing what they had each discovered. They included Joey's notes as well. Once satisfied, Orlando said, "Are you ready?"

Carly took a breath and answered, "I am. Let's get this over with."

They left in separate cars heading for the Farmington PD.

Andy sat at his desk reading the few texts he had taken pictures of. He wasn't exactly sure what was going on, but he was getting the gist of it. And this perception was not good. He wished he had time to read more.

Arriving early himself, but not as early as Andy, Shaker placed the fresh steaming coffee in front of his partner. "Wow, looks like you've been here a while."

Glancing up, Andy said. "Yeah, appears that I've stepped in shit. Take a look at this." He handed Phil his phone with photos displayed on the screen.

"What the hell is this?"

"That my friend, is a text dialogue between Suzanne and someone she calls 'EN'. I'm guessing she's been playing with the bad boys from the sounds of things. I just can't figure out who or why."

"Man, this doesn't look good." Shaker stood and walked to the whiteboard. "Does it fit with any of this?" He said pointing at the facts they had compiled thus far.

"I hate to admit that I think it does. I just don't know how. There's nothing concrete in the text that points to that."

Carly and Orlando entered the police station and checked in with the dispatcher. They said they had come across information that they needed to bring to the attention of the department. Knowing Eric Popper's murder was still under investigation, Orlando requested the detectives who were running the case. They were instructed to sit in the drafty waiting area. Carly noted how intimidating it might be for someone to wait here if they had something to hide.

Shaker replaced his phone in the cradle. "Well, dispatch says we got a couple of people out there who might have information on the Popper case. I'll go out and weed through it before I bring them in."

When he got to the waiting area, he saw Carly glance up to meet his gaze. She smiled and brushed her hair out of her eyes. Shaker noted a look of worry that had her eyebrows knitted together. Then he saw Orlando.

He grinned and shook his hand. "Orlando! Is that really you? It's been ages."

"Phil Shaker! If I had known you'd be here, I would have visited a long time ago." The two men hugged as Orlando quickly explained to Carly that Phil's father was the guy who hired him off the street. He had mentored him, teaching him the ways to make a better life. He had known Phil since he was a boy.

Orlando gave Phil a quick wrap-up of the findings, not wanting to get into detail in the lobby. Shaker acknowledged his reservations and brought them back behind the locked entry.

When Andy saw Orlando, he stood and shook his hand. "Orlando, why didn't they just say it was you?" Andy and Shaker had also worked with Orlando on a few cases in the past. It seemed that Orlando had knack of getting into places for information that they could not access.

They went into one of the interrogation rooms which would afford them privacy. Orlando started the dialogue by saying this really started with Carly. He asked her to start at the beginning. Carly's account of her life with Nick and subsequent breakup was recounted in the condensed version. Her story concluded following the break-ins. She would let Orlando take it from there.

He touched over the lack of response from Officer Zelinsky. He showed them photos of the notes she had received. He said at that point, he began following Nicky. He didn't realize he was dropping a bomb until it exploded. This occurred when he handed them the picture of Suzanne with Nicky.

Andy and Shaker tried to conceal their shock as they listened to Carly's account of her meeting with Suzanne. She added how weird it was finding out his nurse had been to see him. She then explained how she followed Nick, taking more photos with this guy they figured out was Leo.

Orlando stepped in and filled in the gaps with his part of the research. He told them about his past connection to Leo. He expressed his opinion that Leo was responsible for the stuff going on at Carly's house. He was probably operating on Nicky's instructions. Although he was a smart guy, he would only have taken the job if money or his safety were involved. He guessed it was money this time.

He went on to discuss Carly's meeting with Suzanne. He told them he had become very curious about her connection to Nick. It was all so strange. It seemed to start with an angry boyfriend who drank too much and was abusive. Now, it was turning into this tangle of obsession with the past that seemed to overshadow everything. It was then that Orlando revealed the photos and information he had uncovered at the college. Andy recalled from his first meeting with Suzanne, her relationship with Eric was only five years old. This new information would place it over ten. He was dumfounded that Suzanne may have duped him in some way. He still didn't understand the why or how.

Orlando also showed them photos of Eric and Suzanne sans makeover. They scanned the names which clearly listed Eric draped over Suzanne. Then they were shown photos of Carly and Nicky, just to hit the point home that indeed they were identical.

Shaker and Andy were stunned. This information confirmed the conclusion they had reached. Andy could see the puzzle pieces floating around in his brain. He just needed to grab them and fit them together. However, they were just beyond his grasp.

Andy said at this point, he had a few questions for Carly. "First, did Nicky have any facial scars?"

Carly answered, "No, he didn't have any scars for most of the time we were together. Then, one day after he showered and his hair was wet and pushed back, I noticed a small scratch on the side of his face. It didn't look fresh. Anyway, I asked him what happened. He told me that a few weeks ago, when he was moving things around during inventory at the store, a piece of wood had slipped from a shelf. He said when he tried to grab it, it had scratched him. He said it wasn't a big deal, no blood, no cut, just a scratch."

Shaker had something else in mind. "Carly, does Nicky have any other scars? Something not related to his hospitalization."

She answered immediately, "Yes, he had his appendix removed when he was about sixteen. So, he had a scar from that. Why do you ask?"

Shaker was thinking out loud, when he said, "Did you notice that scar when you starting seeing changes in his behavior."

Feeling embarrassed by what the detective was insinuating, Carly replied flatly, "If you're asking me if I recall seeing the scar when he was naked, I can tell you that he had become so belligerent and disgusting, I tried not to be with him in that way. So, no, I can't tell you if I had seen that scar recently."

"Ok, Carly, I'm sorry. I had to ask."

Once their conversation was finished, they thanked Orlando and Carly for coming forward. They cautioned Carly to be careful. Orlando assured them he had all his eyes on her.

Andy walked them to the locked exit door. After organizing these new elements with what they already knew, they would contact Orlando for more assistance if necessary. Once again, he had proven invaluable to them.

After eating lunch and deeply engrossed in his thoughts, Andy glanced at his friend. "Phil, what has Suzanne gotten herself mixed up in?"

Phil Shaker tossed his sandwich wrapper in the trash and looked over. "I don't know, buddy. I'm really sorry about this. I started thinking about those college pictures. It looks like whatever it is, started a long time ago."

"I know you're gonna say I'm in denial, but I can't picture Suzanne being part of this. It's just crazy."

"Yeah, I know. Hey, why don't you do some subtle digging at home? Just remember to keep your perspective. You gotta be objective."

"I know, I know. The other question that comes to mind now is who's the dead guy? Which twin? Too bad, Popper's body was so far gone, we can't find out about a missing appendix or the scar on his face. Maybe we can bring Pellegrino in with a search warrant to look for a scar." Andy said, giving his best effort at humor under the circumstances.

Chapter 92

As she drove away, Carly was feeling good about the meeting with the detectives. She had no idea about the homicide details they were looking into. She was still trying to digest the fact that Nick had a twin from the information that she and Orlando had uncovered. The detectives had validated that fact as well. It still seemed so strange that her problems with Nick were now aiding a murder investigation. Officer Zelinsky would choke on that, she thought.

The very idea that Nicky had a twin was mind-boggling. Especially, since now that twin was dead. She wondered if Nicky knew. He never said anything about it. Then she got to thinking about the insinuations the detectives had made; was Nicky really Nicky or had the twin, Eric, taken his place? She thought it sounded like some crazy TV plot. However, she couldn't laugh about it, because this was happening in her real life.

She decided to make a quick call to Jackson. She wanted to touch base and fill him in. Their conversation was brief and she assured him she would go to the courthouse to apply for a restraining order. Her next call was to her parents. She wanted to stop by on her way home for a quick visit and maybe score some lunch. Quality time with the Mancusos.

When she pulled in the driveway, she saw her dad puttering in the garage as usual. The cold weather didn't bother him.

"Hi dad," she said and kissed him hello.

"Carly girl! I was so excited when mom said you'd being coming over."

"What are you working on now?" She asked, trying to figure out exactly what he was doing.

"Nothing much at the moment. Just straightening up. Look, I got these great little drawers thingies. They're all sectioned off. I'm separating my screws, nails, stuff like that. Trying to organize." He showed her the plastic bins with pride.

"Oh, great idea. It looks like a big project. But way better than the jars you were using before."

"Sure is. Let's go inside. I think your mother said something about lunch."

They were greeted in the kitchen by Carly's mom. Gi gave Carly a nurturing hug and said, "How's my girl?"

"I'm good, mom. Sorry I haven't been by, things have been a little crazy."

"I know honey, what with the shower and your new romance. So do we get to hear more details?" Gi asked. She had set the table with fresh snowflake rolls, grilled chicken breast, and provolone cheese. There was also an assortment of condiments and a plate of lettuce and tomato.

"Oh this looks great!" Carly smiled, thinking how coming home to the comfortable ritual of her family helped settle her and put things in perspective.

"Pass the olives, please." Her father asked. "Thanks." And he piled a few on his sandwich. Carly did the same. They were so much alike in many ways.

When they started to eat, Carly confessed about the problems with Nick. She recapped how he started stalking her when she cut her ties with him. She explained how Jenn's father had taken an active interest in it. She brought them up to speed on the current state of progress. However, she didn't get into the nitty-gritty details because she knew some~~were~~sensitive due the investigation.

"Carly, why didn't you talk to us about this?" Gi asked.

"I didn't want to worry you. At first, it seemed manageable, you know, it was just really annoying. But then, it felt like it was turning into more. That's when I called Mr. Diaz."

"But a twin? This is really possible?" Her mom wondered.

"Gi, remember that movie watched a few months back? It's like that. Only the movie was about a bank robbery. They arrested the wrong twin. Remember that?" Her dad asked.

"I do," Her mom answered. "What was the name of that movie? It was really good." She asked her husband.

"I don't know. I'll google it. I think it had Gerard Butler in it."

"No, no. I think it was Ryan Gosseling. Gerard Butler has an accent."

"Oh yeah, you're right." Sal agreed.

At this point, Carly was just amazed as she looked back and forth between her parents as they debated yet another twin story. They did make her laugh.

He continued, "Anyway, I'll find out the name of the movie for you. It's really good."

Finally, Carly had her opportunity to interrupt. "Thanks, dad, but I think we got a little off topic again."

"Off topic? Oh yeah, well twins are twins, I guess."

"I guess they are, dad." She agreed, although she didn't really know what he meant.

"Well, I'm glad you had the sense to call Mr. Diaz. But from now on, please talk to us too, Ok?" Her mother requested.

"I will, mom." Carly took another bite of her sandwich.

"How's the new beau?" Sal questioned.

Carly felt her cheeks flush as she smiled and answered. "He's really good." She had told them bits and pieces about her time with Jack. But again, she was not really someone who shared every little detail or feeling, even with her parents.

Gi beamed realizing that her daughter was quite smitten with this man. She had met Jack a few times. Something about him had always struck her the right way. It made her happy for her daughter, that she and Rosie had bonded as well. "This is all so wonderful, honey." Her mom commented as she stood to clear the table.

"I'll help." Carly offered.

Sal put on the coffee and grabbed some cookies from the cabinet.

Chapter 93

Things are unravelling. I really need to get a grip again. She pushed me away. I don't know if you'd call what I felt, love, but it was something at any rate. I really don't like rejection. So now, I need to get serious.

The bitch even sicked some detectives on me. I wonder if she realized the error of her ways. She's definitely not taking my warning seriously. Yeah, time to step it up. I can do it myself because obviously, those two other yahoos are watching their own backs. It's mine they should be concerned about. I'm the only one who matters, after all.

Yeah, yeah, we were a team, but I'm the leader. Isn't there a rule or something that says if you protect the leader, the followers will be ok? I don't know, maybe I just made that up. Anyway, it sounds good to me.

Suzanne is letting her own fears get in the way of her normally cool judgement. She really needs to get a grip. She's coming undone and making mistakes. Cell phone charger? I still can't believe that one. If it wasn't such a stupid thing to say, I might be laughing about it. Maybe we'll laugh later.

Then there's Leo. That guy always had my back. I know he's still sticking to the plan. I think he's having fun with it too. But since he didn't want to get involved in the beginning, I'm worried how long it'll take him get careless.

So yeah, it's up to me. Carly Mancuso will pay. She shouldn't have rejected me. I wonder if I can get her back. Sometimes, I get so pissed I just want to kick her in that stupid little face of hers. Show her who's in charge; yeah, let her know that she made huge mistake--huge. I am not to be underestimated. I am the boss, the master in charge. I know what's best. I am always right. I am the sun and they are all inconsequential little planets in my aura.

Chapter 94

A few things had been eating at Andy. He knew his partner was probably thinking about the same details. He realized Shaker was right. The only way to find the truth would be by subtle observation of Suzanne. Confrontation wouldn't work.

At this point, he was aware of more information than she had any clue about. He would use those to his advantage. He decided to play it out as if everything was just hunky-dory in "Andy-Suzanne world". He figured if he behaved innocently, she would behave likewise, thus leading him to other discoveries. That is, if there were any.

Suzanne had an exhausting day at the hospital. However, she was thankful for the intensity it provided her. It kept her focused on more important matters than her own troubles. She cared for a young man in his twenties who had been brought in with what was claimed to be an accidental heroin overdose. The man had been found in his bed in the morning by his girlfriend. He was blue and no-one had any idea how long he had been in that state.

The girlfriend called 911. CPR was started, Narcan was administered, but there was no response. After more than thirty minutes of administering drugs that might jumpstart his heart, they finally had activity on the ECG. The paramedics knew that brain damage occurs after four, but the family implored them to continue.

When they arrived at the emergency room., the young man who had been intubated in the field was alive in body, but completely without brain activity. The family refused to believe that he would be in a persistent vegetative state because he had a heartbeat and appeared to be breathing. They were told the breathing was due to the ventilator; the heartbeat was occurring because the medulla was intact.

It was explained to the family that this portion of the brain stem had only one purpose---to preserve the basic life functions such as heartbeat. It played no role in thought, cognition, or any other purposeful operation necessary for life. The EEG was flat with no response.

Once in the ICU, Suzanne sadly attended to this young man. He lay flaccidly in the bed. His eyes were non-reactive to light; his body had no recoil from pain or touch. His facial expression did not change or grimace with stimulation either. She did her best to make sure he was comfortable until the family came to a decision regarding his future.

Following a clinical assessment which would certify brain death, the results were conclusive. His family finally agreed to withdraw life support. His organs would be donated to young people who would otherwise die without them.

Once Taylor, the respiratory therapist, weaned the ventilator, Suzanne had discontinued the life-sustaining medications. She then, administered medication to be sure the boy remained comfortable. However, as Taylor worked with the machine, the boy never took a breath on his own. It was clear that the vent was the only reason the young man appeared to be breathing. Once off the machine, the boy passed away in under five minutes. The family was relieved to know that they had made an unselfish choice which was the right decision. It had become clear that the only reason he was alive was due to the breathing machine and the drugs that supported his other bodily functions.

By the time she arrived home, Suzanne was spent. It was a tough day, but the outcome was better than subjecting the young man's empty body to a life on machines which would have appeared to keep him alive; his spirit had left him sometime the night before.

She walked in the door to be greeted by a vibrant display of flowers on the table. Her heart melted when she read the card Andy had written. He simply told her he loved her. He greeted her with a mischievous grin and swept her in his arms. Thank you was all she could muster, as the tears welled in her eyes.

"Sit down, babe, I'll make us some coffee. You look exhausted."

He poured them each a cup and joined her at the table. He listened with compassion as she told him about her day. He knew that no matter was else was going on in their lives, Suzanne was a caring nurse who took her job seriously. He understood the sorrow she felt for her patient and his family.

"I've got an idea. I think we should go out for dinner."

"Really? That does sound nice. It's been a while since we did that. We've both been so caught up in everything."

"So where would you like to go? I was thinking that seafood place you like in West Hartford Center. OK, what about the Mediterranean restaurant?"

Suzanne thought about it, "I pick the Mediterranean. I remember how amazing it was."

"Ok Mediterranean it is. I know it's only Tuesday, but I'll call for reservations. What do you think? An hour or so?"

"I think that's good. It'll only take us ten minutes to get there." She kissed him and said, "Thank you. I need this." Eagerly, she scurried upstairs to shower and change.

Andy was feeling good about this. Whatever was going on, he still loved her. A night out would be perfect for both of them. Hopefully, some settlement of the issues would be revealed as well. He joined her to get ready.

She emerged from the bathroom, beaming radiantly. Her blonde curls shimmered around her face. She wore a simple black top with black jeans. For color, she added a jewel-tone green wrap.

Andy couldn't help but notice how stunning she looked all in black. Her blonde hair was accentuated. The shimmery pendant she wore was perfect too. "You are gorgeous." He said, putting on his boots. Just then, he had an idea. "You know what would look great?" She smiled and waited. "Those diamond earrings I bought you a couple of Christmases ago."

Her heart sank. Think quick, don't be stupid this time. "I thought I'd wear dangles. But, yeah, you're right. Let me look for them."

He watched her sift through the jeweler's boxes where she stored her valuable items. "Oh don't worry if you can't find them. The dangles are pretty."

"No, they're here. You know I was always afraid of losing them after that time at work when one slipped out. I haven't worn them much since."

Andy suddenly knew she wasn't going to find them. He remained calm. "You're silly, Suzie Q. What's the sense of having them if you're afraid to wear them. It's ok, we'll look for them another time."

"Yeah, I guess we can. I just thought they were in this drawer. I'll think of where I might have put them."

She grabbed her clutch. He took her hand and said, "I am the luckiest guy in the world. Let's go eat." Inside his heart was shattered.

Chapter 95

Thursday

After a crazy couple of days, Carly knew it was time to get back to normal. Her normal, anyway. It was still dark when she woke at six. Although she loved being up before the sun rose, daylight savings time always took some getting used to. She turned on the coffee, opened the blinds and watched for the first glimpses of sunlight to illuminate the town, house by house.

In the quiet of dawn, she reviewed the events of the past few days. The events centering around Nicky had almost overshadowed the wonderful weekend she had. She was relieved to have left him in the hands of the police. Orlando would continue with his part in it all too.

She had decided that after her morning at Prospect Hill, she would drive to the courthouse to secure the restraining order. At this point, she had enough documentation along with a statement from Orlando which proved Nicky was a threat to her. This time she would have success and some peace of mind.

She left her house earlier than usual and walked up the hill. It was still and quiet all around her. She noticed that lights were just coming on in homes around her as others were beginning to stir. When she approached the house, Carly smiled, realizing that Lucy would be coming home from the hospital with the baby today. She knew in her heart this day would be perfect.

Just as she stepped onto the walk, Jack pulled in. She waited for him to get out of the car. He beamed when he saw her and kissed her hello. "I don't care who sees us. They probably suspect anyway." He laughed.

Jenn replaced the curtain she had been peeking through. "Well, I'll be," she thought. "Finally."

Once inside, they helped with breakfast preparations. Jack decided his office work could wait. While they ate, Jenn announced that she had made a schedule for them to help Lucy with baby Alex. Since she needed to rest, it made sense for the others to pitch in. Jenn had planned times and duties for each of them according to their own schedules. She asked Carly to fill in her own since she had other things on her plate at this point.

"You thought of everything, Jenn." Irene joked. "I think this is great, though. There's a lot that goes into caring for a newborn. If we can help Lucy, I'm in."

Following breakfast, clean-up, and the usual short group session, each of the women prepared for their day. They all wanted to be home by three, when Lucy would arrive.

Parked a down the street, he sat in his car. He mentioned to Nick that he would be stepping things up. He admitted that he was enjoying the game himself. However, he knew that to Nick, it had become more than just a game. He took a swig of his coke. He was startled when he heard a tap on his window. "Shit," he thought as he rolled it down.

"Hiya Leo," Joey said. "What brings you out this way so early in the morning?"

"Hey, Joey, I could ask the same of you."

"Why don't we grab some breakfast and talk about this." Joey offered. "Or we could always take a drive and see Orlando. I'm sure he'd love to see you again too."

Leo started his car. "Listen, Joey, I've got an appointment. No time for reunions."

Joey put his hand through the window. He unlocked the door and yanked it open. "You're not going anywhere, buddy. Not until you tell me what's going on here."

Just then, Carly appeared on the walk and spotted Joey. She couldn't tell what was going on, but from her vantage point, it didn't look good. Joey was distracted when he noticed Carly. At that moment, Leo grabbed the handle and shoved the door hard into Joey, knocking him backwards. Carly reached for her phone and dialed 911.

Leo pressed his foot on the gas and lurched forward. As the car sped towards Carly, she stood frozen. An operator came on the line, while the car was closing the distance. All of a sudden, Carly felt an arm around her waist pulling her to the ground out of the way. Leo's car veered onto the walk where Carly stood seconds ago. It whooshed by.

He kept going until he was out of sight. He realized what a close call that was. But mission accomplished. His intent was to scare her and that, he certainly had done.

Shaken, Carly looked at Jack who had pulled her out of the way. "Are you alright?" He asked.

"I think so. Oh my god, Jack. He would have hit me if you weren't there." Just then, she saw Joey. He was still laying in the street. She ran to him.

"Joey, Joey, are you ok?"

He looked up at her and nodded. "He knocked the wind out of me."

Jackson and Carly helped Joey to sit up. His head was spinning from the blow; he felt woozy and nauseous. That was when the blood seeping from his head, dripped down his back.

When the ambulance arrived, they were able to do a quick patch job on Joey's wound. He was lucky it was just a gash from the fall. They transported him to the hospital to make sure he didn't have a concussion. The police would meet them and take their statements.

Carly was shaken up by the close call. She was unharmed, but she stood watch in the waiting room, eager to hear news of Joey. Jackson stayed with her. He refused to leave until she did.

Even though the Willimantic Police were involved, she called Orlando. He, in turn, notified Andy and Shaker. Shaker called the Willi PD and told them they were investigating Leo and his connection to a guy who was stalking Carly. In a collaborative effort, they agreed to allow the detectives to bring Leo in for questioning.

A young black man in scrubs approached Jack and Carly. He introduced himself as Dr. Lorenson. His broad smile was encouraging as he talked about Joey. The ER physician explained that Joey was fine. He had suffered a laceration to the back of his head which required stitches. The CT scan revealed no bleeding, so that was a good thing. However, he could not rule out a concussion. He was going to keep Joey overnight for observation as a precaution.

Carly and Jack were taken to see Joey. He perked up when he saw them.

"I'm sorry, Carly. I should have had him."

"Oh my god, don't be sorry, I'm just happy you're not seriously hurt." She said. "You couldn't have known what he was going to do. How are you feeling."

"Well, except for a whopper of a headache, I'm ok. I really don't want to stay the night, but the doc says since it was a bad bump, they need to be sure nothing happens in the next few hours. I guess I have to be ok with that."

Jack asked, "Is there anyone you want us to call?"

"Oh yeah, can you let my girlfriend know?"

Thinking it was better if Joey told her himself, Jack handed Joey his cell phone. "Here you go, why don't you make the call. She won't worry as much if she can talk to you." Joey smiled and thanked Jack.

When they were sure Joey was settled in, Jack and Carly left. Instead of going back to the house, Jack drove Carly straight to the courthouse to get the restraining order. It was still early.

She filled out the necessary paperwork which stated her case. She cited examples and attached documentation. After waiting for an hour, it was her turn to see the judge. When she saw him, her heart sunk. It was the same judge she had appeared before the first time a few weeks ago. He had turned her down.

Judge Geary read through the papers carefully. He studied Carly and Jack. Then he spoke. "Ms. Mancuso, weren't you just here seeking a restraining order?"

"Yes, sir, your honor." She didn't add anything further. Her written statement and subsequent documentation would speak for itself. She had also been coached by Orlando only to answer what was asked.

His face was grave when he said, "I'm sure you understand that I had nothing tangible the first time. But now, I see that Nicky Pellegrino is in fact a threat to you. I will grant the order." He banged his gavel and called for the next case.

Carly felt a wave of relief as she and Jack were ushered to the clerk's window. They were told that the local marshal was due to arrive shortly. He would go over the details with them. Nicky would be served the following day since a marshal in the

Farmington area would need to be contacted to serve the order. Once all the details were wrapped up, they left the courthouse feeling exhausted.

Chapter 96

After speaking with Orlando, Andy and Shaker decided to pay Leo a visit. First, they had a few details to go over.

Andy began. "Ok, so here's the deal. Suzanne is in this up to her neck."

"What did you find out?"

"Well, after getting that information from Orlando and Carly. I started thinking about what Bailey told us. And then there were the phone calls and the texts. So, I did what we talked about. I feel bad cuz I kind of set her up."

Shaker watched his friend struggle with his revelation. "Ok, take it slow, what happened."

"Well, I decided to take her out to dinner. I was really thinking about subtly talking about the case. Anyway, my idea changed gears when she came out of the bathroom. She was dressed in all black. Her blonde hair really stood out. All I could think was that Bailey said the woman was blonde. So, I took a shot and suggested she wear the diamond studs I gave her a couple of years ago."

"Oh, don't tell me."

"Yep, she couldn't find them. She gave me a story about how nervous she was that she'd lose them, so she put them away for safe keeping. I knew instantly." He trailed off.

"Man, so we're thinking, Suzanne was the woman in Bailey's account of what happened when Popper went into the water."

"That's about it. Dammit, Phil, what do we do now?"

"Hold on. Let me think." He recapped the scenario out loud. "We now know three of the four. We got Popper, Pellegrino, and Suzanne. We don't know the fourth guy. I hate to say this, but I think we need to bring Suzanne in and confront her. See what happens."

"I know you're right, but this sucks, big time."

"Yeah, it does. Who knows? Maybe it won't be what we think."

"Thanks, but we both know that's not gonna happen."

Phil smiled. "Yeah, I'm just trying to channel your optimism."

"Guess, we should fill the captain in. Then head out to see this Leo guy." Andy said.

It was still early afternoon when Jack brought Carly back to her house. They found Jenn sitting on her front porch. Jenn sprinted to Carly, hugging her. "Are you ok? I'm so sorry I wasn't there when it happened. My dad called me."

"Oh Jenn," Carly said pushing Jenn's jet gelled curls out of her eyes. "yeah, I'm good. Jack got me out of the way. Joey is the one who got hurt. Come on, let's all go inside. I'll make some coffee."

They sat at her dining room table while Carly told Jenn what happened. "The thing is I don't even know this Leo-person.

Joey and your dad say he's bad news. They're pretty sure he's working with Nicky."

Jenn was thoughtful for a minute, then said, "My dad wouldn't want you to know this, but Leo is someone he hung with way back in the day. Every now and then, Leo would show up at our house. Dad would take him outside because he didn't want us kids to know anything. I used to listen at the door. I would hear dad telling him to get lost. He told him he was done with that life. So, I figured Leo kept showing up to suck dad into some scam or deal. Whatever the reason, dad wanted no part of it."

"That explains why he and Joey were so adamant about him being bad news." Carly thought out loud.

"Well, I guess in a way it's good this happened. Now they can charge him with something."

Carly smiled, "I didn't think of it that way. You're so smart, Jenn."

"Yeah, I guess my criminal justice classes are paying off after all."

When Jack was sure everything had quieted down, he stood to leave. Carly walked him to the door. He hugged her and said, "I was so afraid something was going to happen to you. I can't lose you now."

"My hero." She said. "You're not going to lose me."

"Just remember, if anything weird happens, you call the police. If he violates the restraining order, it's a felony."

"Good to know." She said as he kissed her and told her he'd come by after work.

She joined Jenn in the kitchen. She had started cleaning up the mugs but was smiling a broad grin. "So, you and Jack? I love this!"

Carly blushed. "Yeah, me and Jack."

Chapter 97

Suzanne pulled out the box that contained the earring. She stared at shimmering diamond stud resting on the black velvet. It was one of the first gifts Andy had given her. She knew she could have just told Andy she lost one. But she didn't have the heart. Maybe she could replace them. She wondered if he'd even know the difference. That sounded like a prudent plan of action. The problem was Suzanne had no idea why Andy had suggested she wear them. It seemed so random.

Suzanne's phoned pinged to alert her to a text. It was from Andy. He knew she had the day off and was inviting her to meet him at the station. He thought it would be nice to grab a late lunch together. She wrote back that she would love to.

Before Suzanne was scheduled to arrive, Andy and Shaker stopped to see Bernie Falcone, the DA. They explained the situation with Leo to Bernie. Bernie did a quick background check on Leo to see if any priors popped up in the system.

"Ok, here's the deal. He's got no prior arrests, so he's been staying under the radar. Based on the fact that we have multiple witnesses and an actual injury that he instigated, I'd say were pretty lucky. We can charge him with simple assault for pushing the car door into Joey. It's a second degree misdemeanor. He could serve up to a year in jail if he's convicted. We can also charge him with reckless endangerment with a motor vehicle for the near miss on Carly. That's a Class D misdemeanor for a first offense. That would get him thirty days in jail."

"I say let's do it."

"So, here's another thing to consider. He's probably not keen on the idea of going to jail so I'd consider making a deal with him in exchange for information. He may be willing to give it up to save himself the prison time. Let me draw up the paperwork, then I'll get it to the judge. I think it's safe to say we want this to happen sooner rather than later. Come back around three-thirty-ish? I think that should work."

The detectives thanked Bernie and left his office. They knew Leo's screw-up may have just given them a big break. Shaker also placed a call to Orlando to fill him in. He asked Orlando to keep a distant eye on Leo. He didn't want to risk losing him. He further advised his friend to be discreet until they picked up Leo later that day. They didn't want to tip him off.

Suzanne arrived at the police station and was immediately greeted by Andy. She had called ahead to avoid the waiting room experience she endured the last time. He escorted her through the imposing door that had caused her so much panic and followed him down the hall to where Phil Shaker was sitting at this desk.

"Hi, Suzanne, how are you?" He rose and greeted her with a light peck on the cheek.

"I'm good, Phil."

Shaker began the conversation. "Suzanne, before you and Andy head off to lunch, I've got a few questions for you. I just need to clear up a few details. I was hoping you wouldn't mind helping."

Shaker had purposefully left Andy out of the mix. However, Suzanne was confused and shot a condemning glare in Andy's direction. He shrugged his shoulders innocently as if to say "Sorry, I had no idea."

She looked back at Shaker and agreed to speak with him. He suggested they go to the kitchenette, where they could be more comfortable and still be in a private setting. It was his intent to keep this informal. He feared that if she felt intimidated, they'd be at a dead end.

Once they sat, Shaker acted like he was confiding in her. Andy remained silent. "Suzanne, I'm so sorry to put you through this again. I know this Eric business brings back some bad memories." She nodded, he continued. "But, I wanted to share some information that we have. I was hoping you could shed some light on it."

"Ok, if I can help. But I really don't know anything other than what I've told you."

Andy had not said a word, instead he watched Suzanne intently, gauging her reactions. Phil continued. "Did you know Eric had a twin?" She paled at this news. Andy watched her as she blinked her eyes a few times in rapid succession. She was trying to process this information but at the same time attempting to grab a good answer from the different versions floating through her mind.

All she could say was, "A what?"

"I take it, this surprises you."

She glanced at Andy, then back at Shaker. "Phil, what is this all about?"

"Well, we know Eric had a twin. We're trying to find out if and when he discovered that fact."

She relaxed a bit and sat back in her chair. "Oh, well he never mentioned that to me. So, I don't know." In her head, she was screaming, "what the hell is going on here?" She was desperately trying keep her composure. Her rule of the minute— never let them see you sweat.

"Ok, next question. How long did you know Eric before you started dating? I'm asking because I'm wondering about his friends. I probably should have asked you that the last time you were here." He apologized.

Thinking she said, "Um, not too long. We met shortly after I started working at the hospital in New London." She apparently forgot the other rule—only answer what was asked.

Shaker pulled out the photo from Suzanne's yearbook of her and Eric looking rather chummy. "What do you think of this?" He pushed the picture in front of her.

Andy saw her swallow hard. She answered, "Well, it does look like Eric, but who's the women?"

Phil Shaker was quick on the comeback. "Well, according to list of names here at the bottom, it's you. That is, before you got contacts and dyed your hair. And I'm not stupid enough to miss the resemblance." He answered curtly.

"Ok, so I knew Eric in college."

"Why not just tell us that?"

"I don't know. I guess I didn't want anyone to know that I was naïve enough to be mixed up with him for so long." Woefully, she feigned a sniffle and dabbed at her eye.

"Ok, got it." He put the photo aside and reached for a new one. "What about this one?" It was the recent one of her and Nick.

This time she lost it. "What the 'F' are you doing Phil? You're following me?" She scowled at Andy and pointed. "And you? You knew about all this and didn't have the decency to ask me in private?" She was attempting to turn it around in her favor. She tried to play the unsuspecting victim.

"Sorry babe, but this isn't a private thing anymore."

Shaker continued. "So, why were you meeting this guy that, if I recall correctly, was a patient of yours?" He added, "And coincidently turns out to be your former boyfriend's twin, who shows up murdered? Surely, you saw the resemblance?"

She quickly answered. "I was returning a personal item that was left behind after his discharge. I think that clears things up. I'm leaving now." Again, she looked over at Andy. "I'm not hungry, you can have your lunch and shove it up your ass."

"Wait, Suzanne," Shaker said. "Sit down, I'm sorry, I didn't mean to be confrontational. We were just looking for connections."

Reacting only as a guilty person would, she answered defensively, "Well, it didn't feel that way to me."

"Just a few more questions, Ok?"

"Fine, but don't back me into a corner again."

He smiled. He wouldn't engage in her effort to turn the tables and change the subject. He also knew she wouldn't give him much more time to ask the rest of the questions. Her fuse was already lit. Quickly he continued, and as he pulled an evidence bag from his pocket, he asked two questions at once. "Do you recognize this earring? And would you mind explaining the meaning of these texts?" He showed her the copies Andy had on his phone.

Andy finally spoke up, "I saw them by accident when one popped up and you were in another room." He looked down. "They don't sound so innocent, Suzanne."

She sprang from her seat and lunged at Andy. Slapping him hard across the face, she shouted, "You bastard! I'm out of here." She grabbed her bag and slammed the door behind her.

Andy rubbed his stinging face and said in a sullen tone, "Well, that went well."

"I'm sorry buddy."

Andy sighed in defeat. "It's ok, I've already conceded to the fact that it's over. I'm seeing her in a whole new light. Her reactions today were not how the girl I know and love would have acted. She's a whole different person, not even close to what she presents herself to be." Thinking like a cop, he added, "I'm just not sure if we can charge her with anything yet."

Her first instinct was to call Nicky and ream him out for not warning her. However, she decided to hold off on that until she cooled off. She had come to understand that her first impulses of reactivity never turned out well. She had to think.

Orlando checked in with Andy and Shaker. He informed them that Leo had not left his apartment. His car remained in the parking lot and he had not been seen on foot. He did report that Nick had shown up dressed in what appeared to be a disguise of sorts. He didn't stay long. When he left, it was by bus.

The detectives were pleased with this news. Bernie had delivered the warrant signed and sealed. They were on their way to arrest Leo for his little escapade this morning. Hopefully, it would lead to information that would untangle this mess.

They rang the buzzer in Leo's building realizing that of course, it didn't work. They did as everyone else did; they waited and walked in with someone who had access.

Leo answered his door quickly, as if he had been expecting them. "Can I help you?" he asked.

The detectives identified themselves as such. They then showed Leo the warrant, cuffed him, and read him his rights. He was brought to the SUV and transported to the station. There, he would be questioned with an arraignment to follow.

Chapter 98

After Jenn had gone, Carly plopped into the sofa. What a day this had been. She turned on her favorite satellite station and curled up with a photo album. In heart, she needed to know there had been something real and good in the relationship with Nicky. Although, now she was ready to move forward with Jack, she still wanted to validate her time with Nick.

The early days were the best, she concluded. Many of the candid shots captured them in moments of laughter during vacations or family events. She noted that in some of the more recent   pictures, the smiles were forced and unnatural.

The last few photos were from a day at the beach a month or so before Nick had gotten so sick. It had been one of their better days. She recalled that they were actually having fun. She made him laugh when she took a series of shots pretending to be doing a photo shoot on the sand. He went right along with her, posing in silly stances.

She remembered something and looked closely at the pictures. She had stored the originals on her laptop after she downloaded them from her camera. She needed to check this out and getter a closer view. "I can't believe it." She printed out a few photos.

She sent Orlando a text with the photos along with an explanation. He responded immediately. He told her he would contact Phil Shaker with the information, forwarding the text as well. He knew she was seething, so he advised her to sit tight. He was afraid she'd do something impulsive that might put her in danger.

Carly had been through enough because of this man, she couldn't sit back like a good little girl and do nothing. It was time she faced this problem head on.

Shaker looked at his phone when the text from Orlando was delivered. He put up his hand to shush Andy while he examined the photo. Andy had been asking him what was going on. After understanding the gist of it, he passed his phone to Andy so he could read it for himself. Andy smiled. They were pleased that this information arrived prior to questioning Leo. It was a whole new ballgame.

Leo was brought into the interview room. He sat in the chair, waiting for the detectives to make an appearance. He knew this was how it worked. They would make him wait as they watched through the glass. He wondered if they thought he was stupid. He watched TV too, after all.

The state appointed attorney had advised him not to answer any questions until he arrived. However, he was running late. So, Leo sat. He tried to remain calm, but he soon understood that the tactics were having an impact. Finally, the attorney arrived and was escorted in. He introduced himself as Mitchell Rancourt, III. But he told Leo, to just call him Mitch.

Leo looked at him in disbelief. "What are you? Like fifteen? Did you even graduate law school?"

Clearing his throat, and rubbing the barely present peach fuzz beard, Mitch replied. "I understand that I look young, but I've been doing this for a while. Now, let's move on."

After reviewing some of the facts for both charges, Mitch conceded, that the case against Leo was pretty much cut and dried. The only thing in question was how much time Leo would actually do.

The door opened as Shaker and Andy made their entrance. This time they both sat at the table facing Leo and Mitch. Andy turned the recorder on.

"Here's the thing." Andy began. "We have what we call an air-tight case for the prosecutor. The charges will stick and you'll go to prison." Leo flinched, Andy went on. "We also know you've been involved in shady dealings for a long time but never got convicted of anything before."

Mitch interrupted. "Can you get to the point?"

"Just a little background, counselor." Andy continued. "Okay, here's what we've got. The DA has given us permission to make a deal with you. We need information that we think you can supply us with. In exchange, we're prepared to offer you a lighter sentence."

Mitch had a perplexed look come over him. He whispered into Leo's ear. Leo nodded. "Detectives, can you give me and my client a moment to discuss this?"

Once they were alone, Mitch asked. "I take it there's more involved here than just today's charges. Do you want to talk about it?"

Leo said, "Not really, but I might have to, to stay out of jail."

"Go on."

"Well, I think I want to wait and see what they ask me. If I feel like answering, I will." Mitch raised his eyebrows at his client. "Your job is to get me a good deal. I'm not going to jail."

Mitch gave the word for the detectives to join them in the interrogation room. "Detective Gallagher, Detective Shaker, my client is not aware of any information that he may possess.

However, in exchange for dropping the current charges, he is willing to listen. If he can shed light on whatever it is you're looking for, he will answer to the best of his ability."

Andy and Shaker glanced at each other. Shaker spoke first. "Fine, that sounds reasonable. But as we mentioned earlier, our deal will be a lesser charge. We cannot drop the charges all-together. I should also add that it all depends on what your client has to offer in exchange. No information—no deal."

Leo sat back in his chair. "What do you want to know?"

Andy leaned forward and asked in a quiet voice. "Let's start with today. We know you live forty-five minutes from Carly Mancuso." Leo nodded. "So, what were you doing there?"

"I was looking at the houses. The Victorians always interested me. Was thinking about buying one."

"Come on, Leo, you can do better than that." Andy commented. "Did Nicky Pellegrino send you there to scare Carly?"

Leo thought for a minute. He hadn't been expecting this question. "No, this Nicky guy you mentioned did not ask me to do anything."

Shaker then said, "How about Eric Popper? Did he send you there?"

"I told you, I was looking at houses."

Andy took out the photo of Leo and Nicky that Carly had taken. "What about this? We know you've been in contact with Nicky."

"Fuckin' Joey." He pointed at the picture. "I met that guy once, he asked for a couple of bucks."

Mitch stared at this client, then at the detectives. "I'm not sure what's going on here, but can you get to the point?"

"Well, we know that your client knows this guy. We also believe their friendship goes back a long time. We also think your client has been harassing Carly Mancuso on behalf of this guy. We just need to confirm it." Shaker said.

"And if I confirm it, I win a get-out-of jail-free-card?"

"Well, that will be the first step."

"Ok, then, yeah I know the guy. He asked me to do him a favor. It seemed harmless. He just wanted to scare the girl."

It was Andy's turn to pose a question. "Did you also do a favor for him when you pushed Nicky Pellegrino into the river?"

Leo was completely caught off guard. "What the hell?"

Mitch said, "What the hell? Leo, you don't have to answer that."

"Damn straight, I don't. I don't know what the hell they're talking about."

"Or was it Eric Popper who went in the water that day?"

Shaker chimed in, "Leo, we know you were there that day. We have a witness. You might as well tell us."

Leo scratched his scraggy hair and pushed some of the greasy strands behind his ears. "A witness? There was no witness. No one saw..." He stopped and caught himself. "You can't prove it."

"Didn't you hear me? We do have a witness and we have evidence."

Mitch felt like he was watching a ping-pong match. He was having trouble keeping up with the ball. "Wait a minute here. Isn't Eric Popper the guy they fished out of the river a few months ago? My client is here about a motor vehicle incident, not a homicide. What about the deal? You can't make a deal for that."

Looking Mitch squarely in the eye, Shaker said, "We believe your client has information about this homicide. If he comes clean, we can make a deal for a lighter charge. We could probably get an accessory charge or something like that. It's better than murder."

"I got this Mitch." Leo finally said after quickly weighing the odds. "Yeah, I was there. But I didn't do anything."

"Ok, Leo, so how did it go down?"

Leo took a deep breath. "The three of them were arguing when I got there."

"Who, Leo?"

"Suzanne, Nicky, and Eric. They were arguing. Nicky didn't want any part of the scam that Suzanne and Eric were running. Eric thought it would be a perfect set-up, them being twins and all. Things got out of hand and next thing I know, he takes a couple of blows from Eric and goes over into the river."

Andy knew Suzanne was involved, but hearing it, froze his insides. "Leo, it was Nicky who was pushed into the water, Right? Not Eric like we thought." Leo nodded. "Eric took over Nicky's identity, am I right so far?" Leo nodded again. "What were Suzanne and Eric into?"

"Oh man. Listen, I'm already in deep shit. I need to know exactly
what kind of a deal I'm gonna get."

"Well, I'm not sure since it looks like you were knee deep in this too. I think we can get a reduced sentence like I told you. The DA is willing to deal. So, what were they into?" Andy pressed.

"Drugs. They were selling drugs. Suzanne was getting them from the hospital. They were doing some investment stuff too. I don't know much about the details of that. I got nothing else to say. I want to know what kind of deal I'm getting."

Leo was brought back to his holding cell. Mitch expressed his need to speak with Bernie Falcone. He wanted to know what they would do for his client, since he himself, obviously hadn't done anything. He waited for Bernie to meet him.

Andy and Phil finally had confirmation that Nicky was the victim. From the picture forwarded to them by Carly, they had come to the conclusion Eric was posing as Nicky. He had no appendix scar in the beach photos. However, the shock had come when Leo said they were dealing drugs. This brought up a few more questions.

Since they also had confirmation of Suzanne's involvement, they could get a warrant and bring her in for further questioning. Andy would bow out of that session.

When Bernie arrived, he spoke privately with the detectives about the plea deal he had in mind. The three of them then met with Mitch to present the bargain.

"Hi, Mitch, how are you?" Bernie asked as they shook hands. The two attorneys had known each other for a few years.

"Hey Bernie, good to see you. Let's get down to it. What are you offering my client? He spoke freely and gave up some valuable information, so it better be a good one." Mitch said.

Bernie smiled. "Always right to the point, Mitch. Ok, here's the deal. We drop the charges for today. But since he was present at a homicide scene, we have to charge him with something. So, we could look at him as an accessory in which case he could get five years. However, since we don't know if there was intent to commit the crime or if it was accidental, we could probably go for a lighter sentence. Maybe twenty-four to thirty-six months. How does that sound?"

"Well, I think it sounds fair, but I don't think my client will. He's hoping to get off with no time served."

"Come on, Mitch, you know that's not possible. We're talking about a homicide here."

"I know, I agree. Anyway, he's already given the information. I'll tell him it's a great deal. He's really got no choice. Great seeing you, Bernie."

"You too, Mitch. Hey, the offer is still good if you want to come work for me."

"You just keep asking. Maybe someday, I'll take you up on it."

After Mitch left, Bernie gave Andy and Phil the warrants for Suzanne and Eric. They had been prepared earlier after receiving the photos from Carly. They were just waiting for Leo to confirm the details

"Good luck you two." Bernie said as they left the precinct.

The ten-minute drive to Suzanne's house felt more like ten days to Andy. He played out the scene in head. The ending never changed; there was really no good way to do this. When they arrived, the house was empty. Suzanne was not home.

They also had a secured a search warrant, so they were free to look around, even though technically Andy was a resident. The search warrant made everything legal; anything they found would stand up in court. Andy felt a pit growing in his stomach. The only things in the closet were his clothes He found a small wooden box which was left open on the floor. It was empty. He wondered what was in it. He wondered if she stashed some money for an emergency such as this.

Shaker walked in the room and saw Andy staring at the box. "What are you thinking?"

"I'm thinking that she took off. She probably had some cash here to get out quickly. I'm thinking that she played me."

"Come on, let's look some more. Maybe we can find something to lead us where she went."

After two hours of going through the house, including the computer, her drawers, and the mail, they had come up empty. It was almost eight o'clock and they were exhausted. It had been a hell of a day.

"I hate to say this, but I think we should head over to Popper's apartment. If Suzanne took off, he might too. Maybe we can grab him before he does." Shaker opened the car door and started the car.

"Yeah, I was thinking the same thing." Andy said, rolling down his window as he lit a cigarette.

When they arrived at Eric's complex, they knocked on the door. They listened. No sound, no footsteps. Not a damn thing. In defeat, they started to leave. Andy spotted Carly first.

"What are you doing here?" He asked.

"Oh hi." She said surprised to see them at the door. "I just decided to I needed to see this Eric person as Eric and not Nicky. I wanted to give him hell."

"Carly, you could have put yourself in a dangerous situation." Andy led her away from the apartment. "He's not here anyway. Thanks to you, we got a warrant for his arrest."

"So, what happens now, if he's not here?" She asked.

"We'll probably put a watch on the place in case he comes back." Shaker said.

"I want to help. I want him to pay for what he did to Nick. Now I understand Nicky was the good guy I thought he was."

They both smiled at her as they approached the car. "If there's anything you can do, we'll let you know. For now, let us do our jobs. We don't want you hurt."

"What about that other guy, Leo?"

"No worries, he's locked up for now." Andy told her. "Carly, thanks for your help. I mean it. I don't think we could have put all the pieces together if not for you."

"You're welcome. Please keep me informed." She started her car and drove home.

Chapter 99

Suzanne and Eric hurried down the long hallway and pounded on the door. When Millie opened it, she was shocked to see Eric standing there with Suzanne standing off to the side.

"Hi mom." He pushed his way in. Suzanne followed.

"You're alive! I'm so happy to see you, Eric." Millie said with relief and alarm in her voice.

"Cut the shit, you don't give a rat's ass about me. Now sit down and shut up. I need money and I know you have lots of it."

She stumbled on her words, "Eric, no, I don't have any money I can give you. I'm live on a strict budget."

He slapped her across the face. She fell to the side of the chair and rubbed her cheek. "I know you have money. I know the Pellegrinos set up a trust. You were probably thrilled to hear I was dead, so you could keep it all for yourself. Well, mommy dearest, I'm very much alive and I want my money."

"Eric, honey, calm down. We can talk about this." She said as she started shaking.

"Are you afraid of me? What? Am I too big for you lock in a closet?"

"I did the best I could." Millie stammered.

"Shut up, just shut the fuck up! Give me the cash and I'll be out of here."

"I don't have much cash on hand."

He slapped her again. Suzanne spoke up, "Eric, take it easy. We don't have much time." She knelt in front of Millie.

"Listen to me. We need money. How much do you have on hand?"

Millie looked at Suzanne. She began to relax at her calm tone of voice. "I keep a few thousand in a drawer in my bedroom. Just take it and get out of here."

Eric was already on the move to grab the cash. When he returned, he was tucking the money in his pocket. "There's about $2500 here. That's enough to get us where we have to go." He looked at Millie. "Listen to me now. In a few days, I will call you and give you instructions to deposit money into an account. In the meantime, if you say a word to anyone, I'll come back and I will kill you. DO you understand?"

She nodded. Millie Popper put her head in her hands as she heard the door slam shut.

"Ok baby, let's get out of here." Eric said to Suzanne.

"Where should we go?" She asked. "I'm really scared, Eric."

"Well, I think we head back to Stonington. We can stay in the old apartment. I rented it under a phony name a while back and paid the rent in advance. So, we'll be good there for a while until we figure things out."

"I didn't know you did that." Suzanne said, surprised by this news.

"Yeah, after we faked that big scene and breakup, I thought about it. You know, in case something like this came up. No one would ever think to check there."

Suzanne sat stiffly in the passenger's seat as Eric drove. She wished she could turn back the clock to a time before Eric turned up in her ICU. She had loved Eric at one time, but she had gotten over him. They had kept in touch but put some distance between themselves. They had decided to each go their own way for a while. She realized how much she missed Andy.

After stopping at the grocery store, they arrived at the apartment. It was neat and clean. Eric had hired a cleaning service, explaining to them that he traveled extensively. They unpacked groceries. Suzanne pulled out the dark red hair dye. She stared at it and set it on the table with the rest of the food. That would wait until after they ate.

She cut up the rotisserie chicken, tossed a salad, and nuked the store-made mashed potatoes. She was feeling more settled as she sipped her wine. Eric seemed to calm down too after he popped a couple of pills.

He finally spoke, "Listen, you know it was all that Carly's fault. She started it all."

Suzanne looked up and asked, "How do you mean?"

"Well, by kicking me out. Then she started snooping. I really hate her."

"Yeah, you're right. That day she showed up at the hospital, I thought I was going to be sick." She thought for a moment. She couldn't see a way out. She knew Eric always thought of everything. "Eric, where do we go from here?"

He smiled back at her. I have some money in the closet. Actually, it's quite a bit. We'll take that and we're gonna head up to the Cape or maybe the Vineyard. We can get lost there. Use new names, blend in. At least for now."

Chapter 100

Carly pulled into her driveway shortly after nine. She was relieved to see Jack sitting on the porch waiting for her. She had forgotten that he was going to stop by to check on her.

"Hey, I was starting to get worried. You didn't answer your phone." He said.

"I must have left it behind. I ran out in a hurry. That was stupid of me considering everything."

She explained to him how she had been looking at some old photos and noticed that the man she thought was Nick did not have the scar from appendix surgery. This was this final piece the detectives needed. It confirmed that Nicky was the man who had been killed. Eric had taken Nick's place. Yep, the old evil twin switch, she had joked. But she was dead serious when she said Andy had cautioned her it wouldn't be over until Eric was found. She was still an obsession to him. Perhaps, now more than ever.

Jack realized that Carly now might need to mourn for the Nicky Pellegrino that she knew and not the monster she thought he had become. She cherished his empathy for her; she admired his resolve and his consideration for her well-being. Basically, she loved everything about Jackson Foley. So, instead, she invited him in, knowing Rosie was having a sleep-over at his parents.

"It's time to move on." She said and took him by the hand.

Chapter 101

November through March

In the few weeks that followed, the surveillance teams had not observed Eric or Suzanne. A search of his apartment had revealed miles of illegible scribbled notes. Carly's name figured prominently on most of them. The detectives had become worried that the pair slipped away and might not be found. Carly was given frequent updates and still retained Orlando's services for her protection.

One night while having dinner with Jack and Rosie, she looked at the two of them, realizing how lucky she was to have them in her life. She wanted this new family. However, she knew she would not truly be free until she was sure the past could not reach out and grab her.

She had an idea that she needed to discuss with Jack. After she read to Rosie and tucked her in, she told Jack what she was thinking. He saw the determination in her eyes. As much as he worried about the risk, he knew this needed to be settled. He also understood the not knowing hung over her like a heavy fog.

"Carly, I love you. I know this needs to be finished before we can start our life. I'll help in any way I can."

"Thank you, Jack. On so many levels, I need to tell this story. I think I can send a message to women that says, 'you didn't do anything wrong'. These women need to realize they don't have to be victims. I can let them know that abuse comes in many forms; there's no need to be ashamed. It can happen to anyone before you even realize it. They need to hear that there are so many outlets available for help."

"It is a terrific way to open up this issue. Especially, if someone like you can talk about it openly." Jackson agreed.

She threw her arms around him, then made a few phone calls.

It took a few weeks to set everything up, but when the details were in place as December set in, the announcement was made. Carly Mancuso would be performing at Mohegan Sun Arena. There would be two consecutive shows with all the proceeds going to benefit programs for domestic violence and women's shelters.

By January, following that announcement and under the supervision of Andy and Phil Shaker, Carly agreed to do interviews with the local news stations. She would tell her own story, candidly. She would also include some brief statements about Eric and the death of Nicky. Extensive stories also ran concurrently in the papers; one major news magazine even did an interview with her. Pretty soon, her story had been picked up by some of the bigger publications and national news broadcasts. Her concerts were sold out in no-time.

It was a good thing that the grueling rehearsals were paying off. By mid-February, Carly was performing as if she had never left the stage. She was feeling confident that her shows would be a success.

Every time, Eric turned on the TV, there she was. He was incensed. He couldn't get away from it. His face was on the magazine shelves in the local convenience stores, accompanied by some stupid caption. Everywhere, it was everywhere. The lying bitch was taking it too far. She was exploiting him for her own celebrity. He thought he would explode. He just couldn't help himself. He left his apartment with only one thing on his mind.

Chapter 102

Present Day

March

Carly had not expected to be standing face-to face with Eric Popper. He looked like evil if evil had a face. She wondered how she could ever have mistaken him for Nicky. This vile man looked nothing like Nick. His eyes had no sparkle; his smile was flat.

He stood in front of her grinning. He wreaked of stale cigarettes. He stared at her glassy-eyed from the Percocets she guessed he was still taking. "So, how ya doing, Carly?"

"Uh, Nicky. Oh, I mean, Eric. It's been a while." She stammered. In her head, she was thinking that it wasn't supposed to happened like this. She was not prepared. No one was.

"Yeah, it has. We have a lot to talk about." Without warning, he grabbed her by the arm. "Come on honey, let's go home."

She tried to struggle against him, but as frail and out of shape as he appeared, she realized he still had some strength. She attempted a joke to diffuse the situation. "You must be working out, Eric. Using those kettle bells?"

"Cut the crap. Keep walking." He yanked her up the street towards her home and held a knife to her back. "You think you can talk shit about me and I wouldn't come looking for you? You are still so stupid. I should have taken care of you when I had the chance. I'm so pissed off right now, you have no idea. All of this is because of you. You shouldn't have rejected me! Do you know what it feels like to be thrown away? Maybe I wasn't as nice as my dear brother Nicky, but I didn't deserve that. You know what else pisses me off? You and your new guy. Oh wait, now I understand. You were probably screwing him before, that's it, right? I bet you poisoned me to get me out of the way. Oh man," he rambled, "I should have seen that one coming."

Carly knew better than to interrupt his tirade. She kept her mouth shut. He pushed her along, poking the knife harder through the fabric of her fleece jacket. She twinged when she felt the cold tip jab at her back.

When they turned the corner on another isolated side-street, a large woman in leopard spandex, materialized out of nowhere. She pretended not to notice the couple walking towards her. She took out her cell phone and made a call, very casually. She whispered, "Dad, hurry, it's happening. North street." In an instant, she flung the phone and sprung at the tall man coming towards her. She tackled him to the ground, his scrawny body crumbling with the force of the hit. He went down hard. Carly freed herself from Eric's vice grip the moment Jenn made the strike. She grabbed the knife that tumbled onto the sidewalk and stood over him, trembling. When Orlando arrived with the police, they found Jennifer Diaz straddling Eric Popper, effectively restraining him.

Carly hugged Jenn, the protector of all the women. "Your timing was perfect. I love you!"

"I love you, too. We saved each other." Jenn grinned. Carly knew what her friend meant.

When they arrested Eric, they bagged the knife and got him to his feet. He was babbling incoherently as they tucked him in the cruiser. One of the officers present was sure he heard something about Wyle E. Coyote.

Andy and Phil Shaker were notified. They drove with their lights flashing to the forgotten town of Willimantic, Connecticut to get their prisoner.

Chapter 103

Son of a bitch! How did they get me? So yeah, I wanted him dead. I wanted him dead on a whole bunch of levels. I didn't plan it, it just happened. Kind of glad it did. After all, he was the golden boy, living the life I should have had. Instead, they shipped me off with those Popper idiots. Even that name is stupid. They say, 'what's in a name?'. Well, I'll tell you. People look at you differently when your name is weird or stupid. If you have the wrong name, it can make a mess of your life.

Anyway, I hated those people. They acted like they wanted a kid. All they really wanted was the money that came with me. Fuckin' mother Millie locked me in a closet when she didn't know what else to do with me—which was pretty often. I kind of liked Sam, he stayed out of my way. I wish she died instead of him.

I tried to find the family who threw me away but I couldn't get hold of the records. I found Nick by accident. I was tending bar and he walked in. I couldn't get over it. They never said I had a twin. It opened a world of possibilities. My shift ended a little while later and I walked over to him. He was as surprised as I was. We talked a little while and left together.

It was a lucky thing that no one at that bar knew him. While we were talking, I realized that he was everything I wasn't. I wanted the life I was cheated out of. Over a couple of weeks, I had him thinking we could be friends like real brothers. I tried to bring him into my operation, but he was too goody-good. My mistake, I misjudged him. I knew there might be trouble.

I told him too much. I filled him in about the drug deals Suzanne and I were running. She was stealing from the hospital. I was selling them. Man, we made a shitload of money. People love pharmaceuticals. Idiots. They think because they're legal, they're safe. Anyway, I knew he was gonna be trouble.

We met that afternoon down by the river. I had to talk to him. Suzanne was nervous as usual. She tried to get him to calm down. But he wouldn't let up. He was so fucking righteous. I really started to hate him. Finally, Leo showed up. The three of us knew what had to happen. I hit him a few times and pushed him over the bank. The rest, as they say is history. I saw my chance. I took it. I got my new life, or the life I should have had.

It was too bad I got sick. I let the drinking take over. I had a sweet deal with Carly, but she knew something was off. When I almost died, she tossed me out. Who can blame me for wanting revenge? Then the bitch started digging around. Yeah, she needed a taste of her own medicine too. She still does. I'm not gonna let her win—ever.

Chapter 104

Somewhere in Provincetown, Cape Cod, a woman with red hair, smiled as she waited tables. She was content to work in the small restaurant that overlooked the bay. She maintained a low profile, living in an unassuming house within walking distance to the center. Although her tips and earnings provided her with a decent income, she had plenty of money stashed away for a rainy day. She thought to herself that she was finally free of Eric and the past that seemed to haunt her. She saddened when she thought about Andy. But all in all, she was content, knowing that she could be happy in this life---at least for a while.

Suzanne had been keeping a watchful eye on the news about Eric. She read everything. She knew that if she kept to herself, she would never be found. She loaded the plates that were sitting under the warmer and delivered them to her waiting customers.

Carly was proud of her role in the investigation. With her help, the detectives were able to put the pieces together and make a solid case against Eric Popper which consisted of many charges; the most notable being the murder of Nicky Pellegrino.

She was able to stand tall and view her situation from a different vantage point. She felt stronger than ever. After Eric's conviction, she moved on. So much wasted time and energy. Optimistically, she decided that the experience had taught her many lessons about life and about herself. She had discovered some new rules to live by.

Epilogue

Eric was charged with the second degree murder of Nicky Pellegrino. He received a sentence of twenty-five years. The smaller charges added another ten to the total. He knew he'd be able to charm his way into an early parole because he would be a model prisoner, liked and admired by all.

The women of Prospect Hill continued to flourish. Each of them following the path life had set out before them. With the help of Jack and Carly, Irene started a modest catering business. It was growing into a local success. Lucy and baby Alex had settled in. Alex was growing in every way. Physically, he was a big little boy; emotionally, he was a very happy baby. He thrived on the love and attention showered on him from his family.

Jennifer continued her studies in criminal justice. However, she assisted Irene with her business in a part-time role as the party planner. She enjoyed both facets of her life. She was also thankful Carly had come into her life. They formed a special bond and would remain kindred spirits.

Andy struggled with Suzanne's betrayal. He wondered how he got sucked in. In his heart, he would always believe that some part of her really loved him. Amidst his feelings, he and Shaker had searched for her in the places Eric told them to look.

They had no luck. As time went on and new cases needed their attention, Suzanne's importance had faded. They had successfully locked up Eric Popper—that was what counted. Carly Mancuso was their new hero.

Carly's benefit concert was a tremendous success. The money was donated to help fund programs for domestic abuse as well as women's shelters in the state. Her plan to bring this issue to the public eye had succeeded because donations were pouring in from all over the country.

The other part of her plan had also been accomplished. By making her ordeal public, she made herself the bait. From her experience with Eric, she was aware he would not stay hidden too long. His ego drove him to extremes. She was correct in her assumption. He had come after her with a vengeance, as predicted.

Without the threat of Eric looming over them, Carly and Jack were able to properly fall in love. They hadn't spoken of marriage; however, they were relishing every moment they could spend together. Rosie was ecstatic as well.

Following the comeback concert and the publicity she had received, she once again faded from the spotlight. Carly continued to volunteer at the shelter. She treasured every moment of her life. She felt an inner peace that she realized had eluded her for so long.

Her parents and Sally were also a big part of her life. Throughout the drama with Eric, she realized how much she missed her time with them. Her focus had been on him. She discovered how precious every minute of every relationship was. In a heartbeat, everything might change. She resolved to be present in her life from now on.

THE END

Made in the USA
Middletown, DE
25 July 2019